WRITTEN *with* YOU

The Regret Duet (Book 2)

ALY MARTINEZ

WRITTEN

with

YOU

PROLOGUE

WILLOW

"Why?" I yelled, my whole body thrumming with betrayal as Hadley sat across the room, high as a kite. Her green eyes, which were only one shade different than mine, were unfocused, cocaine no doubt coursing through her veins. It was her drug of choice and had been since we were sixteen.

"Could you shut up?" she snapped, draping her legs over the arm of the chair.

"You had a baby!" I waved the journal in the air before I threw it at her. She didn't even try to dodge it.

I'd found it with at least a dozen others in a box she'd mailed to me in Puerto Rico. Was it a gross invasion of privacy to read them? Probably. But after a decade spent with her in and out of rehab, countless nights chasing her down, months where she'd disappear and I had no idea if she was dead or alive, I didn't feel guilty in the least reading them, hoping for even one tiny glimpse into the woman that was Hadley Banks.

She was supposed to be moving in with me.
She was supposed to be getting her life together.
She was supposed to be sober.
And yet…
She'd never used the plane ticket I'd bought her.

She'd run up over a hundred thousand dollars' worth of debt on various credit cards.

And just the night before, when I'd flown back after having my heart ripped out by reading her journals, Beth and I had found her half naked in a glorified crack house in Philly.

It was safe to say that Hadley was not okay.

And the more I'd read, the more I'd realized she never had been.

My twin sister, a mere three minutes older than I was, hadn't walked out of that mall the day our parents were murdered. The innocent eight-year-old little girl on an outing with her family had died in that tragedy. Not physically, of course. She'd walked a lot of steps after that, the majority of them in an effort to outrun the horror of that day. What she really needed though was to follow my footsteps—right into a therapist's office.

Was I the picture of mental health? Hell no.

I'd contemplated ending my life.

I'd done my time trapped in the prison of fear inside my mind.

I'd woken to the agony of phantom bullets ravaging my body.

But I'd never stopped fighting to get better.

Hadley and I had shared a lot of things in life.

A mother.

A father.

A birthday.

A reflection in the mirror.

But our experiences in that mall couldn't have been more different.

Hadley was the last person to be found the day of the shooting. When the first shot had been fired, she'd been standing several yards away, snapping the picture to end *my* roll of film. I'd lost her in the chaos and only later learned that she'd been trampled by men and women alike. Her arm had been broken, but no one had stopped to help her. No one had acknowledged that the terrified child existed. Somehow, she'd gotten herself to the Chinese restaurant where she climbed into a small cabinet, holding the interior latch of the locking mechanism so tight that her fingers became bloody and raw.

She was in agony, but she remained silent long after the police and paramedics had stormed in.

For three hours, she hid in that cabinet.

Alone.

Only a sliver of light peeking through the crack.

Fear terrorized her to the point that she didn't trust the police enough to come out. In the end, it was a female investigator with rich red hair that she'd seen through the crack and mistaken for our mother that convinced her to spring from that cabinet.

Her sudden scream for our mom startled them.

Guns were drawn.

Aimed at her.

Breaking her all over again.

This time irreparably.

While Hadley and I were identical in virtually every way, after that day at the mall, there was one vast difference that changed the path of our lives forever.

I'd walked out of that war zone with my faith in humanity still intact.

I'd had Caven.

And she'd hated me for it ever since.

I shouldn't have been surprised she'd gone after him. I'd never seen him or spoken to him after I was carried away on a stretcher.

But a part of me had always loved him.

And for that alone, Hadley made him pay.

"What did I ever do to you?" I whispered, my throat so thick with disgust I could barely get the words to escape. "Please, tell me. What did I do to you that was so horrible that you felt the need to get back at me by making a *baby* with Caven of all fucking men?"

She shot me a smirk. "Is that what you're mad about? That I fucked your precious *Caven*?" His name was a sneer on her lips, and that shot anger up my spine.

"No. See. I'd expect that from you. Honestly, I'm impressed you waited as long as you did. God knows you've been trying to punish me for not dying in that shooting for eighteen years now. And what better way than having a baby with the boy who saved me and then giving her up without even telling me?" I planted my hands on my hips and fought back the sobs. "I know you hate me. I know you've never forgiven me for being the reason we were at the mall that day. And I know—"

"You know nothing!" She suddenly shot to her feet. "For fuck's sake, maybe it wasn't about you, Willow. Ever think of that? I'm sorry to disappoint, but this wasn't some grand plan devised to torture you. He had Kaleidoscope, plain and simple."

I ground my teeth and it was a wonder I had any left for all the times we'd had this very same argument. "Don't you dare mention that picture. Don't you fucking dare."

She stared at me, utterly unphased. "You weren't there."

I lifted my shirt, pointing to the scar of puckered flesh that had stretched into a spider web over the years. "I was there, Hadley. I was there in ways you will *never* understand. So don't you dare talk to me about that damn picture."

She shrugged. "Then I guess this conversation is over, because without that picture, I can't talk to you about the baby at all."

I took a step toward her, her betrayal igniting me into a fiery rage. "The baby? Her name is *Keira*. Have the decency to at least acknowledge her as a human and not a sack of potatoes you paid a hooker to abandon!"

"I didn't *abandon* her. I left her with *Caven*."

"So that makes it better?"

"I figured you'd be fucking ecstatic. He always kept *you* safe."

I closed my eyes, tears born in frustration flowing down my cheeks.

How did she not understand this?

How could she breathe a single breath knowing there was a little girl out there growing up without a mother?

How did her heart continue beating knowing she'd given up the only family we'd *ever* have?

How could she have closed her eyes at night for over three years without the regret consuming her?

It had only been a day since I'd found out about that baby and I was crippled by those emotions.

She had a daughter. How had she just left her and then gone on with her life?

I shook my head. "If Mom and Dad could see you now…

Jesus, Hadley. You named her after Mom and then gave her away."

Her eyes flashed dark, her hands balling into fists at her sides. "I didn't *give her away*. I gave her to someone who could take care of her."

"*I* could have taken care of her!"

A malevolent smirk pulled at her lips as she stepped toward me. Her hand went to my side, directly over my scar.

I winced, knowing where this was going.

She was high. She had no filter when she was using. But this was a new low.

Thanks to Malcom Lowe's bullet, having children was officially off the table for me. I'd known it since I was a kid myself, but the older I got, the more it seemed to matter. It was the wound that never stopped giving. A scar that wouldn't heal. The loss of a future I never got to choose.

I hated her for what she was about to say.

I hated her for what she knew about me.

But most of all, I hated her because she knew it all and was going to say it anyway.

She gave my scar a squeeze. "I've spent my entire life wishing I could be you. How's it feel to finally wish you could be me?"

"I hate you," I breathed, the gaping hole she'd carved making it nearly impossible to speak.

She released me, stepping away, but her gaze never left mine. "No, you don't. You hate me because I fucked Caven. You hate me for being able to carry a baby. You hate me for seeking the truth. But you don't hate *me*, Willow. And you never will." She lifted a shoulder in a shrug as though she'd just disagreed with me about what to have for dinner that night. "That's your biggest problem. You can't let go because you're scared you're the one who's going to end up alone this time."

She was wrong.

I fucking hated her.

I loathed her.

I wished she'd disappear and never look back.

But I could never let go of the idea that, deep down, my sister was still inside the broken shell of this woman.

Alone.

Scared.

And waiting to be found again.

If there was even a glimmer of hope that she was still in there, I would never give up on her.

Swallowing hard, I pulled myself together. "You're so wrong you can't even see right anymore. I'm not afraid of being alone. I'm afraid of losing *you*. My sister. My best friend. My *family*. I have spent the better part of my life trying to hold on to you. I've been fighting for you, even after you made it clear you'd given up. I gave you money. I bought you a house. A car." I threw my hands out to my sides, allowing them to slap my thighs as they came down. "I started an entire company with the hopes that it would bring us closer again."

She quirked an eyebrow. "Yes, you did all of those wonderful things that only a perfect *loving sister* would do. And then you cut off my bank cards, guilt-tripped me into rehab, sold my car, kicked me out of the house, and fired me. So…"

"You were slowly killing yourself. What did you expect me to do?"

"Let me!" she roared. "Just fucking let me go!"

"You promised me!" I yelled back, my scream so loud that it rattled the windows.

Her mouth clamped shut, the surprise of my outburst momentarily stunning her into silence.

And I pounced. With a long stride forward, I closed the distance between us and stabbed a finger at her chest. "When Grandpa died, you held my hand and promised me that you'd never leave. You swore to me that you'd live forever if you had to so I'd never have to bury anyone else. You sat on that pew beside me and told me that we were two halves to one soul. Wherever I went, you'd be there too." My voice cracked as I forced it through the emotion. I had no idea if I was getting through the cloud of drugs in her system. Worse, I had no idea if she even cared anymore. But, dammit, I had to try. "Where is that woman, Hadley? Just tell me where she is and I will walk through hell to find her."

It was slight at first, the tiniest chin quiver ever witnessed. But my heart soared knowing she was still in there.

I took her hand in both of mine and brought it up to rest on my chest. "It's me and you, Hadley. It's always been me and you. I'm here. Be here with me. I'm begging you. Just be here with me."

I was damn near euphoric as I watched it happen. Her tough exterior crumbling to reveal that familiar broken and scared little girl was the most beautiful sight I'd ever seen.

My sister was still in there, lost in addiction, stolen by an obsession, and shattered by a gruesome past that owned us both.

But she was in there. Therefore, I was there too.

"I'm sorry," she whispered, her eyes filling with tears. "I

should have told you about Keira. I should have..." She didn't finish the thought before pulling me into a hug.

Hadley gave the best hugs. They were just like our mother's—so warm and soothing, like the perfect cocoon of assurance.

"I didn't know what to do with a baby," she confessed. "It was a really...dark time."

I returned her embrace, hoping it was even a fraction as good as hers. "I know I'm a nosy little brat and read all your journals." We both half laughed and half sobbed. "I'm sorry I wasn't there for you. I can't imagine how scared you had to be when you were in labor. I should have been there."

She loosened her hold on me and leaned away to capture my gaze. "Stop. You didn't know."

"I feel like—"

"No. Please. I don't want to talk about this right now. Let me sober up. Let's order some food and then maybe watch a movie? You finally watch TV now, right?"

I laughed sadly. "You'd be so proud. I ordered Netflix and everything."

"Gasp!" she said with a teasing half smile. "You rebel."

I smiled back at her. "We're going to figure this out. Okay? No matter what it takes. We're going to figure this out."

"Okay." She rubbed the pad of her thumb over my tear-streaked cheek. "Go wash your face. Your mascara is running like you were in a horror movie."

Truth be told, our entire life had been a horror movie. It was nothing new. But maybe it could be.

Hadley had a daughter.

We could be a family again.

And that family, in some crazy way, now included Caven Hunt.

I could spend the rest of my life being bitter and jealous that she'd gone after him. That she'd slept with him. Made a baby with him. Given that child to him to raise on his own. But my family was more important than any of that.

Hadley had a daughter.

I had a niece.

Her name was Keira.

That was all that mattered.

And as I walked back from the bathroom two minutes later after washing my face and grabbing my phone to order delivery, I realized that that little girl was all that would ever matter.

Because Hadley was gone.

So were my keys.

My purse.

And my heart.

ONE

CAVEN

Present day...

"Happy birthday to you. Happy birthday to you," I sang as I carried a cake covered with rainbow sprinkles and a bonfire of candles out to the back deck. Rosalee was leading the march, swaying under the sheer weight of the pink gift bag she was hauling with both hands.

I'd felt like an ass for not buying anything for Hadley. But I hadn't even known it was her birthday until the night before. I also hadn't known I was going to end my night fucking us both into oblivion.

Luckily, my girl was the MacGyver of birthday presents. She'd made an entire bag full of gifts for Hadley in twenty minutes with nothing more than the two markers she owned that hadn't dried out, six broken crayons, two rocks, a paperclip, and four cotton swabs she'd snuck out of my bathroom.

Now, what was in that bag? I had no idea. But I knew with an absolute certainty that Hadley would love each and every one of them. For as much as she oohed and ahhed during "art classes," they would be her most cherished possessions for no other reason than Rosalee had made them. I got it. It was the same reason I held multimillion-dollar business deals in my

1

office surrounded by crayon drawings rather than pretentious paintings to impress clients.

When you're a parent, anything your child touches is priceless. It becomes a memory, an age trapped in time. And while I was still struggling with the fact that Hadley was her mother and what that meant for my future, there was no denying that she loved Rosalee something fierce.

"Happy birthday, dear Ha—" I abruptly stopped singing when I caught sight of her standing on the deck.

Standing.

Not sitting and relaxing the way I'd told her to when I'd sent her out back so we could finish preparing the cake. She was tense, her face pale, and her smile so fake it instantly set me on edge. I cut my gaze to my brother as Rosalee and Jenn finished off the final verse of the song. He was grinning, a beer in his hand, nothing out of the ordinary except for the fact that he was alone outside with her.

Still feeling like a dick for not warning her how much he looked like Malcom, I'd asked him to give her space. When I looked at Trent, I didn't see our father anymore. I saw the nineteen-year-old kid who had done his best to protect me when the flames of our father's hell had surrounded us after the shooting.

That's not who she saw when she looked at him though. To her, he had the same dark hair, and looming height of the monster who had killed her parents. I was honestly impressed that she'd agreed to stay at all. Had the roles been reversed, I'd have been peeling out of the driveway. Some memories, no matter how slight, were best left in the past.

For years, Trent, Ian, and therapists alike had warned me about triggers that could possibly set me off. I did everything

I could to figure out what they were and then avoid them at all costs. But Hadley had stayed. Her desire to spend time with Rosalee—and possibly me—trumped her fears. And that fucked with the organ in my chest—as opposed to the one in my pants—that shouldn't have had any feelings other than guilt for Hadley Banks.

But it did. In ways I'd been trying to deny. A connection I'd been trying to sever. And, worst of all, an ingrained need to protect her that I couldn't shake. Therefore, the fact that Trent was well aware that he'd freaked her out and he still managed to find himself alone and clearly freaking her out again pissed me the fuck off.

He didn't like her. He'd thought she was up to no good and biding her time before making a move that would reveal her true colors. All of which he'd assumed were tinted the color of money. He'd stated that numerous times on the phone and then again when he'd shown up that morning and Rosalee told him and Jenn all about the party she was planning. Hadley didn't need my cash any more than I needed his bullshit. As long as he followed through on his promise to treat her with respect in my house, he didn't have to like her.

Rosalee wasn't his daughter. He didn't get to make the hard calls about who was or wasn't involved in her life.

That was my job.

One I took very seriously.

That is if you excluded my desperate need to bury my cock inside her mother.

Fucking hell.

"Blow out the candles!" Rosalee exclaimed, clapping her hands.

Hadley's eyes met mine. Her tangible panic sledgehammered me in the gut.

"Come here, babe," I murmured in a low tone while flicking a glower at my brother.

He replied with a puzzled expression that was about as genuine as Hadley's smile.

She didn't delay in hurrying to my side, her hand fisting the back of my shirt, out of view from Rosalee as she blew out the candles.

"Yay!" Rosalee cheered, hefting the pink bag toward her mother. "Open it."

Hadley took the bag, then peered up at me, something unreadable on her face but panic glistening in her eyes.

"Dry-heave?" I whispered.

She bit her lips between her teeth and nodded.

"Right. Okay. Let's do presents after cake." Pivoting to the long wooden table, I set the cake down. Then I returned to do the same with Rosalee's gift. "You know what? I forgot plates."

"I've got 'em," Jenn chirped.

I ground my teeth. "I meant napkins."

She lifted a stack of pink and purple unicorns left over from Rosalee's interrupted party. "Got those too."

Tilting my head with waning patience, I pointedly flicked my gaze to Hadley. "A knife?"

Jenn's eyebrows shot up in understanding, and she quickly tucked the one in her hand into her back pocket. "Oh, right. Yeah. We'll need a knife. Hadley, you don't mind if Rosalee and I lick the icing off your candles, do you?"

My girl squealed when Hadley replied, "Have at it."

Jenn winked at me, and I spared one last glare at my

4

brother before guiding Hadley inside. If he'd felt its heat, I couldn't be sure because his eyes were locked on Hadley, a satisfied smirk pulling on his lips.

Asshole.

When the door closed behind us, I wrapped my hand around hers. She started toward the hall bathroom, but I guided her up the stairs.

"Privacy," I mumbled, closing the door to my bedroom.

She'd never been in there before, but her eyes didn't wander with curiosity. She stared at me. A trapped urgency showed on her face without a single word exiting her perfect lips.

I rested my hands in the shallow curve of her hips. "Talk to me."

Her teeth trapped her bottom lip, but not like they had all the times she'd stared at me from across the room. This was different—a physical verbal blockage of sorts.

I went for humor. It wasn't a cure-all, but she'd always responded well to a distraction.

Using two fingers, I tugged her lip free. "Go ahead. You can dry-heave on me if you need to." I rocked her toward me. "Hadley, come on, babe. Spill it. Is it Trent? Did he say something? Help me out here. I'm shit at mind reading."

She pressed her lips together as though it were a last-ditch effort to keep the words filling her mouth from escaping.

She probably needed space.

A little air.

Time to gather her thoughts.

But even knowing that, I couldn't convince my arms to let her go.

What the fuck was it about this woman that overrode my brain's ability to process common sense?

Sliding my hands around to her lower back, I encircled her waist, bringing her delicate curves flush with my front. "You can talk to me. He's my brother, but trust me, no one understands that Trent's a hardass better than I do. If he was slinging shit at you for whatever reason, I want to know."

She shook her head.

No words.

No explanation.

No way for me to beat back the hurricane brewing in her eyes.

"Daddy!" Rosalee yelled from downstairs. "Where's Hadley? It's time for cake."

Shit. I dropped my forehead to Hadley's. "I hate to say this, but there's sugar involved. She's going to be kicking that door down like the FBI in a matter of minutes. What do you want to do here? I can go stall her and buy you some time to collect yourself? Or I can make up an excuse if you want to leave? I could also drag Trent out back and beat him like a rug. It wouldn't be our first or last brawl. You say the word—whatever I can do, I'll make it happen."

It was a joke. Sort of anyway. But she gave me nothing. Not even the hint of the smile that always caused my lips to curl as well.

Giving up on me altogether, Rosalee shouted, "Hadley!"

I sighed before calling back. "I'm coming, baby. Go wait outside."

"Is Hadley with you?" she asked on another yell from downstairs.

"Yes. Go wait with Jenn."

"Why is she in your room?"

"She…uh, had to use the bathroom. Go back outside!"

"Number one or number two?"

"Go!" I boomed, my voice echoing on the walls of my bedroom.

For such a serious situation, talking about number one or number two was awkward at best, but that was Rosalee. And I'd never been so grateful for her lack of etiquette as when I felt Hadley's shoulder shake and a soft giggle escape.

Tipping my chin down, I caught her gaze. The pressure in my chest eased at the sight of her ghost of a smile.

"You know, if we wait up here any longer, you're going to have to tell her number two, right?"

Her smile stretched, and I breathed a sigh of relief when the color began to return to her face. Unable to stop myself—or, at the very least, unwilling to *try* to stop myself—I dipped low, pressing my lips over hers.

She didn't kiss me back. Instead, she rested her forehead on my chin, effectively hiding her face from my view.

"Caven," she breathed, the two syllables merging into one.

"Tell me what's going on. Whatever it is, I'll take care of it." I kissed her forehead. It was too close to resist.

She sucked in a deep breath. "I'm going to stay for a piece of cake and long enough to open her present. Then I think I need to go."

"Okay." I ignored the disappointment that rained over me. "Just a heads-up, I'm not sure that I can sneak away to your place tonight after all. Trent was talking about spending the night earlier and—"

"No, I get it. Family first. Maybe another time."

"Maybe?" I teased. Anything to lighten the suffocating weight hanging in the air between us for reasons I didn't understand. "I did not face a horde of zombies to recover the last condoms in existence to hear you say *maybe*."

She laughed, soft and sweet.

But there was something about it.

Maybe it was the way it slid into a pregnant silence.

Or the way she leaned into me, her breasts pillowing between us, her hands going to the back of my neck and holding me tight, as if she could absorb me.

Or maybe it was just the unexplainable string that tied us together being plucked by karma.

But whatever it was, the lull that followed that laughter was utterly heartbreaking.

"Hadley?"

"I love her," she told my neck. "I love her more than anything in the world. Please tell me you know that. No matter what happened in the past. Please tell me you know how much I love her *now*. I only want the absolute best for her. No matter what that entails."

The hairs on the back of my neck stood on end.

She was leaving.

That was the heartbreak I'd heard.

Whatever had happened with Trent. Whatever had been said on that deck. She was leaving.

Again.

I took a sudden step away from her, peeling her arms from around my neck. "What's going on?"

She blinked. "What do you mean?"

"I mean, what *the fuck* is happening right now?"

"N-nothing. I was going to eat cake and then leave."

"And when are you going to come back?"

More blinking from her.

More mounting frustration from me.

Her eyebrows furrowed. "Wednesday? Unless…you need to switch the date for some reason. I'm pretty free whenever. Just tell me when to be here and I'm here."

That was when the alarm bells started ringing in my head.

As I stared at her with her long, red hair cascading over her exposed collar bone and her plump lips parted, all but begging for my mouth to press against them, that alarm became a blaring siren. And it screamed a warning just before a tidal wave slammed into me so hard and so fast that it stole the oxygen from my lungs.

For the first time since she'd reappeared over three months earlier, I didn't want Hadley to leave.

I could bullshit myself and say that was all about my baby girl losing someone she cared about, but the relief singing in my veins told a different story.

That panic.

That anger.

That desperation when I'd thought she was saying goodbye.

That was all about *me*.

"Is…that okay?" she stammered out.

"Yeah. Shit. I'm sorry," I ground out around the knot in my throat. "I misread that situation." I swayed my head from side to side. "Ya know. Assumption. Making an ass out of you and me and all."

She took a step toward me, my body igniting at her proximity. "What'd you assume?"

I could have lied. But not to her.

Hooking her around the hips, I dragged her to me. "I thought you were saying goodbye."

"What?"

"I know. I know. It was stupid, but it felt real. And…" *You're under my skin.* "I overreacted. It's been a long day. I slept for shit last night. There was this insatiable woman who kept me up late."

I expected a laugh.

What I got was a vow.

"I will never leave her, Caven." She held my gaze with an unfettered determination. "I don't care what it takes. What it cost me physically or emotionally. And I don't give a damn who tries to stand in my way. When it comes to Rosalee, goodbye is not a word in my vocabulary. She's my family and I love her. So you can bury that assumption four years in the past where it belongs." And then she was gone. Head held high, marching down the stairs, taking Rosalee's hand before hitting the back door.

True to her word, she stayed long enough to eat cake and gush over some painted rocks with Q-tip legs that Rosalee claimed were llamas. She laughed with Jenn while avoiding Trent's scrutiny, and she'd done it so fearlessly that I couldn't help but feel a sense of pride.

I didn't know what had happened on the deck between her and Trent.

And I didn't know what had changed while we had been in my bedroom.

But as she climbed into her car while blowing kisses to Rosalee, I felt like I was watching an entirely different woman.

TWO

WILLOW

Seven months earlier...

My bedroom was pitch black as I stared up at my ceiling fan. The large blades cut through the humid Puerto Rico air as waves crashed in the distance. My secluded home wasn't on the beach, but late at night, if I opened my windows, the dull roar of the ocean would echo against my walls.

For all the years I'd been living there, the peace and tranquility of those waves breaking on the shore had eased my troubled soul.

Though, for the last two weeks, they had been nothing more than background noise to my turbulent mind.

It had been two weeks since I'd found out about Keira.

Two weeks since Hadley had taken off with my purse and car.

Two weeks of wallowing and trying to convince myself to climb out of bed.

I lived in the seconds. One emotion. One tick of the clock.

But when you were all alone, did time even matter?

I had a good life, though I would have loved it a hell of a lot more with a family to share it with. Hadley was all I had left, and I didn't know how to help her anymore. I'd sworn I would fight for her. It's what my parents would have wanted. But I was at war with a ghost.

Since I'd come home, I'd read her journals cover to cover more times than I would ever admit. There had to be an answer in those pages of how I could save her. But with every sentence, her blistering pain seeped from the words, scorching me to the core.

How had I not known how bad things had gotten for her?

I'd witnessed her struggle with drugs, but the cutting and multiple suicide attempts were news to me.

I told myself not to give in to the anger, but there was a time when Hadley and I had shared everything. In those journals, she was a stranger to me. The façade she showed me was nothing more than an attempt to blend into nothingness.

After two weeks of tossing and turning, my brain desperately needed a break.

But there was no sleep to be found. I had to go back. I had to try.

I had to…

The light to my bedroom suddenly flashed on.

Bolting upright, I threw my arm up to block the light. It was only the sound of her voice that kept me from having a heart attack.

"Are you fucking kidding me? Are you fucking *kidding me!*" Beth roared. There was a crash across my room as the vase I'd filled with shells I'd found on the beach shattered against the wall. "I've been calling you for fucking weeks and you've been hiding out here? Not answering your goddamn phone."

Oh-kay. So, Beth was pissed.

Pissed enough to hop onto a plane to Puerto Rico to give me hell. Surprise visits weren't unusual when you lived in paradise, but the screaming was new.

"Relax. It was two calls. I didn't feel like talking to anyone."

"What is wrong with you!" Her voice cracked as her rage gave way to a sob.

Beth didn't cry.

Beth was an emotional rock who had carried me through the darkest nights when the demons came calling.

The sound of her anguish was like being struck by lightning.

Something had happened.

Something *terrible* had happened.

And there was only one person left the world could take from me.

Dropping my arm as my eyes adjusted to sudden illumination, I shot to my feet. "What's wrong?"

She stumbled backward, the color draining from her face as her mouth gaped. "Wha—"

"What's wrong?" I repeated more slowly, striding toward her. "Beth!" I yelled, attempting to snap her out of her stupor. "What the hell is going on?"

And then, all at once, she exploded off the wall, nearly knocking me off my feet as she threw her arms around my neck. "Willow!" she cried. "Oh, God, Willow. You're alive."

I *was* alive.

I was very, very much alive.

But if she thought I was dead…

"I don't understand?"

She leaned away, palming each side of my face. "I buried you. But you're alive. Oh, Willow." She drew me in for another hard hug. "Oh, God, you're alive."

I pushed her away, my gut sinking to the floor, knowing without knowing. "You buried me?"

I'd never seen such an incredible combination of hysterics and elation as she continued to wail and rejoice. Well, except for that day after the mall shooting when I roused to consciousness for the first time after surgery and saw Hadley sitting at the foot of my bed. I'd assumed she was dead.

I'd assumed wrong.

Beth had assumed I was dead.

She'd assumed wrong.

Which meant…

"Hadley?"

Tears hit my eyes as my knees gave out, sending us both crashing to the floor.

She was gone. They were all gone.

Present day…

I was pacing the polish off the wood floors in my living room as the conversation I'd had with Trent played on a loop in my head.

I'd wanted to tell Caven that I was Willow as soon as he'd led me up to his bedroom. The confession was all but burning on the tip of my tongue, but no matter how hard I'd tried, I couldn't make the words come out—not at the risk of losing her.

I'm Willow, I'd thought over and over, hoping that he could read the truth in my eyes, all the while praying he didn't.

You saved my life at the mall. I'd implored him to hear my silent confession.

But I was such a coward. That was all it would ever be—silence.

There had to be a way to stop this wrecking ball before it destroyed us all.

Trent hadn't said any more about my identity after Caven and I had come outside. I'd waited, expecting him to spill it all at any second. I was ready to lie and deny it with every fiber of my being.

But that hadn't been necessary. Trent had simply sat back, propped his feet up, and sipped a beer as he'd watched his niece fawn all over me.

I'd put on a brave smile as I ate cake with Rosalee sitting on my lap, but as I'd left Caven's house, I'd hugged that little girl extra tight, terrified that it might be the last time I felt her arms wrapped around my neck. Then, on the way home, I'd called Beth in a frenzied panic, giving her the rundown of the latest mountain we were forced to climb. I hadn't been home ten minutes before she came bursting through my front door.

My whole body shook as we made eye contact. There was no denying that I was on the verge of a panic attack—and not the kind a script from my doctor could head off. There was no stopping this runaway train.

"He knows. This is bad. This is so, so bad."

"Relax," she soothed, approaching me with caution as though I were an animal in the wild. "It's not a big deal."

"It's a *huge* deal. He's going to tell Caven that I'm not Hadley. He's going to *tell him*." My voice cracked as the reality of what it'd mean if Trent told Caven crashed over me.

She half shrugged. "What are the chances that Caven would even believe him?"

"I don't know. Trent's his brother. Why wouldn't he believe him? Once he introduces the idea to Caven, that'll be it."

"Be real here." Beth lifted my arms to inspect for bruises. "This asshole cop who doesn't know how to keep his damn hands to himself has no proof. Speculation holds up in court about as well as an eye witness description from a wet dream. He's not dumb. He's not going to spill some crazy conspiracy theory without something to back it up."

I shook free of her hold and raked my hands through my hair. "It's true though. He was totally right, and if he keeps searching—"

"*He can't prove it.*"

"What about my medical records?" I croaked out over the pounding of my heart as it attempted to escape through my ribs. "You said it yourself. They're the only flaw in my plan."

"Yes, but Hadley's appendectomy will explain away your scar. A judge isn't going to order an invasive physical based on hearsay."

I yanked up the side of my shirt. "No one is going to buy this as an appendectomy scar. *No one.*"

"Then I'll make them believe it." Her gaze roamed over my face, her eyes imploring me to believe her. "This is my job, Lo. All we need is reasonable doubt, and we've got that in spades. We've got her journals and details about that night with Caven that no one but Hadley could ever know. I wouldn't have agreed to help you if I didn't know we could handle whatever came up along the way. I'm not worried about one man's hypothesis. You shouldn't be, either." She punctuated each word with a jab of her finger.

I shook my head and resumed my pace. How had this gone from Wednesday and Saturday art classes, birthday dinners where Caven called me his family, and a night of passion and orgasms to being one name away from losing it all?

What a gigantic clusterfuck. It had been from the day I'd decided to become Hadley Banks.

It wasn't hard to become my sister. She'd died in my car, with my purse recovered at the scene of the accident. Her body had been mangled and then burned. Beth had spared me the details, but I knew there were no fingerprints left to be found. All signs had pointed to me. It was why Beth had accepted that I had been in that car for two weeks before flying to Puerto Rico to clean out my house.

Hadley and I had pulled the twin switch numerous times throughout our life, but this was taking it to a new level. However, it was the only chance I had at getting to know little Keira—or Rosalee, as it turned out.

I'd never wanted to hurt Caven. That was always the truth. But I had been too afraid to walk back into his life as Rosalee's *aunt*. If he had slammed the door in my face, there would have been no recourse. I had no rights to her.

But, as her mother, Hadley always would.

Never in a million years had I planned to take her away from him. That wasn't my place. But she was all I had left. All I would *ever* have.

I just wanted to be a part of her life.

I just wanted art classes on Wednesday and Saturday.

I just wanted her to know that she was loved by our family, despite the fact that I was the only one left.

Beth had been the executor of my estate with the understanding that everything would go to Hadley assuming she was mentally sound and sober enough to handle the fortune we'd amassed. Technically, my sister still owned half the business, but after her first stint in rehab, she'd been removed from all the bank accounts. It was her money, and I'd put it in a savings account for her. But she'd been using it for years to fund her habit. I hadn't cared that denying her access to the money made me the bad guy as long as it kept her alive.

In the end, I'd failed.

Everyone.

We were at the mall the day my parents died because of me.

And Hadley was on the road, high and furiously trying to get away from me the day she'd hit that tree.

I vowed not to fail Rosalee.

Though, after listening to Trent accuse me of being the fraud I truly was, I was afraid I already had.

Beth grabbed my hand and guided me to the couch. "Start at the beginning. I want to hear everything Officer Domestic Abuse thinks he knows about you. God, I wish you'd kneed him in the balls."

In hindsight, I wished I had too.

For fifteen minutes, I told her everything. My birthday party. Trent showing up looking just like his father. Being cornered outside. His speculations. My conversation with Caven, then cake, presents, and rushing out of the house.

When I finished, Beth nodded. "I'm only going to say this one more time. Trent Hunt is not a threat. He *thinks* he knows the truth—"

"He doesn't think, Beth. He knows!"

She covered my mouth with her hand. "No. He *thinks*. In order to prove any of this, he'd have to wave his Son-of-Malcom-Lowe flag loud and proud. That is not a risk he can take. Not with his job. Not with his personal life. Not with anything. He and Caven have been trying to keep that shit under wraps for years. If he tells Caven, hell is going to break loose and he knows it. Otherwise, he would have done it today." She dropped her hand and leaned in toward me. "I am telling you one last time: Do not worry about theoretical ramblings from a man who has way bigger skeletons in his own closet. My advice is to steer clear of Trent for, oh, say, forever. And never. *Ever.* Let Caven see your scar."

A flicker of relief washed through me. Maybe she was right. Trent hadn't said anything to Caven. And maybe he wouldn't. Hell, maybe I even passed his little physical assault lie detector test.

But there was something else. I sucked in a deep breath and then told her *everything.*

"I slept with Caven. But I didn't take my shirt off. He never saw my scar, I promise."

She blinked.

Once.

Twice.

Thrice.

She swallowed hard. "Who do you want right now?"

"What?"

"*Who* do you want? Beth Watts, Attorney at Law or your best friend, Beth Watt-a-licious Watts."

It was my turn to blink.

Once.

Twice.

Thrice.

"Which one doesn't involve you yelling at me for sleeping with Caven?"

With a curt nod, she replied, "Watt-a-licious it is. Spill. I want all the dirty little secrets about you losing your virginity to a man who doesn't even know your name."

I shot her a glare. "It wasn't my virginity."

"Sorry to inform you, but Hadley and I voted years ago that ten seconds of *just the tip* when you were seventeen doesn't count."

"It wasn't just the tip."

"Oh, sorry, I forgot it was pencil dick Brad Harris. Just the eraser is more like it."

Another round of blinking later, I curled my lip. "You know what? Give me Attorney Beth. I'm not in the mood for you."

"Not a problem." She shoved off the couch and leaned into my face. "What the hell is wrong with you?"

"I don't know, okay? It just happened. I thought I was texting you, but I was actually texting him. And then he showed up at my door and kissed me. And the next thing I knew, we'd gone through two condoms from the apocalypse." She arched an eyebrow, but I kept going. "He told me he could have handled the woman he'd met at the bar coming back. He was ready for her. But that he wasn't prepared for me. Me, Beth. *Me.* Not Hadley. *Me.*"

"Jesus, Lo," she murmured.

"And it wasn't a one-time thing. He wanted to come over tonight. But then his brother showed up, so now, I don't know when I'll see him again. But today, he kept touching me and holding me and...I felt safe with him. A man who looked just like Malcom Lowe sat across from me, but I was with Caven, so I was *safe*. Do you have any idea how long it's been since I truly felt safe in my own skin?"

She closed her eyes and groaned. "You're making this really hard for me to be Attorney Beth. If he was any other guy, I'd be ecstatic for you. I've always wanted you to be happy. But he's *Caven*."

I knotted my hands in my lap. "You want to hear something crazy?"

"Too late for that. But sure, hit me with something new."

"I think he knows it's me. Deep down. He doesn't realize it. But when he looks at me..." I paused. "He sees *Willow*, Beth. I know he does. And he feels me, that connection between us that can't be broken. He's just confused because he thinks my name is Hadley."

She collapsed beside me on the couch, linking her arm through mine and dropping her head against the cushion to stare up at the ceiling. "So, what if you tell him the truth?"

"I'm sorry, what?"

She turned her head without lifting it. "Tell him the truth."

"Are you insane?"

"Possibly. I'm sitting here, talking to my dead best friend about her daughter who is actually her niece, and listening to her wax poetic about a boy she's been in love with since she

21

was eight years old but he has no idea that he saved her life but she somehow thinks he knows it's her and that's why he came over here and took her virginity. So yeah. I really might be insane."

"Stop saying he took my virginity!" I snapped before groaning. "And there is no way I can tell him the truth now. It's too late. I'm Hadley now. There's no going back."

"Then stop sleeping with him. If you're Hadley, stop making this about *Willow*. Hadley didn't want him. Hadley didn't love him. Hadley *used* him to steal his computer and make her sister hurt."

The hollow ache in my chest intensified. She spoke the truth. Hadley had never cared about Caven. Then again, after the shooting, Hadley hadn't cared about anyone—myself included.

"This hurts," I croaked. "God, why does this hurt?"

"Because love is an impossible game. Especially when only one person knows the rules. We can fight for visitation in court. And we will. One hundred percent to the bitter end. I won't lose her for you. Don't forget how much I loved Hadley too. I'm just as much Rosalee's aunt as you are. But the waters are getting murky now. Clear them up, or we're all going to drown."

"I would drown for them. To have her. *And* him. I'd drown for that."

"It's not going to work that way though. Hadley wouldn't have—"

"She wouldn't have come back." I scrubbed my hands over my face. "But *I* did. And it's killing me because every part of me that's left wants him and that little girl."

"But that's exactly the problem. What if you can't have them both?"

I turned and looked her in the eye, emotion thick in my throat. "But what if I can?"

She gave my side a pointed squeeze. "But what if he sees that scar?"

THREE

CAVEN

My brother was an asshole. And he was the worst kind of asshole. The kind that was *only* an asshole because he was worried about his little brother, so it was almost impossible to really hate him for being an asshole even though he absolutely deserved it.

He'd admitted to cornering Hadley after she'd left. Apparently, they'd exchanged words about her intentions, and I miraculously managed not to put my fist in his mouth as I listened to him talk about it. It was one thing to tell me that he thought she was up to no good. But he knew he'd scared her earlier in the day because he looked like Malcom. Therefore, he knew good and damn well it had not been the right time to interrogate her.

Yet he had. And it pissed me off to no end because it was one more thing I could add to my conscience to feel guilty about. I'd put her in that situation by not rescheduling her damn party. But Rosalee was excited to see her.

And, truth be told, so was I.

By the time dinner time rolled around, I wasn't hungry. I was, on the other hand, about to peel out of my skin if I didn't get away from Trent.

There was only one place I wanted to be.

Me: How ya feeling after today? I'm really sorry about Trent by the way.

Hadley: It's okay. I'm good. I took the night off work and poured a glass of wine.

Me: So you aren't busy right now then?

Hadley: I wouldn't go that far. There is a spot on my ceiling that I'm currently staring at, debating if it's chipped paint that was there when I bought the house or if it's a dead bug.

Me: Oh wow, sorry to interrupt that riveting experience for you, but I have some exciting news.

Hadley: What?

Me: There's a pizza place forty-five minutes across town called The Bistro. It's Trent's favorite, but they won't deliver to my house.

Hadley: That's unfortunate.

Me: Yep. It's going to take me an hour and a half to get there and back and that's assuming I don't hit any traffic. Realistically more like two hours. But you know what I just discovered?

Hadley: That there are at least thirty pizza places closer to your house that will deliver?

Me: Nope. The Bistro delivers to YOUR house. Open the door. I've got nearly two hours to kill before I have to be home.

Her porch light almost immediately came on followed by the click of the deadbolt.

It cracked open an inch and a single gorgeous—and slightly creepy—green eye peeked out. "What are you doing here?"

I grinned, leaning to the side to see what she was wearing. I hoped like hell it was that nearly see-through tank top again. "Waiting for my pizza."

Her lips hitched as she pulled the door open and *bingo!* Different tank top, but it was comprised of even less material than the first, showing not only her hard nipples but also a delicious swell of cleavage.

I shouldn't have come.

But then again, *I shouldn't have* was quickly becoming my life's motto with Hadley. I was past the point of caring.

Tracing my gaze down her body, I gave the door a gentle shove and she allowed it to swing all the way open. *Damn.* Ugly teal pajama pants. *Meh.* You win some, you lose some.

I hadn't been able to stop thinking about her since she'd pulled out of my driveway.

The day had been filled with a myriad of emotions, each one striking me at the bone.

The fear on her face.

The tears in her eyes.

The smile on her mouth as she'd opened Rosalee's present.

The kisses she'd blown to my giggling girl as she'd backed out of my driveway.

I rested my hand on the curve of her hip and dipped to kiss her.

Weaving to the side, she dodged me. "You had your pizza delivered to my place?"

"Don't worry. I got you a stuffed-crust veggie lovers for your troubles." I aimed for her mouth again, murmuring, "But if that is not enough, I have come prepared to offer you the max amount of orgasms you can experience in two hours."

That time, she couldn't escape me. My lips sealed over hers, and as if I'd found the hidden button, her arms came up, wrapping around my neck.

She moaned, backing us both into her house. While our tongues danced, I kicked the door shut and blindly fumbled with the lock. After blindly locking the door, I focused my attention on her round ass.

"Caven, wait."

I opened my eyes and stilled my roaming hands, mumbling against her lips. "For what?"

"I don't know."

"Okay, you think about it for a while, and if you come up with an answer, you let me know." Smiling, I kissed her again.

But it wasn't returned.

I leaned away to get a better read on her face. Body language said she was all in—but her eyes. Fuck. Her eyes told me she was freaked the hell out.

I immediately took a step away. Just enough distance to give her space without having to release her. "Hey, what's going on? Talk to me."

She shifted in closer, plastering her front to mine while saying, "I don't think this is a good idea anymore."

Well, hello there, mixed signals.

"What's not?"

"Me and you."

"What about us?" I wasn't a total dumbass. I knew what she was trying to say, but I wanted her to explain it because it had sure as hell felt like she'd thought it was a fan-fucking-tastic idea the night before.

She put her chin on my pec and stared up at me through her lashes—all innocent and gorgeous. "You're Rosalee's dad."

"I am. And always will be her dad. But unless she snuck into my pocket on my way out of the house, she's not here right *now*."

She. Got. Closer. Her thigh wedged between my legs and her hip pressed against my cock, straining against my zipper. "What if this blows up?"

"Oh, it's going to blow up. Disaster in the making, remember?" I palmed her ass again, rocking her against me. She'd said to wait, but if she could touch me, I assumed it worked the other way around. "I thought we decided what happens when I'm here doesn't involve her."

"We did. But what if we also spent some of our limited time together getting to know each other in non-naked ways so, if and when this does blow up in our faces, we'll know each other and we can say we accomplished something other than tangling the sheets?"

I twisted my lips and squinted one eye. "Non-naked, huh? I don't suppose that means keeping our pants around our ankles while I fuck you against the wall, does it?"

She bit her lip and her face pinked with excitement rather than a blush. "That's…" She shook her head like it pained her to finish the thought. "Not exactly what I meant. Maybe we could just…*talk* tonight?"

She wanted me.

I could feel it like the sun scorching my skin.

But she wasn't wrong about getting to know each other. Hell, I wasn't even sure it was possible to keep my constant need to touch her isolated inside her house. And if anything ever came of there being an *us*—but especially if it *didn't*—getting to know her and feeling comfortable together could possibly help the parts of our life that *did* involve our daughter.

I sighed and released her. It sucked, but not everything I wanted to do to her revolved around being naked. Guiding my hands up her neck, I took either side of her face and brought her mouth to mine. It was deep and hungry, drawing from her throat another moan, and I swallowed it like my favorite elixir.

Finally, when I was done with a thorough, non-naked plundering of her mouth, I performed the herculean task of letting her go. Casually, and ignoring the screaming objections from my cock, I sank onto the tan cushions of her dainty wicker couch and crossed my legs knee to ankle. "So, what are we talking about tonight?"

The way her shoulders sagged was almost comical.

This was what she'd asked for. Clothed conversation.

But her disappointment was suffocating.

I hated it—for her.

But I also loved it—for me. Because it was proof that she was as desperate for me as I was for her.

She walked over to the couch and sat down facing me, one leg curled between us, her shin pressed to my thigh. "If it takes them forty-five minutes to deliver your pizza and you only live fifteen minutes away, we actually only have an hour."

I brushed her hair over her shoulder, allowing my fingertips to sweep down her arms, leaving a trail of goose bumps in my wake. "Yes, but if it took me forty-five minutes to drive home, the pizza would be cold anyway. I show up with piping-hot, fresh-out-of-the-delivery-bag pizza, Trent's going to use his superhuman skills of deduction and know I was here."

She cut her gaze to the door and sniped, "Well, we can't have that."

With a thumb at her chin, I forced her to face me again. "He was a dick today. And I'm sorry I wasn't there. But he and I talked and he's going to keep his own shit to himself from now on. I made it clear that I'm not interested in his opinion on how I run my life."

Her back shot straight, and her eyes flashed wide. "You... *talked*? About...*me*? What did he have to say?"

"Nothing you need to worry about. Trent's all bark. He'll come around."

"I'm not so sure about that. He was pretty pissed today."

"Okay, then let's look at it this way. It doesn't matter if he comes around or not. I can handle Trent." I hooked an arm around her shoulders and pulled her into my side. She came willingly, cuddling in close, resting her head on my shoulder and draping her legs over my thigh. "But I want to make it crystal clear that he's not *your* problem. He's worried, but he doesn't get to take that out on you. Put him out of your mind and leave the rest to me."

She melted into my side, her every muscle relaxing as an audible sigh escaped her lips. It pissed me off at Trent all over again. No wonder she wasn't in the mood for more that night. She'd been alone and strung out all afternoon over the shit he'd said to her.

"Just so you know, there is a good chance I'm going to drop his pizza on the driveway when I get back."

She hummed her approval, draping her arm over my stomach, completing my full-body Hadley wrap. "Let's talk about something else."

"Okay. You want me to come over on Monday and talk to your contractor about why the hell your addition out back isn't finished yet?"

Her head snapped up, an unexpected smile pulling at her lips. "How do you know it's not finished yet?"

"Obviously because I have a drone hovering over your house at all times on the off chance that you decide to walk around your backyard naked."

Her smile grew. "Nah. The one time I tried that, I caught Jerry walking around *his* backyard naked. And let me tell you, an eighty-year-old naked man is not something you can unsee."

"I'll call off the drone immediately."

"Smart man, but I have to say I'm slightly alarmed by your gross invasion of privacy."

I gave her a squeeze. "I've been attempting to stare down your shirt for months while you drew unicorn butts with my daughter. You have no idea the depths of my depravity when it comes to you."

She laughed the way I'd hoped. While Hadley and I had shared quite a few laughs over text messages, this was the first time we'd really been able to talk freely without Rosalee's little ears looming nearby.

This was better. Holding her, cracking jokes while shooting the shit... This could become addicting.

This was Hadley. The most dangerous woman of all. And there I was, sneaking over to her house, volunteering for a crash-and-burn situation. I didn't know what it was about that woman that I found so irresistible. The taste of her both literally and figuratively the night before had been more than enough to have me throwing all caution to the wind to come back for seconds, thirds, and more.

"No. Seriously," she pressed. "How'd you know they haven't finished yet?"

"There's a stack of shingles that hasn't been touched in months in your side yard. What's the holdup?"

She groaned. "I paid them."

"And?"

"And that's the holdup. I made the mistake of paying them in full upfront, and now, they drop by once a week, hammer one nail, then tell me they have to go get supplies and never come back."

My jaw got hard. "First, never pay anyone in full. Half upfront. Half at the end. Second, what day of the week do they stop by to hammer that nail?"

"Usually Mondays. They appear with a whole truck of workers but do nothing. I swear it's like a parade. They all march in at seven a.m. Then they all march out thirty minutes later. It's entirely possible they come over just to have their weekly company meeting. I'm not really sure."

"Okay, then on Monday, I'll be here at seven."

"You don't have to do that. I'm almost to the point of going nuclear on them." She twisted her lips. "Almost. If not this week, definitely sometime in the next seven years."

"Right. Which is why I'm coming over. This contractor thinking he can pull this shit over on you, when he should have finished the damn job months ago, is unacceptable. He shouldn't have taken the money from you upfront, much less billed you for it. I'll be here Monday. He and I will talk and that talk will either end with a refund for shit he hasn't accomplished or a realistic end date I find acceptable for when they'll finish the project. That's supposed to be your studio, right?"

"Yeah," she whispered, her face filled with sweet surprise as she looked up at me.

She had no family. No man in her life. Shit. How long had it been since anyone had actually taken care of this woman? I didn't want to think about it because, in one way or another, all of those factors were my fault.

"Then it's not something you should have to wait on. Is your guest room ventilated properly for you to be painting in there? The fumes can't be good for your body."

That got me more warmth. More adoration. And she added a grin. "It has a window."

"Is your studio going to have a ventilation system?"

She pressed her lips together and nodded.

"Right. Then you know that a window isn't good enough. So I'll be here on Monday to talk to this contractor and get things worked out so you don't have to listen to his bullshit for seven years or however long it would take you to go nuclear on him."

"You're a really sweet guy during non-naked time, Caven Hunt." Her hand drifted up my abs and my chest to my neck, where she curled her fingers around the back of it and pulled me down for a lip touch.

Teasing her waistband, I spoke against her mouth. "I can be sweet during naked time too. Here, let me show you."

She playfully slapped my hand away.

I lifted my hands in surrender. "Okay, okay. I'll stop. But if you truly want to talk, I'm going to need you to crawl out of my lap and back up a few feet, possibly a few states."

Laughing, she pushed to her feet and extended a hand down to me. "I want to show you something."

"Is it your bedroom?"

Her glare made me chuckle. I took her proffered hand and allowed her to pull me to my feet, purposely stumbling into her to steal another lip touch. She laughed against my mouth, forcing me away with some seriously half-assed effort.

"You're terrible."

"The worst," I agreed with her, slinging my arm around her shoulders. Together, we walked down the hall to her make-shift studio.

We'd barely rounded the corner when I stopped dead in my tracks.

I'd seen Hadley's art before. It was hard to miss since the images of trees and tropical flowers hung all over her house. But this… This was unlike anything I'd ever seen before.

On the easel in the middle of the room was the picture of Rosalee I'd given her months earlier. That small pocket-size image had been blown up and cropped so it was just her face, and it was no longer a picture. She'd applied paint over the lines. Thick waves of various shades of red curled over her hair like highlights while her lips were the perfect shade of pink to match her cheeks. My girl's smile was bright and white, and the green of her eyes popped from the canvas, bringing it to life.

Rosalee was gorgeous, but this… This was stunning.

"How much?" I asked as I walked over to it, fighting the urge to trace the curve of my daughter's jaw because I was fear-ful I'd mess it up.

She moved a cup filled with paintbrushes to the table on the other side of the room. "Oh, it's not for sale."

"Bullshit. Everything's for sale."

"Not that one. Though I took some really cute pictures at her awards ceremony. If you're nice, I might be willing to make you an R.K. Banks of one of those."

I didn't need it to be an R.K. Banks original.

And I didn't want one of the others.

I wanted this one.

"Five hundred thousand dollars."

She crossed her arms over her chest, and her lips tipped up in a crooked smile. "It's not for sale, Caven."

"Six hundred."

"Not for sale."

"Eight."

"Not for sale."

"A million dollars. Cash. I'll have it wired to you first thing in the morning."

She laughed and shook her head. "Not. For. Sale."

And then I made her the one offer I knew for certain she would never be able to refuse. "Mondays."

Her smile fell, and her back shot straight. "What?"

"Mondays. You come over. No art. Just hang out. Eat dinner. Paint her nails. Chase her around the backyard. Whatever the hell you want to do. I get that painting and you get Mondays."

She pursed her lips and stared at me. I might not have known her well. But I knew that look. She wasn't considering whether or not to accept my offer; she was trying to figure out how to keep herself from bursting into tears when she did.

Honestly, it was wrong of me to use more time with Rosalee to obtain the painting. Though I'm not too proud to admit that it was a wholly selfish offer. I knew without a shadow of a doubt she was going to accept. Thus earning me the painting *and* more time with her.

I prowled toward her. "Do we have a deal?"

She tilted her head to the side and extended a hand my way. "Shake on it. You get that painting and I get Mondays."

I didn't back away as I took her hand, which made for an awkward shake in the small space between us.

She sucked in a sharp breath and then finally grinned. "Would you like to take it with you tonight, or shall I have it delivered after it's framed?"

"Depends. Is the frame going to be an atrocious tropical color like the ones in your living room?"

She narrowed her eyes. "I'm surprised you noticed. As a side note, I'd like to advise you to never invest in art again."

"Oh, I don't know. I think I got a pretty good deal."

"No, what you got was a painting that I messed up and was using as scrap to practice the technique for the highlights I used in her hair." Pointing to the wall behind her, she finished with, "That was what I wanted to show you."

And I'd be damned. It was the same picture. The same strokes and colors, but everything was better. Rosalee's eyes were brighter, and her vibrant curls blended together in a waterfall of color. Even the crop of the photo was better, slightly off center so her smile was the main focal point.

My mouth fell open and she let out a loud giggle.

"Before you say a word, I tried to warn you about it not being for sale. But you insisted and shook on it and everything. So, now, I have Mondays and you have my practice canvas."

"Hadley," I rumbled, but she kept right on laughing.

"I'll get this boxed up for you."

She didn't make it to the painting before I bent, put a shoulder to her stomach, and lifted her off her feet.

"Caven!"

I started back to the living room. "You know what? I don't think I like getting to know non-naked Hadley."

Her laughter got louder. "But you got a beautiful painting. Truly. All the smears and smudges. It's my best work yet."

I slapped her on her ass. "Liar."

"No, really. The trashmen are going to be devastated when I don't put it at the curb this week."

My smile was unrivaled as I deposited her on the couch, the whole thing creaking as I followed her down, my mouth finding hers before my body did.

She opened her legs, allowing my hips to fall through. Then she let out a sigh that erased whatever anger I'd been pretending to carry.

Truth be told, I still got the better end of our deal.

My painting was gorgeous.

And *I* got her on Mondays.

Fucked up as it was, I'd have happily paid a million dollars for the same outcome.

We made out on that couch until the pizza arrived. Technically, we'd stayed clothed the entire time, but it was far from the get-to-know-you session she'd suggested at the beginning of the night.

By the time I forced myself out her door an hour and a half after I'd arrived, both of our lips were bruised, my face hurt from smiling, and Trent's pizza was stone cold—just like he deserved.

FOUR

WILLOW

Caven: Let's play a game of Would You Rather?

I grinned and put my paintbrush down.

Me: You have my attention.

Caven: Would you rather eat cheesecake or tiramisu?

Me: I'm not sure you understand how this game works. It's supposed to be two difficult choices both with pros and cons.

Caven: Okay. Let me give it another go. Would you rather eat cheesecake in twenty minutes or tiramisu in twenty-one?

Me: Oh wow. That's tough. On one hand, it's tiramisu. On the other, I'd have to wait a whole minute longer to eat it. How will I ever decide?

Caven: What if I tell you I will be accompanying the dessert so you'd have to wait a whole minute without me?

Me: You'll be accompanying the dessert? Why? Are they out of ranch?

Caven: I'm getting both because you suck at this game. Alejandra asked if she could take Rosalee to a movie. So I decided to order dessert and crash whatever you had planned for tonight.

True to his word, bright and early on Monday morning, sexy businessman Caven Hunt had arrived wearing a mouthwatering suit and a grumpy scowl that almost made me feel bad for my crappy contractor. I wasn't sure what happened in my backyard that day. From my vantage point of the upstairs window, peeking through the blinds, I saw Caven standing stoic as ever while the contractor's mouth never stopped moving. Caven said no more than three sentences before turning on a toe and marching to my back door. I opened it. He told me that my studio would be done in ten days, they would be upgrading my flooring and windows free of charge, and he had an inspector that would come by a few times to make sure they weren't rushing through the process. After that, he kissed me on the cheek and informed me that we were having tacos for dinner at his place. Then, just as quickly as he'd arrived, he was gone.

No smiling.

Or lip twitches.

But damn if Businessman Caven Hunt wasn't sexy as hell.

It was now Friday night. And while I'd seen Caven on Monday night for tacos, then again on Wednesday while Rosalee and I played with potato stampers, and I was slated to see him again the next day for Rosalee's art class, the idea of him coming over to spend time with me, *alone*, was more than enough to send me sprinting up the stairs for a shower. But as I ran, I typed out my reply.

Me: Lucky for us both I have no life and I love cheesecake.

Caven: I guess I'll be seeing you in twenty minutes then.

I'd decided to slow things down with Caven after my conversation with Beth in hopes of us developing more than just a physical connection—and also to buy myself time to figure out how in the hell I was ever going to explain away my scar.

It was hard. Excruciating, really. While he'd more than proven that he wanted me physically, I'd been in love with that man for the majority of my life. It didn't matter one bit that I didn't know his favorite color or what he did in his spare time. I knew that he was good, honest, caring, and kind. I knew that he'd risked his life for a little girl. And I knew his world started and ended with his daughter. I didn't need to know anything else.

But I did need to shave my damn legs because, while slowing down meant not stripping his clothes off the second he walked through the door, it thankfully didn't mean he would keep his hands to himself.

Twelve minutes later, I pulled the door open and found him standing on the other side. It was Casual Caven in low-slung jeans and a T-shirt that hugged his broad shoulders and showed off that sexy tattoo.

"What happened to my twenty minutes?" I asked, securing the end of my wet braid with a hair tie.

He grinned and gave me a quick head-to-toe, the wolfish curl of his lips signaling his approval of my sleep shorts and tank top.

"You sounded desperate for me in your text, so I came as fast as I could."

My eyebrows shot up my makeup free face. "Oh, did I now?"

He walked in carrying a paper bag in one hand, trailing his

fingertips across my stomach as he passed. He set the bag on the bar in my kitchen, and removed two white boxes, and two sets of plastic cutlery.

I went straight to my pantry and pulled out a bag of pretzels before dumping them into a bowl.

He eyed me curiously. "What are those for?"

"To dip in the cheesecake."

His eyes did a slow blink. "What is it with you and dipping random food?"

"I think I have lazy taste buds. I don't taste sweets after the first bite unless I mix it with something salty." I lifted a pretzel in the air and scraped off the top of the New York-style cheesecake. Then I popped it into my mouth. He watched in disgust as I chewed with a grin. "Don't look at me like that. Pretzels covered in pretty much anything are widely accepted. It's not like I'm dipping my pizza in birthday cake or anything. Though you should be warned that's another favorite of mine."

"Have you always been like that?"

I shrugged. "As long as I can remember."

His lips twitched as he crowded me in the best possible way. His hand went to my hip. "Ice cream is the only exception, huh?"

"Nope. I use pretzels for that too."

He gave me a squeeze, a shadow fluttering across his face. "You didn't seem to have a problem while we were sharing that carton of Ben and Jerry's back in the day."

Oh, shit.

Oh, fucking shitty shit.

And this was precisely the problem with giving him Willow while pretending to be Hadley.

Hadley had always gagged at my crazy food combinations. She was a simple girl who ate meat and loved ice cream. I had been a vegetarian since I was ten and a salt and sweet mixer since…well, forever.

I picked up my bowl of pretzels, stacked the box with the cheesecake on top, and carried it to the coffee table in front of my couch. "Well, I wasn't about to expose that level of crazy on the first night."

"You were naked and planning to steal my computer. Pretzels and ice cream would have been a drop in the bucket."

My stomach rolled. It was a joke, and I applauded him for his ability to even speak about that night without seeing red. But he was teasing me about the night my sister had gone above and beyond to shatter my heart. It was the reason we had been fighting when she'd sped off in my car, ultimately hitting a tree and losing her life. And it was the reason the last thing I ever said to her as I screamed into her voicemail was, "You were wrong. I will *always* I hate you."

I didn't know if she ever heard that message.

But I'd said it. I'd left those words dangling in the universe just moments before she took her final breath.

Maybe I deserved the slash through the heart he'd caused with his little stroll down memory lane.

I avoided his gaze by retrieving my remote from the drawer and then a blanket hanging on the ladder across the room. "Anyway. You want to watch a movie or something?"

"Shit. Hadley."

God, I'd have given anything to hear Willow roll off his tongue. Just once. But that was the price I had to pay to keep Rosalee.

She was worth it all.

He set the tiramisu on the coffee table and sank beside me on the couch. "You know I was kidding, right?"

I nodded and clicked the button to turn the TV on, desperate for a distraction.

He plucked the remote from my hand and set it on the table. "Look at me."

I swallowed hard.

I was Hadley.

I had a daughter who deserved a mother who loved her.

He wasn't the boy who had saved my life.

He was just Caven. Nothing more.

I plastered on a smile that I hoped looked more genuine than it felt and turned toward him. "What kind of movie are you in the mood for? Action? Suspense? Comedy?"

"I shouldn't have called you crazy," he rushed out, taking my hand in his and intertwining our fingers.

I willed my smile not to falter. "You didn't call me crazy, crazy."

"I did and I'm sorry. You told me you were in a bad place the night we met, and I know how brutal the memories can be sometimes, and finding a way to survive is *never* crazy."

I could have lived the rest of my life in complete and utter happiness if I never heard another apology from Caven Hunt again. "It's okay. You weren't wrong. That night *was* crazy."

"Still." He sighed and sagged against the couch. Lifting his arm, he silently invited me into his side. "I shouldn't have brought it up."

It was an offer I would never refuse. He could call me Hadley every day. But in his arms, I would always feel like Willow.

Tucking my legs up beneath me, I settled into his curve and dragged the blanket on top of us both. "You don't have to censor yourself with me. I know we have a past. It sucks. But it exists. I'm not upset."

"That night sometimes feels like the elephant in the room with us. I thought maybe, if we could make light of it, it wouldn't feel so damn awkward all the time. I still remember so much from that night, but at the same time, it feels like it was a different life."

Because it was—at least for me.

"Elephants were meant to live in the wild. Maybe we should let this one go."

He kissed the top of my head. "I like how easy you make everything sound."

"Good. I like the way you bring me cheesecake."

He laughed, and it finally broke the fog of regret swirling all around us, but as I traced my fingers over the black tattooed feathers on his forearm, an awkward silence settled in its place.

We needed a subject change. Something light. Something innocuous. Something…

"Two of those are for your parents."

My fingers stilled, and my stomach churned. I had no idea what he was talking about, but if the gravel in his voice was any indication, I didn't want to know, either. I'd told him once that time only marched in one direction. But Caven was clearly headed back to the past.

"My mom…" He paused to clear the emotion from his throat. "When I was ten, my mom died of cancer. She knew her time was coming, so she started talking to me and Trent about it a lot. I guess to prepare us. She never used the word 'dying' though. She would say things like soon she was going to get her *angel wings*."

I sucked in a sharp breath, dread rolling in like a thunderstorm as I waited for the part where this sad story from his childhood somehow converged with my parents and his tattoo.

"After the mall, I tried to go on with my life. Trent didn't really understand what I was going through. I pretended a lot. Pushed the guilt to the back of my head. Compartmentalizing." His lips curled in a devastated smile. "It didn't work. When I graduated high school, I went off to college and met Ian. He was the first person to see how bad things really were inside my head. He forced me into a therapist's office, and day after day, for years, he went to war with me. It took a lot time for me to be able to face what Malcom did that day, and to a certain degree, I will always blame myself for what happened at that food court. But forty-eight people gained their angel wings that day. And it seemed like a tragedy to allow guilt to steal a life that had been spared. I got this as a reminder that I have a lot of angels I need to live for."

I physically ached, and tears welled in my eyes as I silently counted each feather, ticking off all the names I'd memorized shortly after the shooting. My therapist had told me that it wasn't healthy to obsess about the victims. But how could I not?

Caven turned his arm over, palm up, as I gently tapped each one, working my way around.

My parents would be last. My father was the first to die in that shooting, but as a girl, when I fell asleep at night reciting that list of victims like most people would count sheep, I'd hoped that somehow, someway, when I got to the end, my parents' names would no longer be there.

They always were.

And it was no different as I got to the last few feathers on Caven's arm.

Robert.

Keira.

I stilled my finger, lingering over the longest feather that ran from wrist to elbow on the blade of his ulna. I'd seen that tattoo countless times over the last few months, but for the first time, I noticed that this particular feather was a deep red instead of black.

"Forty-nine," I whispered, peering up at him in question.

His face warmed as he stared down at me, his blue eyes twinkling with unshed emotion. "That one's for a different kind of angel."

"Your mom?"

He shook his head. "I tried to help this little girl when the shooting first started, but she ended up saving my life. I've always thought of her as my guardian angel of sorts."

My.

Heart.

Stopped.

I couldn't breathe. I couldn't think. My entire body felt like it was shutting down.

Everything except for my head, which was screaming for him to say my name.

But if he said it, I'd be forced to take the final plunge. Dive into the deep. Past the point of no return.

There was no hiding that my supposed sister's name was Willow. When I'd told Beth that I wanted to come back for Rosalee, she'd argued with me tooth and nail, determined to point out every possible angle in which my plan would fail.

She came up with nothing.

But the one thing she'd repeated over and over again as we flew back from Puerto Rico was that if I went to Caven—if I became Hadley Banks—Willow would have to be gone. *Forever.*

And that meant, if the day came and Caven realized Willow Banks was the girl from the mall, I was going to have to sit back and lie to the only man who ever deserved the truth.

At the time, I didn't think it would matter. As far as I knew, Caven had never thought of me again after that day in the mall. I'd spent the better part of my adolescence trying to get in touch with him, but he'd never reached out to me. I'd gambled on coming back thinking he wouldn't even make the connection with my last name. And for months, he hadn't.

But there it was.

A red feather on his arm.

Proof that he remembered me.

Thought about me.

Cared about me.

He thought I was his guardian angel.

A pained chill traveled down my spine.

I had known that this day would come, but I wasn't ready.

I wasn't ready for Willow to be gone forever.

I wasn't ready to lie and watch the man I owed everything mourn for the girl sitting directly in front of him.

If he said her name, I'd have no choice but to tell him. And that couldn't happen. Though I wasn't sure what was going to come out of my mouth if and when I opened it.

My mind told me to stay on track. To focus on Rosalee.

But my heart—it screamed at deafening decibels to confess it all.

I'm Willow.

I'm *Willow.*

I'm *Willow.*

In the end, I said nothing.

"Christ, do I know how to ruin a night or what?" He dragged me on top of his lap, cradling me as tears dripped from my chin. He lifted the bottom of his shirt, bringing it up to wipe my face. "You know, one of these days, we're going to hang out and I'm not going to make you cry."

I wasn't so sure about that.

"Good tears," I lied.

He shot me a side-eye. "Bullshit."

"You have feathers for my parents on your arm," I choked out. But what I really wanted to say was, *You have a feather on your arm for me.*

"I wish I didn't," he confessed with a heartbreaking regret that wasn't even his to own.

"I wish that too."

"You should hate me, ya know," he murmured, nuzzling me with the scruff on his cheek.

"No more than you should hate me."

His forehead crinkled as he screwed his eyes shut. "It's not the same."

Wrapping my hand around his tattoo, I lifted his arm and hugged it against his chest. "What if we let all the elephants go? The whole damn herd. What if we just become two strangers? What if you just fall in love with your daughter's art teacher?"

His eyes flashed open. I hadn't meant to say *love.* We weren't even really dating. But as much as I wanted to take it back, as much as I knew it was an impossibility, we were wishing—and that was my greatest wish of all.

He kissed me. Slow and sad. It was moments like these where he was that teenage boy again, lost in emotion and remorse, bearing the crushing burden of a sociopath he couldn't control.

And I was lost in a little girl's fairytale where they all live happily ever after.

I remained in his arms for over two hours.

Part of that time, we talked.

Part of it, we kissed.

Part of it, we sat there allowing the silence to say more than we ever could.

As I cuddled in close, listening to the staccato of his heart—the very pulse he had risked in order to keep me safe—I came to the realization that I couldn't keep lying to him.

I couldn't tell him his guardian angel was dead.

I couldn't hurt him more than Malcom already had.

But I had no idea how I would ever tell him the truth.

FIVE

CAVEN

"**A**re you allowed to take things out of Hadley's purse?"

"No," Rosalee replied sheepishly, refusing to make eye contact with either of us.

"Go wash your face, brush your teeth, and then get in bed. No TV tonight."

Her head popped up. "That's not fair!"

I waved my hand out to the lipstick handprints smeared on the bathroom wall. "Need I say more."

"Fine," she muttered.

"Don't you *fine* me," I scolded as she marched up the stairs. "And hold onto the rail!"

She snaked a hand out to catch the wooden railing while huffing, "Fiiiiiine."

I wasn't going to make it through the teenage years. No ifs about it.

I looked at Hadley. She had her hand over her mouth, hiding what was no doubt an epic grin.

It had been three weeks since Hadley had scammed me into buying her painting.

And, well, three weeks since I'd scammed Hadley into spending every Monday night with me.

We'd yet to have sex again. She'd made it clear that she

50

wanted to slow things down. I understood—*hated* it, but understood it nonetheless.

We were learning to be friends. Something I never would have dreamed possible only months earlier. But I had to admit: She made it easy.

Well, as easy as it could be when kinda-sorta, not-really falling in love with the mother of your child.

The one your child didn't yet know was her mother.

And the very same one that was probably going to file for at the very least partial custody in two months when our supervised visitation agreement expired.

Yeah. Nothing about that was easy.

However, denial was a hell of a drug.

"What are you laughing at? That was your lipstick she ruined."

She moved her hand. And… Yep. Epic smile. "I can buy new lipstick. The look on your face is priceless."

"The last time she colored on the wall, I had to have the entire hallway repainted because the guy couldn't match the color."

She curled her lip. "It's masking-tape beige. How hard could it be to match that?"

I scowled and that epic smile of hers somehow stretched. I fought the urge to kiss it off her damn face, but with Rosalee awake and upstairs, my lips were required to stay on their own face for a while longer.

We'd been doing our best to keep our…whatever the fuck was happening between us a secret from Rosalee. She'd more than likely still caught the occasional eye-fuck exchange, but without preschool Love Expert Jacob to explain it to her, I felt we were reasonably safe that she wouldn't catch on to the rest of… Shit, maybe I needed Jacob to explain to *me* what was happening.

I was addicted to Hadley and the absolute comfort she provided our family. It was funny how natural it felt having her around. I was trying hard to live by the rules Monday, Wednesday, and Saturday. But the hollowness from knowing she was fifteen minutes and a phone call away on all the other days of the week was starting to wear me down.

If she were any other woman, I wouldn't have been staring at my ceiling every night, my fingers aching to connect with her even if it was only through text.

Sure, I had a daughter, but she had a bedtime of eight.

I could have seen Hadley every night of the week. I could have taken her to nice dinners, bars—whatever people did on dates nowadays.

But she wasn't any other woman.

She was Rosalee's mother.

And I was starting to feel like we needed to let my daughter in on that secret sooner rather than later.

"Welp. I should really get going before you ask me to stay and help you clean," Hadley announced.

"Smartass."

She gathered the scattered remnants of her makeup bag off the floor and tucked them into her purse. "You want me to bring over a Magic Eraser tomorrow? It should save you the trouble of calling the painter again."

I *wanted* her to stay and get naked, though I'd have to settle for a kiss and a few gropes on the front steps—the only place we were sure Rosalee wouldn't catch us—when I walked her out. "Trust me, I own stock in Mr. Clean." I turned the light off and shut the bathroom door. I'd have to clean it before I went to bed, but first… "Come on. I'll walk you out."

I swung the front door open and waited for her to exit first, but she came to an abrupt stop, mumbling, "Oh, goodie."

Peering around her, I saw Ian leaning against the hood of his car. He wasn't headed up the walk or climbing out. He was just sitting there as if he'd been waiting for a while.

I'd yet to tell him about the change in my relationship with Hadley. It wasn't that I was keeping it from him exactly. I was just…keeping it from him in general.

"What are you doing?" I called.

He looked to Hadley then back to me. "Stopped by to talk to you about the Goodman account."

"You know there's this little button next to the door that you can press to let me know you're here, right?"

His disapproving gaze drifted to Hadley as he stated, "I didn't want to *interrupt*."

"Ooookay. That's my cue to leave," she whispered, starting down the steps.

Nope. Ian could be as pissy as he wanted, but no way I was letting him rob me of one of my three weekly opportunities to taste her. Catching her arm, I spun her around, my mouth sealing over hers. As always, her lips were pliable, but this time, her body stiffened. She gripped my bicep for balance, both of us teetering on the top step. But despite Ian's no doubt murderous glare heating her back, she opened her mouth, welcoming me in for an all-too-brief tongue sweep.

She pulled away first, burying her forehead in the curve of my neck. "I think our plan not to tell Ian has been foiled."

"Strong possibility."

"Well then. I'm going to leave you to clean up *two* messes tonight."

"Chicken," I murmured.

When her head popped up, she was wearing that epic smile again. And it hit me just as hard as it always did. Warming me in a way Ian's icy glare could never cool.

"I'll see you Wednesday," she whispered.

I nodded and dipped for another lip touch.

Ducking, she dodged me and laughed as she trotted to her car. "Night, Ian."

His dark gaze tracked her until her taillights disappeared into the distance. Only then did he turn his attention back to me. "We're keeping secrets now?"

I shrugged. "So, funny story. Turns out you were right and I have a thing for Hadley."

He strolled up to the door. "Shocking. I'm especially impressed with how you were so mature and upfront, telling me about it so I didn't have to show up at your house unannounced to find out."

"Don't give me that guilt trip. You know why I didn't tell you."

"Because I would have told you, *again*, that it was a stupid idea?"

I swayed my head from side to side. "More or less."

He followed closely as I walked inside, heading straight for my downstairs office. I didn't work from home much anymore, but when Rosalee had been little, I'd claimed that glorified closet so I wouldn't wake her up while on the phone. Nap time was too precious to take chances.

That space had once been a mudroom, but I'd added a wall and a door. It was just big enough for a desk and two leather chairs, but it was quiet and far enough away from the action that I rarely heard Godzilla knocking down Rosalee's building blocks.

And given that Ian was prepping to give me an earful about Hadley, we needed all the privacy we could get.

"Rosie in bed?" he asked, sinking into one of the chairs.

I walked around the desk and sat down. "She's supposed to be. But I took away her TV time because she smeared lipstick all over the bathroom. So she's probably up there destroying something else."

He chuckled before letting out a resigned sigh. "Good, then you have plenty of time to fill me in on what's going on between you and Hadley. Are you sleeping with her? Trying to sleep with her? Copping feelings? What?"

"Is there an 'all of the above' option on this quiz?"

He pinched the bridge of his nose. "Jesus, Cav. What the hell? This isn't like you."

He was beyond right. This rash and emotionally driven guy was *nothing* like Caven Hunt. I liked women—a fuck of a lot— but I always had my priorities in check. Ever since Rosalee had entered my life, she'd been at the very top of that list. But there was something about Hadley. Something that had me taking risks. Something that didn't date back to our one-night stand but rather to the bond we'd formed over the last few months.

"She makes me feel."

"Feel what? Please tell me what the hell this woman makes you feel that approximately one billion other women on the planet couldn't?"

The corner of my mouth hiked up. "That was the end of my thought. She makes me *feel*. And it's crazy given who she is and her parents and... Well, you know the rest. But I don't know. Having somebody who understands me on this level is like feeling the sun for the very first time."

"Oh, for fuck's sake, Keats. Are you writing poetry over there?"

I barked a laugh. "I'm serious. She's different. I'm not a wolf in sheep's clothing when I'm with her. She's seen the skeletons in my closet, and she gets them because they are the same ones hanging in hers. And I fucking hate that she gets it. But Christ, there is something to be said about not having to fillet myself open to explain every excruciating detail of my past with a woman. I've never gotten serious with anyone because opening myself up and airing out the dumpster fire that is my life seemed like a nightmare...but she already knows."

"You let this one go and I'll personally sit down with the next woman and explain everything about your past. Deal?"

I shook my head. "As very appealing as having a mediator in my relationship sounds, I think I'm going to pass."

He groaned, crossing and uncrossing his legs. "When are you going to tell Rosalee?"

"Tell her what? That I have a thing for Hadley? Because I gotta say, I'm not sure I'm obligated to reveal that information to a *four-year-old*."

He stood up and quickly peeked out the door to make sure the coast was clear. Then he dropped his voice so low that it was almost inaudible. "I'm talking about telling Rosie that Hadley is her *mother*. She's spending a lot of time here these days. Are you even the least bit concerned that she's going to slip and tell her before you have the chance?"

I reached into my desk and pulled out the paper I'd had Hadley sign the first night she'd come over. The one that outlined exactly what she wasn't allowed to discuss with Rosalee including but not limited to the fact that she was her mother. I slid it across to him. "I had her sign that as an insurance policy. She breaks it and you might get your wish because, feelings and understanding notwithstanding, she tells my daughter anything without discussing it with me first, we're going to have problems."

He lifted the paper and scanned over it.

I'd known Ian for a lot of years. He was my best friend and more of a brother to me than Trent in a lot of ways. It was because of that that I sensed the exact moment he went on alert.

He blinked several times before shaking his head as though his mind were an Etch A Sketch he was trying to reset.

I inched forward to the edge of my chair, trying to see the paper in his hand. I'd read that damn thing a dozen times after Doug's assistant had emailed it over. There was nothing on there that would be news to Ian.

"What?"

He looked up at me and I could almost see the gears turning in his head.

When I was ten, the death of my mother had changed my life.

A few years later when I was fifteen, a single bullet had changed my life again.

At twenty-nine, a shrill cry from an abandoned newborn had flipped my life on end.

At thirty-three, in the middle of my daughter's fourth birthday party, Hadley Banks had changed my life once more.

But in that tiny office, with my daughter upstairs and her mother—the woman who was stealing my heart—on her way home, Ian changed it all over again.

"Who the hell is Willow Banks?" He turned the paper around and pointed to the signature line.

Clear as the day is long, it read *Willow Banks.*

Willow.

Willow.

Willow.

My head got light as all the blood drained from my face. There was only one person I'd ever known named Willow.

A terrified little girl.

A terrified little *redheaded* girl who had haunted me for the majority of my life.

I shot to my feet and snatched the paper from his hand. Turning it at different angles, I tried to see the word Hadley in the perfectly formed W-I-L-L-O-W.

It wasn't possible. I'd seen Hadley sign that paper. She had been standing in my kitchen.

"Wasn't Willow the name of the—"

"Shut up," I snapped. "She has nothing to do with this. This has to be some sort of mistake."

I couldn't even think of that kid without feeling like a spike had been driven through my heart. Fighting to stay in the present, I was overcome by an onslaught of memories. The last time I'd seen my Willow, she was being wheeled out on a stretcher with a bullet hole in her abdomen. It didn't matter that I was bleeding to death, barely able to lift my head off the ground—I watched her until I couldn't see her anymore, and then I stared at the door they'd taken her out of her long after she was gone.

I was a wreck, drifting in and out of consciousness, but every time I would rouse, her green eyes were the first thing I saw on the backs of my eyelids.

I'd contemplated reaching out to her over the years. But what would I ever say to her? *Gee, thanks for saving my life, but I'm sorry my father shot you in the stomach?* She'd sworn that she'd forgive me as long as I didn't die. But those were nothing more than the words of a frightened child. If she knew me— the real me—she'd hate me for the rest of her life.

And it made me a coward of the worst kind, but I didn't want her to know that side of me.

Because then she'd know that it was all my fault.

The kindest, most generous thing I could ever do for her was let her forget. Let her move on with the rest of her life.

Even if I never could.

She deserved that.

But that didn't stop me from thinking about her. She would have grown into a woman over the years, and in the back of my mind, every redhead I ever passed was always Willow.

If a redhead was smiling, I'd smile too because she wasn't crying and covered in blood anymore.

If a redhead was walking down the street, I figured that meant she had a life she needed to get to, one that didn't involve pain and fear.

But every so often, my curiosity trumped my conscience and I'd stop a redhead to ask her name.

None of them were ever Willow.

But one of them had been Hadley. Her cascade of deep-red hair had caught my attention the moment I'd walked into the bar that night. I'd held my breath as I'd made my approach. And as she'd told me her name, much to my disappointment and relief, she hadn't been the little girl who haunted my dreams.

Ian stood and walked around to me. "Was there any way Hadley knew about Willow?"

"How the hell would she know that?"

"Well, she knew *something*, because she signed the name Willow Banks to fuck with your head."

"She's not fucking with me. Maybe it's her middle name nor something?" I rasped, my voice not quite working properly. "Get Doug on the phone. Now."

I stared at the paper as he pulled out his phone and called up our attorney.

Willow was not a common name by any stretch of the imagination, but it wasn't impossible that two complete strangers could have shared it. And that was exactly what they were. Strangers.

Who had both been at the mall that day? *Fuck.* There had to be a logical reason for all of this.

"Here." Ian handed me the phone.

"Tell me everything that was in the file about Hadley," I demanded. "What's her middle name?"

"Why? What's going on?" Doug asked.

"What's her fucking name!"

He paused. "Hang on, hang on. Let me get into her file."

Exiting the office in exchange for more room to pace, I listened to his clicks on a keyboard, which were not nearly fast enough to tamp down the panic racing through my veins.

Finally, on an exhale, he only confused me more. "Hadley *Marie* Banks. Now, tell me what the hell is going on?"

"She signed the nondisclosure agreement Willow Banks. Please tell me there's something that I'm missing?"

"Her sister's name is Willow."

My stomach rolled, and as I threw out a hand to brace myself against the wall, Doug's words crashed down over me like a boulder caught in an avalanche. This couldn't be happening, but I had to ask anyway. "Was she at the mall that day?"

Ian let out a loud cuss behind me, but I didn't have the emotional bandwidth to spare him a glance.

"Was she?"

"Who? Hadley?" Doug asked.

"Willow!" I boomed. "Was she at the mall too?"

"Jesus, Caven, what the hell is going on over there? Hold on and let me see if it says anything about her sister." There were several seconds of silence. "News reports mention that they were at the mall as a family that day. Why does this matter? The sister passed away a few months back."

My vision tunneled as that little girl from the mall flashed on the backs of my eyelids. I'd done everything I could to save her that day, and the thought of her being gone now nearly brought me to my knees. The phone fell with a clatter as her voice from all those years earlier played on a loop in my head.

"Let them help you, Caven, and I'll forgive you. I promise. I will."

She was Hadley's sister.

My daughter's aunt.

My guardian angel.

And she was dead.

Ian retrieved the phone from the floor. "Talk to me."

Not including the thundering of my heart, there was silence as Doug filled Ian in on my latest nightmare.

"Shit. Right. Okay. Email me that report. I'll get back with you in a few. Yeah. He's… I'll call you back." Ian ended the call and stepped in front of me. "What are you thinking right now?"

"I don't know. I honestly don't know."

"Did she ever mention this sister to you? Is it possible she knew your connection to Willow the whole time?"

I scrubbed a hand over my face, trying to ignore the gaping hole in my chest for a kid I hadn't seen in over eighteen years. "I don't know."

"Why else would she sign Willow if she didn't know?"

Denial broke inside me. "We don't even know if it's the same Willow. It's completely possible that there was more than one Willow that day. Maybe it wasn't her. Maybe she's still alive. Maybe—"

"Caven, stop."

But I couldn't stop. It couldn't be true. And there was only one person who would know the truth.

"Stay with Rosalee," I barked as I darted toward the front door.

Ian followed, matching me stride for stride. "Where the hell are you going?"

"Hadley will know if it was her or not. I need to know, Ian. I have to know if it was her."

"What makes you think she's going to tell you the truth?"

"Because she will."

"She signed a dead woman's name on a damn contract. I'm doubting she's going to—" He abruptly stopped talking, his footsteps no longer echoing on the wood behind me. "Oh, fuck," he groaned and then repeated, "Oh, fucking fuck."

I was a man on a mission, but there was something in his tone that caused the hairs on the back of my neck to stand on end. I put my chin to my shoulder as I reached the door. "What?"

"Did Doug have *our* lab pull DNA on her, or was it her lab?"

I shot him an incredulous glare. "Of course we had one done."

"They have to be identical, then." He raked a hand through his hair, his gaze flicking around the room at nothing and everything. "Holy shit," he whispered. "Where's the note? The one that was in Rosalee's blanket. Where is it?"

I had no clue what was going on, but it wasn't often Ian got worked up about something.

"In the safe. Why?"

I'd considered lighting that damn note on fire at least a dozen times over the years. But at the time, I'd thought it was all Rosalee had left of her mother. It wasn't mine to burn.

He turned on a toe and hurried back to my office. I was emotionally hanging on the edge of a cliff, but I trusted Ian enough to follow.

He knew the combination and was already cracking the door open when I entered the room. There wasn't much in there—some cash in case of emergency, our passports, Rosalee's birth certificate. But I'd find what he was looking for far more quickly than he would.

Reaching over his shoulder, I pulled the manila folder out.

He snatched it from my hand, peeling the brass clasp back

before sliding it out and carrying it to my desk. He placed it next to the nondisclosure agreement signed as Willow and then stepped away like a fucking detective examining evidence.

One read:

Caven,

I'm sorry. I never meant for this to happen. This is our daughter Keira. I'll love her forever. Take care of her the way I can't.

Written with regret,

Hadley

The other: *Willow Banks.*

Not exactly the best handwriting sample to compare.

But it was enough.

The Ls didn't match. The two in *Willow* were loopy and large. The one in *Hadley* was nothing more than an angled stick. The slope of the letters was different too. Hadley's note was slanted hard to the right and messy to the point that it was almost illegible.

Willow Banks was clean, bubbly, and defined.

But it wasn't fucking *possible*. Instinct told me to argue. Hadley's note had been written within hours of her having a baby and in the middle of a PTSD episode. If there was ever a valid reason to have jagged and unusual handwriting, that would be it.

But what I couldn't figure out is why she had signed Willow's name.

Her sister's name.

Her *twin* sister's name.

Who had been at the mall.

"Tell me you see that," Ian whispered. "Tell me you know that's not the same handwriting."

"This doesn't make sense. None of this fucking makes sense!"

"Think about it. What if she didn't sign the wrong name?" His dark gaze came to mine. "What if she accidentally signed the *right* one?"

"That's impossible. Willow was shot at the mall. She would…" Oh, fuck me. This was not happening. This was *not* happening. My throat closed, oxygen becoming trapped in my lungs like poison.

She would have a scar.

A scar I never saw because the night Hadley and I had sex, she'd refused to take off her shirt.

SIX

WILLOW

The banging on my front door was so loud that I jumped, nearly dropping my laptop. I hadn't been home long, but I'd decided not to paint that night in lieu of editing the photos of Rosalee I'd taken at her awards ceremony. I had big plans to make a painting for Caven using one of the images I'd snapped of the two of them together. It was an adorable picture. She was sitting on his hip, both hands on his cheeks. I'd lucked out and caught one just before she'd squished his face together, making him look like a fish. Though that one was pretty great too and I'd more than likely print it out for Rosalee. She'd get a kick out of it.

After setting my computer aside, I walked to the front door and peeked through the side window. At the sight of him, my lips curled into a huge smile, warmth engulfing my entire body. I loved when he did this. The random showing-up or text messages out of the blue with excuses for why he was going to come over. We both knew the truth was he couldn't stay away from me any more than I could stay away from him.

I ran my fingers through my hair and smoothed my shirt down before opening the door. "Well, hello th—" The words died on my tongue the second his tormented gaze met mine.

His jaw was hard, but his face was a heartbreaking

66

combination of confusion and betrayal. He was holding a piece of paper in his hands, fidgeting with the seam where it had been folded. My stomach dropped, and he silently walked inside.

He didn't kiss me.

He didn't touch me.

He just walked inside and stood in the center of my living room, his eyes locked on me like the points of a thousand daggers.

I shut the door, the anxiety in my chest becoming heavy as I turned to face him. "What's going on?"

"Lift up your shirt," he rumbled.

I laughed awkwardly to hide the pure and utter panic that blasted through me.

He knew.

Oh, God, he knew.

Trent had told him and he was there looking for proof.

I sucked in a shaky breath. "What for?"

He looked at the paper. Then back at me, anger rising to the surface with the tick of his jaw. His voice got louder as he demanded, "Lift up your shirt."

My heart was waging war with my rib cage as I inched deeper into the room, careful to keep my distance. "What's going on, Caven? Everything okay?"

He shook his head, but then he thrust the paper toward me. "Lift up your fucking shirt!" he roared, his pain echoing around the room, slicing me from every direction.

I startled, raising my hands up in defense. He wouldn't hurt me, at least not physically. That wasn't to say he couldn't destroy me. "Look, I don't know what your brother told you. But it's not true."

"My *brother*?" His head jerked to the side as if he'd been slapped. "Trent knew?"

Fuck. I shook my head rapidly. "No. I mean… There's nothing to know."

He swallowed the distance between us in three long strides. "Except for the fact that you have a twin sister named *Willow*. Who was also at the mall that day. Who happens to have the same name as the little girl who saved my life." He thrust the piece of paper in my face. "The same fucking name I watched you sign months ago. Now, stop fucking with my head and lift up your goddamn shirt and tell me what the hell is going on."

My mouth dried. I'd signed my real name. Nobody had told him. There was no speculating like Beth had insisted. No evil brother hell-bent on ruining me.

I'd made a mistake. Plain and simple.

I'd been trying to figure out for weeks how to tell him the truth. But it was an unforgivable confession. One that would cost me everything. There was no way out of this. No magical fix-all. No amount of words in the English language could make this right.

My hands shook.

It was over.

The masquerade.

The dreams of watching Rosalee grow up.

The unexpected benefit of falling in love with the boy—now man—who had once been my hero.

I could continue lying. But he didn't deserve that. He didn't deserve any of this.

Not from Hadley.

Most of all, not from me.

And for that reason alone, with tears welling in my eyes, I finally gave up on having a family. "I didn't save your life, Caven." I lifted the hem of my shirt, revealing the spider web of puckered flesh caused by Malcom Lowe's bullet. "You saved mine."

The paper fell from his hand like a feather caught in the wind. But his knees went straight to the floor.

I slapped a hand over my mouth and fought the overwhelming need to go to him.

But that was no longer my right.

And if I was being honest, it had never been my right.

"Who are you?" he rasped, the words sounding as if they had been filtered through broken glass. "I need you to say it."

I'd often imagined the moment when I finally told him the truth. Though, in those daydreams, it had never felt like a knife through the heart. "I'm Willow."

He peered up at me with the most beautiful and soul-crushing awe. "And who is Rosalee's mother?"

My chin quivered. If there was one thing I could change about the entire situation, that would be it. I would never want to go back in time and erase the incredible little girl who now existed only because my sister had had an ingrained need to break me. But I wished like hell I could answer this question differently. "Her mother was Hadley. My deeply, *deeply* troubled sister."

His eyes scanned my face. Looking for something he'd missed. Some way he should have known I wasn't her.

Or worse—at least for my aching heart—searching for some way he should have recognized that I was the girl he'd once met.

"You couldn't have known," I whispered. "My own grandfather couldn't tell us apart when we were growing up."

Slowly climbing back to his feet, he looked at the door and scrubbed a hand over his jaw. "You gotta help me here. You gotta help me make sense of this. Because I feel like I'm losing my mind. I don't know whether I'm relieved that you're alive or livid that you've been playing me."

"I wasn't playing you. Everything I told you was the truth."

"Except the fact that you aren't her mother! And that you aren't Hadley. You're…" His breathing shuddered. "Oh, fuck, I gotta sit down." He moved to the couch and sank down, putting his elbows to his knees and looking about as comfortable as if he were sitting on a bed of nails.

"Okay," I breathed, wringing my hands to keep from reaching for him. I was a nervous wreck, but on the inside, I was just was so damn happy that he wasn't racing from my house like a man on fire.

He used his thumb and his forefinger to rub his eyes. "Start from the beginning. And how about, for once, you don't fucking lie to me."

"Okay. Okay." I swallowed hard. "Hadley never recovered from the shooting. After the first bullet was fired, she was trampled, her arm was broken, and she hid in a cabinet for hours, all alone, terrified out of her mind. After she heard my story about you, she became obsessed with all things Caven. You were the hero she'd needed."

He tugged at the top of his hair. "Don't call me a hero. Don't you *ever* fucking call me a hero. Do you understand?"

He'd never been more wrong, but arguing with him about

technicalities wasn't going to keep him from leaving. Then again, when this conversation was over, nothing would.

"Sorry," I whispered. "She was alone. I had you and she hated me for it. She talked about you all the time growing up. Any time she wanted to hurt me, she'd tell me that she'd found you or had run into you or…whatever lie she could think up at the time." I shrugged, fighting back tears. "And I, uh…guess, one day, she got sick of threatening me and she followed through on it."

"Why did you care?" he asked, the confusion so genuine that it made me sad.

"Because whether you like the word or not, when I needed a hero, you were there for me. And my eight-year-old heart fell in love with you before you ever said the word *go*."

"Jesus Christ," he cussed.

"Yeah. So. I did lie to you about some things, but the majority of it was the truth. She did steal your computer for Kaleidoscope. Just not to look up pictures of our parents." I walked over to the couch and sat on the other end, tucking into the corner to give him as much space as I possibly could. His eyes tracked me every step of the way. "My father was the first person to die. And when it happened, Hadley was taking a picture of me with my parents. She was looking through the lens of a disposable camera, but she swore it was a woman who fired the gun. The picture even showed a blurry woman in the background, but there was no gun or anything to back up her claim. Honestly, it could have been anyone. The police wouldn't listen to her, and in true Hadley fashion, she became obsessed with figuring out who it was."

His brows drew together. "Malcom worked alone. There was no woman."

"I know. *Everyone* knew. A therapist once said her brain was creating a story of the woman to block what she had really seen. You know…of my dad dying. I saw him fall, but she got a front-row seat. We were very different people before the shooting, but after that, it was like night and day. I struggled a lot for a long time. But Hadley, she was…gone. She had no interest in figuring out how to survive. By the time we hit high school, she'd gotten into drugs and started stealing things. I tried really hard to help her. She was the only family I had left. I would have given up everything to make her better. But there was no saving her. She died in a car accident in November."

The guilt was written all over his face. I swear, blaming himself was Caven's favorite pastime, but at the moment, he had bigger problems than booking his tattoo artist to add another feather of responsibility.

"Then why the hell does everyone think Willow died?" he asked.

And I guessed guilt was one thing Caven and I would always have in common. "Because we got into a big fight because I'd read her journals. She'd described everything about the last few years of her life. Including every excruciating detail of her night with you and then giving birth to Rosalee. I'd never been so hurt in my life, but we were going to fix it. We were going to be a family the way we were supposed to be. She was all I had left. But it was nothing but another one of her games. The second I turned my back, she stole my car and my purse and took off."

I rolled the hem of my shirt between my thumb and my forefinger, desperate for a distraction from the gut-wrenching pain in my stomach. "It was the proverbial straw that broke the camel's back. I was done. Done trying to save her. Done letting her hurt me. Done trying to stop the inevitable. I took her purse, used her ID, and caught a flight back to Puerto Rico. She could keep my car and all the money she could get from my accounts. But I was done with *her*." I swiped a stray tear away. "When the wreck happened, all signs pointed to it being me in the car. Beth didn't even question it. Not surprisingly, nobody could get in touch with Hadley, so Beth buried me. Well…she buried *Willow*. Two weeks later, she found *me* when she came to clean out my house in Puerto Rico."

With my every word spoken, his face filled with another emotion.

Most of them conflicting.

All of them heartbreaking.

"Why pretend to be her? Hadley came back and I was ready to wage war. But you… You're Willow. Do you understand me? You. Were. *My Willow*. But the lies? What the fuck?"

My Willow.

I was his Willow.

Devastation shook me to the core and my lids fluttered closed as I imagined that alternate universe. "I didn't know I was anything to you. When we left that mall, I never heard from you again. I tried to reach out over the years. I wrote letters every night when I'd wake up in a cold sweat. I rode my bike to your old trailer in Watersedge when I thought I was breaking. I even called once when I couldn't breathe anymore."

"What makes you think I could breathe! You were a kid. When I was eighteen, hiding under beds because of fireworks, you were eleven. The best thing I could do for you is let you forget that day in hell."

"People don't forget, Caven. They learn to live with it."

"Nobody fucking lives with this. They live *around* it. They learn to not let it dictate their lives. That's what I wanted for you. It wasn't about if I thought about you. Or if I wanted to reach out. It was about not *reminding* you of all the ways I had ruined your life. I was there the day you saw Trent. You were clinging to the edge of reality with those memories. I didn't want to be something else you had to live *around.*"

My breathing stammered, and I was unable to find oxygen in the pain hanging between us. "That was why I stopped trying to get in touch with you too. If you had moved on, I didn't want to drag you back. I'm not blaming you here, Caven. You did nothing wrong. I'm just trying to explain why I pretended to be Hadley. I can't have kids, at least not biologically speaking. The bullet that went through me—"

He shot to his feet like the same bullet from the past had just gone through him. "Jesus Christ. What the fuck?"

I lifted my hands in surrender and quickly amended that with, "That's not your fault. I'm not in any way putting that on you. It's just Rosalee is the last remaining part of my mother, my father, and my sister that will ever exist. I couldn't chance that you'd shut the door in my face. Willow had no rights to that child. Not as her aunt. But Hadley... She was her mother. So, when she died and then Willow was declared dead, it felt like a sign. I didn't lie to you when I said I wouldn't take her away from you. I would have been happy being her art teacher forever. I never wanted to hurt you. I swear."

He rubbed his chest. "Oh, good, because this feels fucking amazing right now."

I inched toward him but remained seated as he loomed over me. "I'm sorry. I'm so sorry."

"You're sorry," he whispered ominously. "You're sorry about what? That you lied to me? Manipulated me? Made me feel like I was falling in love with you? Was that part of your plan too? Capitalize on whatever you think I felt for Hadley in the past to get your way in the present? Because I have news for you. I felt absolutely nothing for your sister. But *you*... You had me. Hook, line, and sinker. Bravo. Truly. Good job."

My whole body blanched. He was falling in love with me. It was what I'd always wanted to hear from him. But, now, it just felt like a slap in the face.

"Caven, please." Unable to resist any longer, I stood up and reached for him.

He backed away, each step crumbling my heart. "No. Don't touch me. I don't even know who the hell you are."

"I'm me." I patted my chest, my voice breaking with desperation. "I'm Willow. The girl from the mall. The woman who believes you were her hero. I eat brownies with ranch and spill glitter all over your floor. I love your daughter with my whole soul, and I'm more than falling in love with you. I'm *in* love with you. And not because of our past. But because of the man and father you are in the present." Tears were pouring down my face, and I used my shoulder to attempt the futile task of drying them. "After I told you Hadley's truth that night at the diner, the things I'd read in her journals about the darkness that surrounded her the night she had Rosalee? After that, I always gave you Willow. You know me. You know me better than anyone else in the world."

"And I'm supposed to believe you now. It's convenient. Your sister is dead. No one to back you up. Just your word about having a baby in the middle of some epic PTSD episode, making me feel like I somehow caused it."

"You didn't cause it. But it is the truth. And for the record, I didn't do any of those things, but I would have taken responsibility for every single mistake Hadley ever made to be a part of Rosalee's life."

His eyes were hollow as he stared back at me. The emotion was gone. The confusion. The betrayal. He just looked... empty. "You know what? I don't even care about the bullshit you fed me. I can handle it. But I have a daughter. And I trusted you enough to let you into her life, and now, I have to break her heart and tell her you're *gone*." He let out a loud growl. "I'll never forgive you for that." And with that, he turned and marched out the door.

"Caven!" I called, hurrying after him. "Please don't do this. Please. She's all I have left."

He stopped when he reached his SUV, his angry, blue eyes finding me with the burn of a laser.

And then Caven Hunt landed a blow far worse than the bullet that had pierced my stomach. "Then you have *nothing* left."

SEVEN

CAVEN

I cut the engine and watched in the rearview mirror as the garage door slid down behind me.

Everything hurt.

My body.

My heart.

My brain.

Rosalee's mother was dead.

The woman I was falling—oh, fuck the bullshit. The woman I was *in* love with was Willow. The kid who had saved my life. The girl who had forgiven me even when I couldn't forgive myself. Now, she was the woman who had lied to me and dragged my daughter into the middle of it.

I wanted to be pissed. I wanted to be a vortex of rage. I wanted to hate her the same way I'd been able to hate Hadley.

But this fucking hurt.

I'd expected her to follow me when I'd left or, at the very least, blow up my phone with texts of explanation and profuse apology. But her silence spoke the loudest.

Movement from the interior door caught my attention. Ian was standing there, concern etched on his face. But it was my daughter sitting on his hip that got me to climb out of the car.

"Hey," I called, doing my best to sound normal even

though it felt like I was being torn in half on the inside. "Why isn't she in bed?"

Ian half shrugged. "She said she missed her daddy. So I distracted her with a movie."

"What happened to no TV?" I asked her.

Rosalee might as well have had *Busted!* painted across her forehead. "It was Uncle Ian's idea."

"It sure was," he boasted. "And as we all know, you can't punish me."

Rosalee giggled and it nearly stole my breath.

From the day I'd brought her home from the hospital, the longest I'd been away from her was three nights. It was a business trip to LA when she was two and it'd nearly broken me. I'd watched her for hours each night on the camera I'd mounted in the corner of her room while I'd sat alone in my hotel room. Ian had been out painting the town an extremely light shade of red. Meanwhile, I'd been counting down the hours until I could get back to her. It was a tad obsessive; I'd admit it.

It was only three days, but I swear, when I got back, she looked like she was a full inch taller. As far as I knew, she wasn't akin to a giant, so it was probably just my imagination. But when you see someone every single day, you don't notice the subtle changes.

I'd never noticed the individual centimeters of her hair growing from peach fuzz to ringlets.

Or when her chunky baby feet had thinned and elongated.

Nor did I remember when each of her freckles had appeared across her nose.

It had all just happened sometime over the last four years.

I could see that she looked like her mother.

But it wasn't until that moment that I realized just how much she looked like the little girl from the mall—how much she looked like *Willow*.

My chest got tight and I forced a smile around the emotion as I reached out and brushed her cheek with my knuckles. "I love you. You know that, right?"

She grinned. "I know."

"Good. Now, get your booty in bed and let me talk to Uncle Ian for a little while. If for some miraculous reason you're still awake, I'll stop in for a story when he leaves."

Her face lit and it slashed through me like the hottest knife. Jesus, how was I ever going to tell her?

Not just about Hadley the art teacher leaving, but Hadley her mother.

And Willow her aunt.

And how Hadley had died.

And why I'd kicked Willow out of her life.

And… And every other fucked-up piece of the puzzle that had created this clusterfuck of epic proportions.

Ian put her down, and she gave my legs a hug before taking off through the kitchen and up the stairs.

"Jesus, Cav," he breathed, his hand landing on my shoulder. "Come on. Get inside. Tell me everything."

———◆———

After leaving no less than twelve scathing messages on Trent's voicemail trying to figure out exactly what the hell he knew, I told Ian every mind-boggling detail of Hadley…er, Willow's deception. He nodded a lot but otherwise kept his opinions to himself. Part of the reason Ian and I got along so well was because I was the basket case and he was the basket. Though, that night, there would be no preventing the dam from breaking inside me.

My emotions were an ever-swinging pendulum.

The highs were high when I found relief in the entire situation. Willow wasn't Rosalee's mother. She couldn't take my daughter. It was everything I'd feared since I'd seen the woman at Rosalee's birthday party.

The lows on that pendulum were so low that I swear I could feel my body being raked across the gravel. Those were the moments I realized that not only had I lost the first woman to truly make me feel, but I'd also lost Willow, the girl I owed my life.

And then like someone had broken that pendulum and thrown it off the edge of a mountain, I'd had to accept that Rosalee's mother was gone, and in a roundabout way, it was my fault.

However, with the exception of the highs, lows, and all-consuming guilt, the rest of my emotional grid was filled to the brim with anger.

After Ian declared he was spending the night, I went to bed. Well, I went to pace my bedroom, anyway. I'd hung Hadley's—shit, I was never going to get her name right—*Willow's* painting of Rosalee on the wall in my bedroom. I immediately took it down. Considered breaking it because she had made it. Considered not breaking it because it was of my daughter. Hung it back up. Felt like I was going to implode. Took it down again. Considered breaking it again. Then, finally, I hid it behind a row of suits in the back of my closet.

I didn't sleep at all that night. Partly because adrenaline was almost as good of a drug as denial, but predominantly because Ian cracked the door open every few hours to check on me. He didn't come in or try to strike up a conversation; it was more like a drive-by health-and-welfare check. What he thought I was going to do, I had no idea, I didn't even have the balls to break a fucking painting she'd made. But that didn't stop him from making sure I was okay. He was a worrier and I had always provided him with more than enough product to feed his habit.

It was around five in the morning when I finally gave up on sleep and decided to distract myself with coffee, work, and absolutely nothing to do with Hadley—dammit, *Willow*.

I stopped in my tracks when I got downstairs and saw Ian sitting at the dining room table with a stack of spiralbound notebooks in front of him.

"What are you doing? What's all that?" I asked, heading straight for the coffeemaker.

"Hadley's journals."

I froze, my hand hanging in midair as I reached for a mug. "I'm sorry, what?"

"Willow left them at the gate a few hours ago."

I couldn't deny the flicker of disappointment when I realized she'd been there and I'd missed her. I didn't want to see her. I didn't want to be around her. I didn't want to even think about her. Or so I told myself. The tightness in my chest told a different story altogether.

"She looked like shit if it helps at all?"

It didn't.

It made it worse.

"I don't care what she looked like. Did she say anything? Did you talk to her?"

He leaned back in his chair and shot me a side-eye. "Yeah, you sound like a man who doesn't care."

"Fuck you. I'm just curious."

"Okay, then I didn't talk to her. She only stopped long enough to slip the notebooks through the gate with a note that said, *I gave you my truth. This is Hadley's.*"

"Jesus," I breathed.

"Do you want me to tell you what she was wearing, or has your curiosity been quelled and we can move on to the portion of the program where we discuss a mentally ill woman's notebooks and the relief I feel that she can never get anywhere near Rosalee?"

I bypassed the caffeine and headed straight to the table. There had to be at least a dozen notebooks, and as I flipped through the pages, I found them filled back and front with sloppy handwriting, making the pages more black than white. "What the hell are you doing reading these? This is none of your business."

"Somebody had to read them. And I needed to know how much clothes to pack if I was going to temporarily move in as an emotional support dog. After reading this shit, I scheduled my U-Haul for tomorrow." He reached around me and started lining the notebooks down the length of the table. "She was not a stable woman, Caven." He pointed to the first with a blue cover. "This is your notebook. It starts when she was fourteen and carries on until she was around twenty or so. I don't even know what half of this shit says because it's mostly incoherent ramblings. But the gist is she both idolized and hated you."

My stomach wrenched as I picked up the notebook, but just as quickly, Ian plucked it from my hand.

"Nope. She was a selfish kid in a lot of it. Her thoughts were not rational or realistic. You do *not* need to add that to your conscience. Take my word for it." He slid over a stack of at least five notebooks. "From what I can tell, these are mostly about Willow. A lot of stories from when they were kids. Good times. I'm not sure when they were written, but there are subject starters at the top of a lot of the pages, so I'm thinking homework from therapy." He pushed the pile to the back and slid forward an even bigger pile. "These are all dated a year ago, and she talks about being in rehab. They start with the night she tracked you down at the bar in hopes of accessing Kaleidoscope. She had this picture of a woman she wanted to see if she could find a match to. It continues to finding out she was pregnant and debating whether she was going to keep the baby, right up until the night Rosalee was born. You want to know something I found interesting?"

My heart was in my throat. This was too much. All of it. My quota for bombshells had been met for the next century. I had the sudden urge to box those journals up and toss them into the trash bin. Trash—not recycle. Because my pettiness at the moment had no boundaries.

But I knew myself, and they'd just end up in my closet, next to the painting of Rosalee, because as much as I didn't want to think about the Banks twins, one day when Rosalee was at a hundred and five and finally mature enough to handle this level of insanity, she would want those journals. God knew I'd clung to as much of my own mother as I could and I'd had her for ten years. Rosalee hadn't even had her mother for ten minutes.

"No. I don't want to know what you found interesting. I don't care. I don't care what Hadley had to say. I don't care what—"

He suddenly pushed to his feet. "Nothing. I found nothing interesting. Willow told you the truth about pretty much everything."

"Well, ya know. *Except for her name.*"

"Except for that. But the rest of it was all true. She sat in front of you and took responsibility for every off-the-wall, morally wrong, and utterly unforgivable thing her sister had ever done. She let me blame her. She let *you* blame her. And from what I can tell, she was ready to let the law blame her as well."

"Well, it's not too late for that," I snarked.

"Oh, really? You've been having a nervous breakdown all night, but not once have you mentioned calling the cops or even Doug. You got big plans to hit up the FBI tomorrow? I'm sure we could get her on some kind of fraud." He retrieved his phone from his pocket. "Say the word, Cav. I'll call it in myself."

That would have been the right thing to do. She was fucking with people's lives—my daughter's life. But I didn't want Willow in jail.

I wanted this to be one big fucking nightmare.

And I wanted to wake up.

My only response was to clench my teeth.

"Right?" he mumbled. "So, as I was saying, if her attorney hadn't been able to get her off on that theft of property charge and you had pressed the issue of child abandonment, she could have been sentenced to years in prison. Why would someone risk that?"

I didn't want the answer to that question. I wasn't to the

point where I could see any positive in this kind of mind fuck-ery. For all I knew, those notebooks were filled with more lies. Shit, maybe Willow had written them herself. Maybe every single thing that had ever come out of her mouth had been a lie.

Maybe her promise to forgive me while we had been at the mall was her biggest lie of all.

"No," I stated matter-of-factly while collecting all the note-books and stacking them into a pile. "After months of hating Hadley, you do not get to read a fucking diary and decide that she's some kind of martyr."

"Whoa, slow down. First of all, I still hate Hadley. She was exactly the manipulative and dangerous woman I was afraid she was when she came back. The one that I thought was pull-ing the wool over your eyes, playing on your emotions, biding her time, and warming your bed until she could get her tal-ons into your back. But I gotta say: That's not who we got." He leaned toward me. "And all I'm saying is I'm *relieved*. I don't know Willow's next move. I don't know your next move. All I know is that I can sleep at night knowing"—he poked his finger at the notebooks—"she's not *that* woman."

"Who knows? Maybe she's worse."

"And yet hours ago you were waxing poetic about how she floats on rainbows and makes you *feel*. I thought she was just a good con woman, but this makes more sense."

Losing my tempter, I barked, "None of this makes sense! Okay? Nothing in my entire life. Not since the day I was fifteen and found Polaroids buried under the floorboard in my dad's closet."

I watched in horror as confusion crinkled his face. "What the hell are you talking about?"

Okay. So, maybe Ian didn't know *everything* about me.

Shit.

"Nothing," I groaned, turning toward the kitchen, desperate for an escape. This was not a conversation for tonight. This was a conversation for when I was six feet under the ground. "Go home."

"Caven—"

"Go home, Ian. I can handle it from here."

He cussed under his breath, but eventually, he relented and left me alone.

The way Hadley had been at the mall.

And, if I stayed true to my word, the way Willow would be forever.

EIGHT

WILLOW

"What is this?" Beth snapped as she walked into my spare bedroom-slash-studio.

The backyard studio was almost finished thanks to Caven's "chat" with the contractor. But it had been hard to get excited over anything in the week since Caven had stormed out of my house. I set the paint down and checked my phone for the five millionth time.

He hadn't replied to the one text I'd sent him when I'd missed her first art class.

Me: Please tell her I'm sorry and that I love her very much.

I didn't figure that would get relayed to Rosalee, but it was worth a shot.

I missed them. A lot. But I had no tears left and the pain in my chest had become so constant that I didn't feel it anymore.

I'd failed.

Glancing over at Beth, I saw she was holding a cardboard cylinder and guessed, "An empty toilet paper roll?"

"Exactly. Now, do you know where I found it?"

I blinked up at her, not in any mood for a guessing game. "Go away."

"In the trash, Lo. In. The. *Trash*. The Earth is crying right now."

"If the Earth is crying, it's because you've driven over here fifteen times in the last seven days."

She dragged an extra stool over, so close that it was nearly touching mine, and plopped down. "Yes, remind me to bill you for mileage this month."

"Is there a purpose to this visit?"

She grinned. "Depends. How was your day?"

"Well, let's see. I ate granola and raisins for breakfast."

She nodded approvingly. "Good, good. Food is good."

"I cussed out Hadley twice in the mirror."

"More good. Get that anger out."

"Then I cried in the car when I convinced myself it was okay to ride over to his house, but then I wouldn't allow myself to actually leave my driveway."

Her smile fell. "Shit."

"Pretty much." I blew out a ragged sigh. "What about you?"

Her smile returned, but it was nothing more than a pretty hood ornament for the discomfort in her eyes. "I talked to Caven's attorney today."

My heart sank. "Oh, goodie."

Her proximity made more sense when her hand landed on my back for a soothing rub. "He's agreed to add Hadley Banks to Rosalee's birth certificate."

I shot to my feet, a tsunami of hope flooding my veins. "What?"

"Under the condition that *Hadley* waives her parental rights."

And there it was—the bittersweet end. He wasn't going to

turn me into the police for lying about my identity. He wasn't going to make this a media spectacle. He just wanted it over. And despite the way my heart was breaking, I couldn't blame him for that one bit.

My whole body sagged with defeat. "Okay."

It was Beth's turn to shoot to her feet. "Okay? After all of this, you're just going to give up?"

"I'm not giving up. He knows Hadley is gone. So signing this piece of paper means nothing, but the fact that he's willing to add her to the birth certificate means *everything*. It's a compromise. Not exactly the outcome I would have liked. But if it's this or nothing, I'll take honoring my sister every day of the week."

"We don't need his permission to add Hadley to the birth certificate though. We have DNA."

I walked to the bathroom across the hall, and she propped her shoulder against the doorjamb as I washed my hands. "He knows that. He's waving the white flag. I push this, he's going to push back ten times harder. I gave him all of Hadley's journals. One handwriting sample and he'd have all the proof he needed."

Her mouth fell open. "You *what*?"

"I'm done!" I exclaimed, my voice echoing around the bathroom. "I knew when I hatched this plan that it was wrong. It was selfish and careless. I just didn't care what it cost me. I didn't care if I had to take responsibility for Hadley's crimes. I didn't care about anything except for Rosalee. But, now, I've lost her and hurt Caven in the process. I was wrong, Beth. I *am* the villain in the story. I always said I was going to make this right—for Hadley and my family. But the only right in this entire situation is for Rosalee. It's time to make things right *for her.*

"Before I came along, she and Caven were living a blissfully quiet life. She might not have a mom, but peace and safety are a hell of a lot more than Hadley and I ever had. She'll grow up one day. Only"—my voice cracked with emotion as I did the math—"fourteen more years before she can do whatever she wants. With Hadley on her birth certificate, she'll always have a link to me. And if she wants to find me, I'll be there waiting and ready to tell her all about the other side of her. If not..." *Oh my God, why does doing the right thing hurt so fucking bad?* "Well, then, at least I know she's happy."

"Willow, honey. Come on. We can fight this."

"No. No more fighting. Someone has to win here. After everything we've been through, someone deserves to be happy. I want it to be Caven and Rosalee." My chin quivered, but there were no more tears. Resolve settled heavily in my veins. "He's a good man. She's safe with him. What more could I possibly ask for?"

Beth let out a sigh and then pulled me into a hug. "Please tell me you realize that this isn't the end for you. You'll find a man and start a family of your own one day. You can adopt a whole herd of babies. And, until then, you have me. I'm a way better sister than Hadley anyway. She didn't even like wine."

I laughed, but it was sad even to my own ears. Pain in the ass that she was, I missed my sister. I missed my mom. I missed my dad. I missed my grandpa.

And most of all, I missed Caven and Rosalee.

It was over, but as selfish as it made me sound, I didn't regret any of it.

It had been the happiest four months of my entire life.

I had pictures of her.

Memories of her laughter.

Silly art projects to remind me how lucky I'd been.

And, now, I knew what loving a man was supposed to feel like.

I didn't know if I'd ever find that with anyone else. The rational side of me told me I would. The broken shards of my heart weren't clinging to much hope. But I'd had four incredible months with Caven. So what that he'd spent over half of them glaring at me from across his dining room table. That had all been erased the second his lips had touched mine.

It was enough.

It would have to be enough.

"Get me the paperwork. I'll sign whatever he wants me to."

NINE

CAVEN

"Did you know it was Willow?" I rumbled into the phone as I watched Rosalee run through the sprinkler.

It took nine damn days for my brother to finally call me back. And when he did, it wasn't necessarily by choice. I'd called Jenn, sent text messages, and finally tracked him down at work, leaving a message that he had twenty-four hours before I would beat down his door in Pennsylvania.

"Did I have my suspicions that she was a woman named Willow? Yes. But did I think she was the girl you met in the mall named Willow? Hell no." He sighed heavily into the phone. "I spent three years before you went off to college begging you to tell me about what happened inside that food court. All you ever gave me were a bunch of grunts and door slamming. How was I supposed to know?"

"You still could have said something though. You at least knew she wasn't Hadley."

"What did you want me to say? 'Oh, by the way, I'm not sure the woman you're fucking is actually your baby mama'?"

"That would have been a start."

"You were in too deep to see anything but her. I saw the way you looked at her. If I came to you with no hard evidence, you would have told me to fuck off. I see it every day on the job.

You can't make people believe the worst in someone when all they've ever shown them was the best."

I scoffed. "She's shown me plenty of bad."

"No, she didn't. *Hadley* did. The woman who came back was the Crown Princess of Perfection. She didn't push the custody shit with Rosalee. She asked your permission for everything. She made you comfortable, and then she made you happy. Rosalee loved her. You loved seeing Rosalee love her, so you turned into some kind of puppy on a chain. And I'm not going to lie, Caven. I didn't exactly hate seeing you happy, either."

"Bullshit. You hated her."

"Yes. *Her.* Because she was playing you for a fool. So I told *her* my theory. Worst case, I was wrong and she got pissed. What the fuck did I care? Best case? I was right and I saved you from heartache down the road. And I was right. I could see it the minute I brought up her twin sister. But all that aside, I like the idea of you having a woman. You can put your dick wherever you want, but maybe next time, let me give the stamp of approval before you bring her home to meet the kid? Yeah?"

"It's hard to get a stamp of approval when it takes over a week to get in touch with you."

He groaned. "Give it a rest, little brother. I already told you I didn't have any cell phone service while I was camping."

"You were camping for four days."

"Oh, right." He chuckled. "I forgot you talked to Jenn. Yeah. Okay, fine. All the other days, I was trying to avoid this bitchfest."

Yep. That was Trent. My life was in shambles and he was trying to avoid *a bitchfest.* He cared just enough to corner a frightened woman who he thought might be scamming me, but not enough to have a conversation with *me* about it.

"Right," I drawled before shooting a placating smile at Rosalee as she aimed the sprinkler in my direction. Luckily, it was far enough away not to reach the deck, where I was sitting fully clothed and not particularly interested in joining in her water day. "Anyway, she signed the paperwork. It's done."

"I cannot believe you're going to let her walk away scot-free. This has fraud and prison time written all over it."

"Yes. Just what I want to tell Rosalee one day. My dad killed your grandparents, which ruined your mother's life, led to your conception, then her death, and then I had your aunt put in jail for pretending to be someone she isn't because she loves you. No, thank you. My conscience is currently full. Willow can take a number and wait for her spot to come available."

"You didn't do any of that shit though. People make choices, Caven. Willow made hers."

"Kinda like the choice we made not to tell the cops about those pictures after the shooting?"

"Shut your fucking mouth," he hissed. "We did what we had to do after he left us to clean up his mess. You think for one second we'd have the lives we do now if they knew what a sick fuck he was?"

"He killed forty-eight people. I think the general consensus is he was a sick fuck."

Frustration seeped from his voice. "I'm not talking about this shit with you again. He's dead. He got a fucking bullet in the chest. The whole fucking world can sleep better knowing he's gone. The rest of it doesn't matter anymore."

"It might for the families."

"You know what? Fuck you. I'm done having this conversation. Your life is falling apart and you're trying to take it out on me for decisions *we* made eighteen years ago. Go take your bullshit out on Ian. I gotta get back to work."

I clenched my teeth. I wasn't being fair. But with all the shit about the mall and Malcom coming back up recently, I was once again struggling with the decision we'd made not to tell the police about the pictures I'd found that morning after the shooting.

But Trent was right. That maniac was dead.

He ended the call without so much as a goodbye.

As I set my phone down, I attempted a sigh of relief, but there was no solace to be found in any of this.

Hadley…Willow…whoever… That woman had no rights to my daughter. But for all intents and purposes, I'd taken away her last blood relative.

I should have been celebrating, not feeling like an asshole. But then again, guilt was my forte.

I'd taken off over a week from work to stay at home with Rosalee, and each and every day, she'd asked about Hadley. I'd put her off by telling her that Hadley was sick. Christ, I didn't know how I was ever going to explain this to her. Alejandra had been badgering me to tell her the truth, but I didn't have the right words. I wasn't even sure the right words existed.

Our story was too complex. Too traumatic. Too depressing. Too much for me to handle, much less my four-year-old daughter.

But it was the betrayal that I couldn't seem to get over. Given enough time to mull it over, I felt like a part of me understood why Willow had done it. I'd lie, cheat, and steal my way back to Rosalee if someone tried to keep her from me. But I couldn't get over the fact that she'd done it to *me*. A person she claimed to *love*. What a load of bullshit. Lies upon lies upon lies until the truth became an abstract concept. I wasn't sure I would ever get over *that*.

But then I looked at Rosalee. And I remembered the terrified and bleeding little girl who told me that she'd forgive me.

My father had killed her parents and she'd forgiven me.

And there I was, fuming because she wanted to know her niece.

But fuck, she had *not* handled it in the right way.

After hearing what Ian had to say about the journals, I'd been too big of a coward to read all of them.

But I'd read one.

One about Willow.

According to her sister, they had once been best friends. Willow was the smart one. The pretty one. The kind one. The *honest* one. She made friends wherever they went but preferred the quiet of being at home. After the shooting, she diligently went to therapy and tried to drag Hadley with her. In her own words, Hadley referred to herself as the bastard of the family despite being a few minutes older than Willow. She was bitter that Willow had "had it easy" during the shooting. Angry that she'd found "ways to deal with the aftermath of that day at the mall." And resentful that Willow was able to carry on with her life while Hadley was still stuck in that cabinet for years to come.

And all of this was just on paper. I couldn't imagine how often she'd taken her emotions out on Willow. Or how hard it must have been to fight for a survivor who didn't want to survive.

I ached for them.

For both of them.

But most of all, I ached for...

"Daddy?" Rosalee called, trotting toward me.

"Right here, sweet girl."

She snagged her towel off the chair beside me and then held it out to me in a silent order. I wrapped her like a burrito, only her wrinkly little toes sticking out, and then settled her in my lap.

Her bright, green eyes peered up at me as she asked, "Is Hadley coming over today?"

I flinched. With the ink drying on the paperwork, Hadley would never be coming over again. I pretended like that didn't feel like a punch to the gut.

I needed to tell her. I needed to find words and break her heart—quick like a Band-Aid.

But she was four. She shouldn't have to deal with this kind of bullshit. Her only concern should be rainbows and butter-flies and how she was going to afford her llama farm one day.

That wasn't her life though. That wasn't any of our lives.

And it never would be.

I could give it to her easy. Offer her the bare minimum of facts and ease her into the cold, hard truth as she got older. Just my luck, the first of the five Ws was *who*.

"No, baby. She isn't coming over anymore. Not today. Not ever again."

"What?" she shrieked, fighting out of her towel. "Why not? Is she still sick? We should take her some soup. We should take her some of Ale's soup. Hers is better than yours."

Alejandra also had better parenting instincts than I did,

because I now had to explain that *Hadley* had never actually been sick.

"She's not sick." I shifted her in my lap, her wet bottom soaking through the towel to my shorts. Okay. I'd started; now, I just had to keep going.

"Is Hadley dead?"

My back shot straight. "What? No!" *Well, technically, yes. But...* "Why would you ask that?"

"Because Jacob's grandma got sick for a really long time and then she died. He said they planted her in the ground like a seed." Her red brows furrowed. "Is Hadley going to be a flower?"

I made a mental note to bribe Jacob's father to take a job out of the country before once again gathering my nerve. "No. She's *not* dead. As far as I know, she's at her house right now, painting pictures or doing whatever she does. But we still can't see her. I need to explain to you a few things about that and I need you to really listen because it might be hard for you to understand, okay?"

"Sure," she chirped, already wiggling in my lap.

I had about three minutes before she got bored of talking to me. I had to make them count.

Dread pooled in my stomach. Once I told her, there was no going back. No pretending. No ignoring. No figuring out how to build a time machine. Nothing. Once this clusterfuck hit her ears, it couldn't be unsaid.

Even if there was a part of me that would always wish it could be changed.

"The lady who comes to teach you art, her name isn't really Hadley. Her name is Willow and she's your mommy's sister."

A slow smile split her face. "I have a mommy?"

My stomach wrenched. "You had a mommy, yes. Her name was Hadley."

"Hadley is my mommy!" she shrieked.

Technically, the answer was yes, but she wasn't talking about the real Hadley.

"No," I stated firmly. "Her *name* was Hadley, but she died, kind of like Jacob's grandma."

Her smile fell so fast that I could almost hear the crash.

"But I'm sure she loved you and was sad that she didn't get to meet you." I wasn't sure if that was true or not. But it seemed like the right thing to say at the time.

She stared at me, almost emotionless. I hadn't expected her to crumble at this news. For kids, missing something they never had was a hard concept. I had a feeling losing her beloved friend and art teacher was when the emotions were going to come into play.

"So, the thing is, *Willow*, the lady who was teaching you art, she lied to us. And it was a bad lie. So, we can't see her anymore."

I waited for the fallout. Braced for the tears when her mind finally wrapped around my words.

Instead she gasped, full-on soap opera mode. "Hadley knew my mommy?"

"Yes. But remember, her name is actually *Willow*. They were sisters. Twins, actually."

Another gasp. "Twins like Molly and Gabby?"

I nodded.

Gasping wasn't enough that time. She palmed either side of my face, squishing my cheeks together as she often did when she got excited, and then yelled, "My mommy looks like Hadley!"

I pried her hands away. "Rosie, baby, listen for a second. Her name is *Willow*." Why did I have to keep saying her name? It felt like a rusty blade from the past each and every time. But if I was being honest with myself, it was a rusty blade from the present too. I missed her.

Hadley.

Willow.

Whoever the fuck she was.

I missed *her*.

Rosalee hopped off my lap. "Can we go tell Hadley? She's going to be so excited."

Shit. This was going downhill fast. It was time to stop this runaway train. Blunt. And to the point. That's what kids understood. "We can't see Willow anymore. She lied to Daddy about a lot of stuff. I'll get you a new art teacher. I'll—"

"What? Why? You lie all the time. You told me I didn't even have a mommy. Just a daddy. And you told me that you rescued a seal on Rosie Posie Day."

I sat up straighter in my chair. She had a point. "I did do that. I was trying to protect you though. Except for the seal. That was a joke."

"Maybe Hadley was joking."

"She wasn't."

She planted her hands on her hips. "You don't know that."

"Yes. I do."

"You could be wrong. Did you ask her?"

"Sweetie. Rosie. Listen. There are good lies and bad lies. Hadl—*Willow* told bad lies. The kind that are not a joke. The kind that are not funny. The kind that could hurt people. I get that you liked her. I liked her too. But—"

"What kind of lies?"

"Bad ones."

She stomped her foot. "Like *what*?"

I sighed. "It doesn't matter. It's my job to protect you. And—"

"What kind of lies!" This was yelled at exactly one decibel below a dog whistle.

There it was. The confusion. The surprise. The anger. The rage. All the emotions I'd been feeling since I'd found out that the woman I was in love with was...well, not the woman I thought I was in love with. But this time, the hurt was ten times more potent because the emotions were ravaging my baby.

I scooted to the edge of my seat and plucked her off her feet, settling her on my lap again. "She told me she was your mommy. She tricked me so she could spend time with you."

Her eyes lit. "But that's a good lie. Uncle Ian does it all the time to spend time with me. He told you he needed my help at the bank, but we really just went to get ice cream."

"Yes, but Ian was joking, and he's not a stranger. He's Daddy's best friend."

And then she backed me into the corner that I knew existed. The one that had a blinking neon sign over the top of it. The one that had two stools and a craft table. The corner that had absolutely nothing to do with me and the betrayal I felt.

"But Hadley is my mommy's sister. She's not a stranger."

"Rosie."

Big, fat tears rolled from her eyes. "She draws really good. And she's fun. Please let her come back, Daddy. Please."

I didn't have much of a heart left, but it was breaking all the same.

Her bottom lip pouted. "When I lie, you just put me in timeout. Maybe you can put Hadley in timeout and she can come over next time."

I wanted to say yes. I wanted to take it all away from her.

I'd caused this. I'd allowed it to happen. I'd let my defenses down, *assumed* that the cloud of chaos was done with me. I put my trust in a woman and ended up with not one, but two broken hearts—three if you counted Willow's.

God. Willow.

I was pissed. I was hurt. I was bitter.

But every single one of those emotions was mine.

Yes, it was my job to protect Rosalee. But what was this protecting her from? Glitter? Smiles? A piece of her family that was nearly extinct?

Willow had wronged me.

Me.

But she'd never once done anything but the best for Rosalee.

"Please, Daddy," she repeated.

I sucked in a deep breath and looked down at my baby— who was no longer a baby—as tears dripped down her cheeks.

When a man did stupid shit, it could usually be traced back to one of three things: a woman, alcohol, or *his kid*.

As it turned out, this one was two out of the three.

TEN

WILLOW

"I'm coming!" I yelled, walking to my front door as my bell rang for the third time in less than ten seconds.

It was probably Jerry dropping off his recycling again. Apparently, his son had started bringing his recycling to his father's house so he too could use the magical recycling bin. I was all for helping the environment, but this was getting ridiculous.

I ground my teeth when the bell rang again just as I hit the foyer.

I will not cuss out an elderly man.

I will not cuss out an elderly man.

I snatched the door open and my heart came to a screeching halt as I took in Caven standing on the other side, sporting the world's darkest glower.

But the little girl standing at his side was what ripped the breath from my lungs.

"Hadley, guess what?" Rosalee exclaimed. "Your name is Willow and you were my mommy's sister. You look just like her because you were twins! Isn't that cool?"

I sucked in my lips, biting them as I tried and failed to hold the emotion back. Tears sprang to my eyes, and my chest clamped down until I feared that my ribs were going to break.

103

He'd told her.

He'd told her and they were standing on my front porch. Both of them.

And while my whole body ached at the sight of Caven Hunt, I didn't give the first damn that his eyes were boring into me with a contempt that would have made Ian proud.

He'd brought her. Knowing everything. He'd brought her.

"Hey, Rosie," I managed to choke out, dropping into a squat.

She wasted exactly zero seconds before throwing her arms around my neck and squeezing tight.

I was going to die. That was all there was to it. I was going to burst into tears and cry until there was no moisture left in my body and then I was going to die from dehydration.

With her red waves tickling my nose, it was a hell of a way to go.

She leaned away. "Daddy said we can only stay if you aren't busy. Please don't be busy."

Oh, God, they were staying. I slanted my head back to look up at Caven, but he had his hands shoved inside the pockets of a pair of khaki shorts and was blankly staring at the brick exterior of my house.

Every instinct I had told me to dive into his arms, but every instinct I had had been wrong more than once recently.

Instead, I looked back to Rosalee and croaked, "I am actually free every day for the next twenty years."

"What do you have to do in twenty years?"

I shrugged. "Probably get dentures since I didn't go to the dentist for two decades. But it'll be worth it. Come on in."

She did not need a second invitation. I'd barely risen to my full height before she'd squeezed past me.

"Oooo, your house is pretty!"

"Thanks," I called over my shoulder, unable to tear my eyes away from her father.

The hum I felt when I was with Caven was as present as ever, but when his steely gaze finally came to mine, it was my nerves that buzzed the loudest.

"Thank you," I whispered.

"Don't thank me," he said tersely. "I didn't do this for you. It's Wednesday and she wanted to see you. I told her about Hadley. I told her about you lying. But I haven't mentioned anything else about our past together. I'd appreciate it if you would do the same."

I swallowed the lump in my throat. "Of course."

His face remained hard and stoic. It was the angry man from her birthday party who could barely look me in the eye, not the man who'd held me and kissed me and made love to me.

I'd come to terms that that man was gone forever.

But this was agony all the same.

"I gave you Mondays as a part of the deal for the painting," he continued, gruff and to the point. "I'm a businessman. I'll keep my word. Pick another day of the week that suits your schedule and I'll bring her over for you to teach her art. I don't want you at my house. I don't want you texting me. I don't actually want anything to do with you. But she does. And despite your absolutely asinine stunt over the last four months, I love my daughter. So here we are. No need to thank me. No need to even acknowledge that I'm here at all because I assure you I wish like hell that I wasn't."

And with that, he followed his daughter into my house, sliding past me without so much as an *excuse me*.

Half of my heart was singing grand hymns of praise.

The other half was withering into nothingness.

This wasn't about Caven. It wasn't about the way I longed to curl into the safety of his arms. It wasn't about the way I missed his smile or his tender touches.

I'd gotten what I'd wanted: time with Rosalee. And while I was grateful beyond all measure for his generosity, two days a week with Caven sounded like absolute torture.

But, for her, there was nothing I wouldn't endure.

Closing the door, I squared my shoulders, pasted on a halfway-real smile, and said, "At my house, we paint, Rosalee. Fingernails, toenails, pictures, and all."

She let out a loud squeal that immediately transformed that halfway-real smile into something so genuine that I felt it in my bones.

This was enough.

This would always be enough.

"That's me!" Rosie exclaimed as I walked her into my spare bedroom studio—Caven only one step behind us. "Daddy, you used to have that picture in your room."

Used to. I didn't know that my stomach could sink any lower. I'd wondered if he'd kept it. Clearly, he had not, and I had no idea why that hurt as much as it did. I should have been immune to the pain by that point. But not when it came to Caven.

He grinned down at her. "Yep." When his head lifted, the grin was gone and he avoided my gaze by retrieving his phone from his pocket and propping his shoulder against the wall.

Right.

He didn't want to be there. He'd only come for Rosalee.

I walked over to the shelves lined with tubes of paint and

grabbed two pinks, a white, and three purples—the palette of princesses everywhere. "So, what are we painting first?"

"A flower like my mommy."

I froze and, without moving my head, shifted my eyes to Caven. I wasn't sure what she was talking about, but I was even more unsure of what I was allowed to say to her in regard to Hadley.

Caven looked at his daughter, his face so soft and so gentle that I was jealous of its warmth. "When people die, they don't really turn into flowers, baby."

"But they get planted in the ground, right?"

He took a step in her direction and used his large hand to smooth the top of her hair down. "Kinda, but it's called being buried, not planted."

I held my breath as I listened to them discuss Hadley. In some way, it felt strange to talk about her. In other ways, it felt liberating. She wasn't a dirty little secret anymore. Hadley and I had more issues than I could list. But she was my sister. And I missed her.

"Oh! What kind of berry?" She looked at me. "Is she a strawberry? We picked strawberries one time."

God, I loved that kid. I bit my bottom lip to stifle a laugh.

"Buuuuuried, Rosie. Not berry." His gaze finally lifted to mine. Just like the grin, his warmth was gone. "Maybe, instead of painting, Willow could show you pictures of your mommy when she was alive."

My lungs seized, and my eyes flashed wide. I'd never dared to dream of a day where I could break out the old photo album with Rosalee. I had a million stories I wanted to share with her about Hadley. From both before and after the shooting. And thanks to Caven, no matter how much he hated me, I now had the chance.

"I can do that," I breathed. "I have lots of pictures of her."

"Can I see? Can I see?" Rosalee begged.

"Absolutely," I replied, setting the paint down. "I'll be right back."

I rushed from the room, pausing as I passed Caven.

He turned to stone when I wrapped my hand around the feathers on his forearm. His eyes flicked from my hand to my face, his jaw getting harder by the second. He already hated me though, so I had nothing to lose.

I kept my voice low so Rosalee couldn't hear me—and also to keep from revealing the tremble of emotion. "I don't care if you did this for me or not. She looks like my mom. Laughs like my dad. And argues like her mother. For however long you stay tonight, and any night in the future, my family will be alive again. This is truly the greatest gift anyone has ever given me. And I will never stop thanking you for that, regardless if you want me to or not."

I didn't wait for a response. I simply released his arm and walked away.

But I did it with a huge smile on my face for the first time in over a week.

ELEVEN

WILLOW

"What the hell?" Caven rumbled as he finally looked up from his phone. He was precariously perched on the edge of my bed, a far cry from the last time he'd been in that room—when he'd been naked and sprawled out beside me.

For three weeks, Caven had kept his word. He brought Rosalee over to my house every Monday and Thursday—the day I'd picked to spread out her visits, never wanting to go too long with seeing her. He always stayed within arm's reach, sitting at the end of my table as we rolled vases in glitter or hovering in my new studio once it'd been finished as we painted a unicorn mural on the wall.

He didn't look at me or speak to me if he could avoid it. He didn't even crack a smile when Rosalee and I were giggling ourselves sick.

From what I could tell, hate from Caven Hunt only came in one form, because he was right back to treating me like he had the day I'd arrived as a total stranger at his house for Rosalee's first art class.

He didn't trust me. I got it. I deserved that. And as long as he kept bringing her back, I was willing to accept it.

But it was getting worse. His hate for me was growing

instead of fading. It had only been three weeks; I didn't expect him to be my best friend or anything. But he never missed the opportunity to throw out a snide remark even if it was mumbled under his breath. He'd bitten my head off when they'd arrived an hour earlier because I'd prepped slime for our nightly craft. Apparently, they were going to dinner afterward and he didn't want her to get messy. I'd offered to give her one of my T-shirts to cover her clothes, but he leaned in close, his nose nearly brushing mine—and not in a good way even though my nipples reacted all the same—and seethed, "This is a privilege I'm letting you have. Pick another project or we're leaving."

I enjoyed taking his shit about as much as I would have enjoyed a root canal, but I had no leg to stand on. So I'd packed the slime away and instead broke out the photo albums. Not surprisingly, Caven sat on the other side of Rosalee on the couch, busy with his phone and ignoring my existence as I showed her more pictures of Hadley.

Looking at pictures was her favorite thing to do when she came over. And not just pictures of Hadley. She wanted to see pictures of me and my parents too. I thought Caven was going to have a nervous breakdown the day I told her that they were in heaven with her mommy. Of course, he'd been able to mask his emotions from Rosalee, but I'd seen the straining of the muscles at his neck and the sweat beading on his forehead. He'd said nothing though. He'd actually looked me in the eye for a second, making me feel like we were rebuilding a semblance of trust when I'd managed to redirect her interrogation about how my parents had died by showing her an old home video. I regretted it immediately, because the moment my mother appeared on the screen, Caven stood up and stormed outside. It was the one and only time he'd left me alone with her.

I'd started to go after him but that wasn't a demon I could beat back. At least not for him. I would have only made it worse. The memories. The guilt. The pain. While Caven's presence made me feel safe and calmed my ever-brewing anxieties, Willow did *not* do the same for him.

To Caven, I represented the past.

I was Willow, the little girl from the mall.

He was always on edge when he was around me. His jaw hard, his lips tight, and he fidgeted like it was either that or tear out of his own skin. He didn't want my reassurances and not just because he was pissed that I'd lied. He saw me in a different light now, which was almost worse than being Hadley the Terrible in his eyes.

He hated her.

But the sight of me wrecked him.

Which, in turn, wrecked me too.

But just like he'd said the night he'd brought her over, these visits were about Rosalee. And while Caven and I were dancing the world's most awkward tango, young as she might have been, Rosalee was thirsty for knowledge about the Banks family.

She had her favorite pictures of Hadley that she insisted I show her every time she came over. One was a photo that my mother had taken when Hadley had been jumping rope as a kid. Her mouth was so wide that the laughter was almost visible. Rosalee's other favorite was one of me and Hadley together. We were fifteen, and it was April Fool's Day at school, so we'd broken our rule of individuality and dressed exactly the same to confuse people. The irony was not lost on me or Caven. He'd cussed under his breath the day Rosalee had shoved that picture in his face, exclaiming, "Look! They are exactly the same!"

It was that same picture that was about to get me in trouble. Again.

"Can I get a word with you?" Caven flicked his gaze at Rosalee, sitting on a stool in front of my bathroom mirror, then back to me. "In private."

I flashed a pair of wide eyes at her in the bathroom mirror, unplugged the flat iron, and tucked it under the sink before leaving the room. "Uh, yeah. Sure."

We met in the hallway, where he quietly closed my bedroom door.

"What the hell are you doing?"

I pursed my lips to the side. "Her hair and makeup?"

"You said lip gloss and hair?"

I rubbed my chin, pretending to be deep in thought. "Okay, you got me. It was tinted Chapstick."

"I'm talking about her hair, Willow."

He didn't say my name often, but each time, no matter how coarse or how short tempered, it caused a chill down my spine.

"What about her hair?" I asked, genuinely confused.

"It's straight. Why is it straight? Her hair is curly."

"Right. But she asked if I could do her hair like Hadley's and you said yes. So I'm doing her hair like Hadley's. I'm not completely sure where the problem lies?"

"Hadley's hair wasn't straight."

I arched an incredulous eyebrow. "No. But she always wore it that way. Rosalee showed you the picture of us when she asked if I could do her hair."

His jaw ticked as he cut his gaze down the hall. "I didn't inspect the damn picture. Her hair was full of thick waves the night I met her. I just figured—"

Confusion hit me like a Mack truck. "What? That's impossible. She hated when it looked like mine."

He leaned in close. "You want to know something I've learned recently? *Nothing* is impossible when it comes to you and your sister. Stalking me down. Stealing my shit. Fucking me as a distraction. Leaving babies on doorsteps. Screwing with people's heads. Pretending to be someone you are not. The list goes on and on. Don't talk to me about impossibility, Willow. My entire life is currently an impossibility."

Okay. Whoa.

I shouldn't have said it. I was toeing the line. His line. But damn, I was sick of keeping my mouth shut for the sake of not making waves. I wasn't Rosalee's mother, but he was allowing me to be a part of her life. We hadn't talked about long-term. We hadn't actually talked about anything past Mondays and Thursdays. But he was coming to my house twice a week and something had to give.

Snaking a hand out, I grabbed his forearm. "You know what? I was willing to accept all of your hate when you thought I was Hadley. She deserved that. But now that you know I'm Willow, you are not allowed to throw in my face the things *she* did. I couldn't control my sister any more than you could control your father."

His eyes flashed wide, and I knew I'd cut him deep, but it had to be said.

"I am sorry, okay?" I continued. "I can't say that enough. What I did was wrong. But I did it for the right reasons and you will never be able to convince me otherwise. So, if you want to hate me, go for it. Hate me for *me*. Hate me because I remind you of that terrible day. Hate me because—"

He moved fast. His hand went to the back of my neck, his fingers sifting into my hair. I stumbled back and his large body pinned me against the wall. I ignited with need as his head dipped low, his mouth only a breath away.

"The only reason I hate you is because I can't figure out how to fucking hate you at all."

I sucked in a sharp breath, chills exploding over my skin as his words sank in soft as a feather and sharp as a knife igniting a wildfire of hope inside my hollow chest.

He didn't hate me.

I'd cried myself to sleep more times than I could count, missing him and wishing I could fight for the only man I'd ever wanted, but he was always so stoic and angry. Sure, he'd said that he was falling in love with me, but I'd assumed that my deception had made it just as easy for him to fall out of it.

But maybe that was our biggest problem of all.

Assumptions were made based on how a person perceived something.

And never, since day one, had Caven and I perceived things in the same light.

"Caven," I whispered, gripping his hips. "Please. Just talk to me. If you don't hate me, then—"

"I don't *want* to talk to you," he seethed, his mouth inching impossibly closer like a magnet that had met its polar opposite.

His hand came up, cupping my jaw and forcing my head back. I gasped and his gaze immediately dropped to my mouth.

"I want to *hate* you," he hissed. "I want to stop thinking

about you. I want to stop fucking staring at you for two god-damn nights every week." His mouth hovered over mine, not touching. Nothing but an exchange of air as I panted, thick with desire. "I want to forget the way you felt. I want to forget the way *I* felt. I want you not to have lied to me. And I want to stop feeling so fucking guilty because you had to."

My body sagged, and I forced my mouth closed, fearful of what was about to come out. It was going to be some variation of *Caven, I love you* and then a tear-filled plea for him to give us another chance. But I couldn't stand the idea that it was only going to be one more thing to add to his list of what he wanted to forget.

The hope that only seconds earlier had sung in my veins turned into a toxic sludge, poisoning me with every beat of my shattered heart. In a lot of ways, it was easier to accept that Caven and I were over when I thought I was the only one hurting. I'd spent a lifetime in agony; I could handle it. But seeing him there, so close, his anger nothing but a mask to hide the pain—it was a blistering torture I never could have prepared for.

I had no way to fix it. This was my storm. My disaster. All I could do was let him know that I'd be waiting in the rain if he ever changed his mind.

I gave his hips a squeeze. "I'm here, Caven. If you want to call. Text. Come over. Yell at me. Whatever you need. I'm here. But I am begging you. Please, whatever you do, just don't forget how it felt when we were together."

His gaze once again found my mouth, his fingers biting deliciously into my jaw as he held me in place. "Oh, don't worry, Willow. Forgetting you has been an eighteen-year-long process

I've never been able to master. I'll remember you until the day I die. At this rate, it might even be what kills me." With that, he suddenly let me go, opened the door, and walked into my bedroom, calling out, "Rosalee. It's time to leave."

I stood there, my chest heaving as I watched him exit my bedroom with his hand wrapped around his daughter's. It was all I could do to follow them downstairs on shaky legs. He didn't look at me again as I hugged her goodbye.

He didn't even acknowledge me as I waved and called out for them to have a good night.

And four days later when he brought her back, he pretended nothing had happened. Which just meant he went back to pretending he hated me.

TWELVE

WILLOW

"Shit. Sorry," he said as my face collided with his chest. I winced and not because my nose had taken the brunt of the full-body collision, but rather because my already shitty day had taken a turn for the worse.

That morning, a week after Caven had shredded me with the joyous news that he didn't actually hate me, I found myself in need of a mop and a metric shit-ton of bleach. Why a mop and enough bleach to burn the hairs off my nostrils ten times over? Because my incredible finished studio complete with a unicorn mural and every single piece of art work Rosalee had ever made was covered in shit. Literal *shit*.

It was just a regular Friday morning when I'd woken up, still high from my visit with Rosalee the night before and broken from Caven's *Sixth Sense* ghost routine. But it was Friday. People were happy on Fridays. Well, people who didn't work around the clock painting pictures that would never be good enough to sell because their sister who had been a total pain in the ass but the most talented painter in the world had passed away—those people were happy on Fridays anyway.

I, on the other hand, hated Fridays because it kicked off the longest stretch of the week before I could get my Rosalee high and Caven low again. It also sucked because Beth would no doubt try to drag me out to some god-awful happy hour or speed-dating nightmare. And I'd have to make up a ridiculous reason why I couldn't go.

But not that night. Because, that night, I had a valid excuse.

My studio was filled with shit.

At some point overnight, the toilet, shower, and both the sinks in my studio had backed up with enough sewage to fill a swimming pool. Okay, maybe that was an exaggeration. But it was *a lot* nonetheless.

I'd called the plumber out and he'd taken one look at my pipes and laughed.

No, literally—*laughed.*

It seemed my contractor had done just enough to pass inspection, but not enough to keep gallons of sewage from pouring into my house any time it rained.

A small fortune and six hours later, he was able to fix my problem and pump out the inch of vomit-inducing filth that had been pooling on the floor.

Cleaning the aftermath was up to me. I'd called around and found a company that could come first thing the next morning to rip out the majority of my floors, but I needed to get it cleaned as much as possible so it didn't start seeping up the sheetrock.

Hence why I'd been hurrying through the grocery store in search of a mop and my body weight in bleach when I'd run face-first into none other than Ian Villa.

Why hello there, Karma. So good to see you again.

"Shit. Are you okay?" he said, recognition hitting his dark-brown eyes.

"Just dandy," I replied, swiping at my nose to see if it was bleeding. It wasn't. Though, for a moment, I wished it were so I had an excuse to make a break for it. Stepping away, I aimed an awkward smile up at him. "Hi, Ian."

"Hey," he replied, curt but upbeat. Like maybe he was one of those people who got excited about Fridays.

"Sorry about that," I mumbled, starting around him. I didn't know Ian. Not really, anyway. Most of what I knew about him I'd learned when Beth and I had done our research before I'd come back as Hadley. We'd spoken a few times, during most of which he'd glowered and grumbled. He was Caven's best friend, but that hardly obligated me to stand in the grocery store and have a chat. "Have a good weekend."

"Willow, wait. Can we talk for a minute?"

I stilled, my eyelids fluttering shut as I internally groaned. No. The answer was no. We had nothing to talk about. Nothing left to say. No apologies left to issue. I was a horrible person. I got it. I didn't need another reminder.

So I craned my head back, opened my mouth, and chirped, "Sure, what's up?" *Damn my manners to hell!*

Much to my surprise, he smiled down at me. I'd seen a lot of frowns from that man, so the smile took me off guard. And it should be noted that it was a gorgeous smile. The kind Beth would lose her mind over, but since he was holding a basket with nothing but a box of condoms inside, I figured some other woman would be losing her mind over it later that night.

"He's confused," he stated, thus making *me* confused.

"Huh?"

"Caven. He's confused. He misses Hadley. Well, he misses *you* when you were Hadley. Now, he has these different versions of you. Willow the little girl. Willow the woman who lied to him. Willow the sister of his daughter's mother. And he can't figure out what compartment to put *you* in in his head."

I blinked at him. "What are you talking about? All of those people are me."

"Right. But Caven doesn't live his life that way. Ever since..." He glanced around the cleaning aisle then lowered his voice. "Ever since *that day*, he lives his life in neat little mental boxes. He has one for work. One for Rosalee. One for me. One for Trent. One for the mall. And every box has its place. Because inside those boxes in his head, he doesn't just get to decide what goes in them. He decides what stays *out*."

He popped his eyebrows pointedly. "But *you* were different. I didn't understand it while it was happening, but when you were Hadley, Caven started this one big box for you in his head. You were Rosalee's mom, the one thing he'd always wished he had growing up. And you knew about his past, so whether he wanted that to be in your box or not, it didn't matter. And then there was just *you*. The beautiful woman who made the Tin Man *feel*." He grinned. "Now those people all live in different compartments. He's mad at the woman who lied to him. He misses the woman he was falling in love with. And he is damn near paralyzed by guilt when he's around the girl from the mall." He shrugged. "He's confused."

I shifted my eyes from side to side, waiting for the music from *The Twilight Zone* to start playing. "I'm sorry. Don't you hate me?"

He laughed. "No. I hated your sister. I hated her for getting pregnant and never telling him. I hated her for dropping the baby off on his doorstep. And I hated her for never looking back after she abandoned the most incredible child I have ever met."

I opened my mouth, but he lifted his hand.

"I read the journals. I know she had her reasons. But I've seen Caven with Rosalee, so I know there is a difference between struggling and giving up. Several times since she was born, Caven has needed help, but you would have to pry that child from his lifeless arms before he'd ever let her go."

My chest got tight. He definitely had a point there. Hadley had had her problems, but she'd absolutely given up on her daughter. She hadn't spent the four years after Rosalee was born lost in the past, unable to see through the fear. She'd laughed. She'd painted beautiful pictures. She'd had boyfriends. She'd gone to rehab. She'd relapsed. She'd been obsessed with the nonexistent woman from the mall. She'd traveled to and from Puerto Rico to visit me. She'd lived a full life, all while her child had been out there living one without her.

His hand came down on my shoulder. "You didn't do those things, Willow. You could have come back like a raging tornado, fighting for custody, dragging Caven through the mud, and using every resource you had to take Rosalee. But you didn't. You tiptoed in and made paper flowers at his dining room table. I don't like the lies you told, but I don't have any reason to *hate* you, either."

I bit my bottom lip. Damn, why did that feel so good? "Thank you. That means a lot."

"He doesn't hate you, either, ya know."

"Yeah. He's mentioned that. But then, shortly after, he said he wanted to forget me, so I'm not holding out hope that things between us are going to change any time soon."

He shrugged. "With fifteen years of experience dealing with Caven Hunt, I can tell you that you need to pick a box.

Your name is Willow, but you're still the Hadley that came back. Make him remember that. He's confused." He smiled again, his hand leaving my shoulder to tuck inside the pocket of his slacks, and he lowered his voice to a whisper. "Un-confuse him."

"How?" I begged. "Just tell me how?"

"Now, that I don't know. I've personally never tried to make him fall in love with me." He winked and dipped his chin. "Have a good weekend, Willow."

"You too," I managed to croak as I watched him walk away.

He'd said a lot of words. Most of which I understood, but the concept of un-confusing Caven after all the hell I'd put him through seemed impossible.

But maybe he'd said it best…

Our entire lives were one impossibility after another.

I could make him remember that I was still the same woman who eye-fucked him from across the room, curled into his lap every chance I got, and laughed with him over cheese-cake. I could fit into whatever box he wanted me to as long as it got me him.

Things might have changed, but I was still me.

Only, as I walked out of the store that day with renewed hope infusing me, I realized that I'd never truly be me while the world still thought I was Hadley Banks.

I'd just loaded the final gallon of bleach in to my trunk when a man's hand collided with my throat and shoved me into the back of my car. The mop jabbed me in the side as I crashed down, but I couldn't even scream around his hold on me.

"You fucking cunt," he rumbled. "What did you tell him?" Panic consumed me, but from his blond goatee to his buzz cut, he didn't trigger the first memory for me.

"Let me…go," I grunted, clawing at his wrist.

He gave me a hard shove, my head banging against the tire well on the inside, but he finally released me.

I gasped for oxygen. "I don't know what you're talking about."

He laughed without humor. "After everything I did for you. This is the way you fuck me over? Well, guess what, Hadley? I can fuck you ten times harder."

Hadley.

Of course.

He loomed over me as I balanced half in and half out of my small trunk area.

"Where is it?" he growled. "Where the fuck is it?"

My pulse thundered in my ears as I shook my head. "I don't know. I'm not Hadley. I'm—"

"Swear to God, woman. Don't try this bullshit with me. Your fucking sister is dead. I checked. You can only pretend to be Willow so many times before your act gets stale. I let you drag me into this, but I'm not letting you hang my ass out to dry." He picked my purse up and dug through my wallet to remove my ID. "Yeah right, you're not fucking Hadley."

I let out a scream, lifting my hands in defense as he reared back and threw my purse at me. It hit me square in the face, the buckle on the front clocking me on the cheek.

"Hey!" a man yelled. "Get away from her."

My attacker looked up and quickly started to shuffle away as he shoved my ID into his pocket. "I'll swing by your place on Sunday, and I swear to God, if you don't have that fucking flash drive, it's your head that's going to roll, not mine." His feet beat the pavement as he took off at a dead sprint.

Almost immediately, another man appeared. But this one I recognized. As soon as I saw Ian, whatever strength I was holding on to crumbled.

"Oh, God," I croaked.

He helped me to my feet and pulled me straight into a tight embrace. "Shhh, it's okay. Just relax. He's gone." His hand glided up and down my back. "Do you know who that was?"

I shook my head and swallowed hard, doing my best to keep the tremble out of my voice. "He…he thought I was Hadley. I think she stole something from him. I don't know."

"All right. Okay," he mumbled, and I was vaguely aware of him pulling his phone out. "Just breathe. I've got you. It's all good."

THIRTEEN

CAVEN

"She's fine. She's fine. She's fine," I chanted to myself as I white-knuckled my steering wheel.

I'd just gotten home from the office when Ian had called to tell me that a man had mistaken Willow for Hadley and assaulted her outside the grocery store. He'd assured me that she was fine, but she was Willow. *Fine* was not fucking good enough. Leaving Rosalee with Alejandra, I'd darted out of the house, and the worst-case scenario played in my mind as I'd all but peeled out of my driveway.

Because Ian knew me so well, I received a text a few minutes into my drive, warning me that an ambulance had arrived, but it was only a precautionary measure. In all caps, he repeated that Willow was fine.

It was crazy how a mind worked sometimes. I was ready for the ambulance, had mentally prepped for it the entire fifteen minutes it took me to arrive. However, the second it came into my view, a savage anxiety slashed through me. With nausea rolling in my stomach, I frantically searched the area for any sign of her red hair. It wasn't until I caught sight of her sitting in the back of her Prius with the hatch open, shading her from the sun, that my pulse slowed a fraction.

She was okay.

But as I took in the fact that she had an icepack pressed against her face, I was not.

My car was barely in park before I was out the door, storming her way. The thunder of my steps caught her attention and her head slowly turned my way. The surprise that hit her face might as well have been a sledgehammer to my gut. Things were bad with us at the moment, but what the hell? Had she really not thought I'd come when I found out some idiot had attacked her in the parking lot?

Or maybe she'd hoped I wouldn't.

"Nooooo," she moaned, swinging a glare at Ian. "What did you do? I don't want to be in this box, Ian. I don't want to be in this box."

He shrugged. "A man puts his hands on you and I'm there to see it? I'd end up in a *pine box* if I didn't tell him about it."

I had no fucking clue what the two of them were talking about. Nor did I care. My only concern was making sure she was truly okay and my swirling mind wouldn't still until I did a full inventory of her injuries. I rested a hand on her thigh, the other going to her hand holding the icepack as I squatted in front of her.

My throat was gravel as I ordered, "Let me see."

She sighed. "I'm fine, Caven. Really."

"Fantastic. Then let me see."

She stared at me, her chin quivering and her green eyes sparkling with unshed tears. "Please don't. I don't want to be in this box."

"What are you talking about? What box?"

She glanced over at the cops, who were congregating behind a cruiser, then whispered, "The one in your head where

I'm the girl at the mall who you have to rush in and save all the time."

"Babe, I have no idea what you are talking about right now. But I really need to see what's going on beneath that ice because the shit in my head, seeing you surrounded by police and paramedics again, it's not pretty. Okay?"

Her face got soft. "God, I'm sorry. I didn't think about that."

As she moved her hand, revealing nothing but a quarter-size bruise on the apple of her cheek, I physically swayed with the movement of my world tipping back on its axis. All the garbage from the past crashed into place, hidden in the recesses of my mind where it belonged, but it left the most beautiful woman sitting in front of me. Despite everything that had happened between us over the last month, I didn't think twice about kissing her forehead, allowing my lips to linger as my anxiety ebbed, leaving me lighter than I had been in weeks.

Nothing like an overdose of fear and adrenaline to put life into perspective.

"Caven," she whispered, covering my hand at her thigh. "I'm okay. Really."

And she was.

This time.

Using her wrist, I guided her hand with the ice back to her cheek and rose to my full height. "I'll be right back, okay? Shout if you need anything."

She nodded, and I felt her gaze track me as I walked to the front of her car with Ian on my heels.

Careful to keep my voice low, I rumbled, "What the hell happened here?"

His jaw got tight. "Some douchebag Hadley stole a flash drive from wants it back. Snatched her ID, roughed her up, then took off when he saw me."

"He took her ID?"

"Gave her two days to find the flash drive. My guess is he plans to pick it up in person."

Molten lava hit my bloodstream. "Fucking Hadley."

"Basically." He moved in close. "Look, we have to figure out this shit with her identity. After this crap, it's not safe for her to be walking around as Hadley Banks. Who the hell knows who else that woman could have pissed off. She's been dead for over eight months and this guy is just now coming back for something she took? For all we know, it's going to be a never-ending parade of idiots wanting their shit back."

A heavy weight settled in my stomach as I looked at her back through the windshield. "She told the cops she was Hadley, didn't she?"

"Legally, that's who she is now. The cops are pulling security footage of the attack, but Willow doesn't know who he was and he took off on foot. I'm not holding out a lot of hope they are going to catch this guy. At least not in the next forty-eight hours. She can stay with me for a couple nights, but—"

My head snapped back to him. "The fuck she can. You've lost your damn mind if you think I'm letting her go home with you."

The side of his mouth hitched. "Wow. Do I sense some jealousy there?"

"It's not jealousy, you ass. The woman has just suffered a traumatic event. It would be cruel to let you bore her into a coma."

His smile flashed full blown. "What are you going to tell Rosie about her staying the night?"

"You think she's going to ask any questions when I tell her Willow's coming for a sleepover? We'll all be lucky if we escape with our eardrums intact. Besides, it's not Rosalee I'm worried about convincing."

As though she'd heard our conversation, she turned and looked at me through the car. Her gaze hit me like a tangible weight, but it was the anxiety carved in her face and the cop standing beside her that got my feet moving in her direction.

"What's going on, officer?" I extended a hand his way. "I'm Caven Hunt. A friend of Ms. Banks."

He shook my hand but looked at Willow. "We don't have a lot to go on here. We've put his description out to the city and all the surrounding counties. I'm going to be real honest with you here. The fact that he didn't take anything other than your driver's license is what I find the most worrisome. We can increase patrol through your neighborhood in case this guy decides to pay you a visit, but I'd highly advise that you don't go home for a few days while we try to figure this out. Do you have somewhere safe that you can go for a few nights?"

I slid my hand under the back of her hair and curled my fingers around her neck. "She can stay with me."

"Caven, no. You don't have to do that. I can stay with Beth."

I gave her neck a squeeze. "You could. But remember what I said about you being surrounded by paramedics and police. I'd feel a lot better if you were under my roof with my security system tonight."

She bit her bottom lip and looked to Ian.

Ian. Like he was suddenly her keeper and not mine.

He winked and tipped his head toward me. "I don't think this is the box you think it is."

What the fucking hell were these boxes they kept talking about? And when had they become winky, she-can-stay-at-my-place friends? What the hell was he even doing at the grocery store with her that day?

I swung a scowl between the two of them, but it was erased when Willow lifted her gaze to mine and asked, "Can we grab some things from my place first?"

It should have been relief that swelled in my chest.

Relief that she wasn't going to argue.

Relief that I might actually be able to sleep that night without having a nervous breakdown.

And relief that I wasn't going to have to kidnap her and hold her hostage at my house for a few days.

But fuck me, all I felt was excitement that I'd get to spend more time with her. I hated the reason, but while having her in my house for a few days sounded like torture to one side of my brain, it also felt like a winning lottery ticket to the other.

"Yeah, babe. We'll swing by your place."

The cop nodded. "I'll have a cruiser follow you. Just in case."

We waited twenty minutes for the police to finish up with the paperwork. Willow alternated between hanging her head and forcing a smile for anyone she caught looking her way.

She was shit for an actress though. She wasn't going to make it much longer without breaking down. And damn if I didn't want to get her the hell out of that parking lot so she could have that moment in private.

Well, private with me.

When it was all wrapped up, at least temporarily, Ian offered to drop Willow's car off at my house and catch a cab back to get his own. She didn't argue or offer anything more than a resigned, "Thanks, Ian."

In a true show of maturity, I only contemplated breaking his fingers for a second as he pulled her in for a side hug and whispered something into her ear. She smiled up at him, sad and wholly broken, then gave him one of her signature forearm squeezes that were usually reserved for me. Okay, so I'd lied. I'd contemplated breaking his fingers for *two* seconds. But I didn't follow through and that's all that counts.

The police had bagged her purse as evidence, so when she climbed into the passenger seat of my SUV, she did it with nothing but her phone, a small makeup bag, and an empty expression.

"You okay?" I asked as I pulled out of the parking lot with a police car on my tail.

"I'm gonna need to get back to you on that."

I grinned. "You need to dry-heave?"

"Ummm…" She dropped her head back against the headrest. "That has yet to be determined. But have no fear—I promise I won't do it in your car."

I chuckled, thankful that she at least still had a sense of humor, one that I'd missed greatly over the last month.

"My studio is filled with shit," she told the windshield.

"What?"

"Yeah. My contractor sucks and sewage backed up into my studio this morning. I had a plumber come out and fix it, but it's still a mess. And it's going to smell like shit forever because Hadley was a klepto who couldn't keep her damn hands off people's stuff. Now, I have to go to your house and I won't even have a chance to clean it, which means I'm going to have to tear out the entire mural of unicorns Rosalee helped me make. I don't believe in ghosts, Caven, but I think there is a very real possibility Hadley has come back from beyond the grave just to screw with me."

"Okay," I said calmly.

She turned to look at me. "None of that's okay, Caven."

"Yeah, it is. *All* of that's okay. Because right now, you're sitting in my car a little banged up, a little shaken, but you're safe. And we're going to get your stuff and head back to my place. Rosalee is going to summon all the dogs in the neighborhood with her scream when she finds out you're spending the night. I'm gonna order dinner from somewhere that has brownies and ranch, and we're going to sit on the couch and not talk about Hadley or the mall or anything else for one goddamn night, because tonight, we are living in the seconds. And in this second, Willow, *you* are okay. We can fix the rest of it."

As I rolled to a stop at a traffic light, I propped my hand on the center console and turned to face her, daring her to argue.

She stared back at me, her eyes filling with tears.

A million words hung in the air between us.

Apologies.

Accusation.

Blame.

Guilt.

Love.

But all of that could wait for another second.

Because right then, for the first time in over a month, I had hope that maybe we really could fix the rest.

"Okay," she whispered, sliding her hand across the console and inching under my index finger so just the tip rested on the top of hers. "But I want carrot cake and french fries."

I tapped the top of her finger. "Then tonight, while you eat carrot cake and french fries, I will be the one dry-heaving."

She smiled with quivering lips. "Who said anything about dry-heaving?"

FOURTEEN

WILLOW

"**D**addy says you have to hold the rail when you go down the stairs," Rosalee said so close to my face that her eyeball was all I could see. She leaned to the side to get a better view of my bruise. It had to have been at least her tenth inspection of the night.

"And clearly he's right."

I hadn't been sure what to say to her when we'd arrived and she'd asked me what had happened to my face. The last thing I wanted was for Caven to see me lie again. But the kid was four. She didn't need to know that some guy had attacked me in a parking lot. Or that he was looking for her mother. And she definitely didn't need to know that there was a very real chance that he was going to come looking for me again. Thankfully, Caven had jumped in with an elaborate story about shoestrings and tripping down the stairs. It ended with a moral and everything. Seriously, his dad level was epic.

"Did you get to pick purple?" she asked.

"No. That's just what color bruises are. Black, blue, purple, and sometimes green."

"No pink?" she whispered, thoroughly offended as she lifted her finger to trace around the edge. *Again.*

"Don't do it," Caven scolded as he walked into the room

wearing the universal hot-guy sleeping attire of gray sweats and a plain white tee. He set a glass of water and two Tylenol on the end table next to me and hooked his daughter around the stomach, plopping her on the middle cushion of the couch while he settled on the other side of her. "Quit touching her face. A bruise is an ouchy. You wouldn't like it if I was poking at your ouchy, would you?"

"I was being careful."

"Careful is not touching it." He kicked his feet up onto the coffee table and nabbed the remote. "What are we watching tonight, Willow?"

It was a miracle, but I wasn't even breathy as I replied, "Oh, um, it doesn't matter. Whatever."

He shot me a teasing glare. "You do know that if you don't pick something we have to watch the Animal Channel, right?"

"Yesssssss!" Rosalee hissed.

God, I loved her.

I loved this.

The casual comfort of three people just lounging on the couch. In recent memory, I'd never been that happy before.

I wasn't hiding a ticking time bomb.

I wasn't pretending.

I wasn't lying for the sake of someone else.

I was Willow Banks sitting on Caven Hunt's couch. With his daughter. My niece. The only remaining member of my family. It was all so perfectly boring that it wasn't even worth noting.

And that might have been what made it the most noteworthy of all.

"Then I guess we're watching the Animal Channel," I said,

flashing him the most genuine smile that had ever crossed my lips.

She bounced in her seat as Caven groaned. He wasn't the least bit annoyed though. Based on his subtle smiles, he loved the monotony almost as much as I did.

We were absolutely living in the seconds that night.

I'd thought it would be strange to be at his house again. But from the moment I'd walked through the door, everything had felt right.

After inspecting my face the first time, Rosalee had cornered me with a box of crayons and a mountain of coloring books. Caven had attempted to come to my rescue, but after the day I'd had, sitting at his dining room table and quietly coloring with the girl I loved most in the world seemed like the best way to unwind.

Much to my surprise, Caven didn't hover. Well, at least not over Rosalee. I'd caught him creeping on me several times when he'd thought I wasn't looking. I had no idea how he did it, but the moment my ice pack would start to warm, he'd magically appear with another one. Thanks to his constant care, the swelling on my cheek was minimal. But given the ache behind my eye, I had a sneaking suspicion the bruising wasn't going to cooperate as nicely.

Hence the Tylenol and water—another of his magic tricks.

Caven proved his experience by clicking exactly two buttons on the remote. When two lizards duking it out appeared on the screen, Rosalee squealed almost as loudly as she had when she'd learned we were having cake and french fries for dinner.

Caven grinned down at his daughter before he turned his attention on me. "Did you talk to Beth?"

Boy, had I talked to Beth. First, she'd screamed at me when she found out I'd gotten attacked and hadn't called her. Then she'd screamed in surprise when she found out Caven showed up pulling the Alpha routine. Then she'd screamed again when she found out I'd agreed to stay with him and hadn't packed the first piece of lingerie. Then she'd told me to call her the minute we finished having sex. I assured her Caven and I weren't having sex that night, or likely ever again. So *then* she screamed at me for being so blind. Finally, I hung up on her and put my phone on silent. I did not need to be reading into his White Knight act and this sleepover any more than I already was.

I avoided eye contact as I replied, "Yeah. We…uh…*talked*."

"Good, I know she was probably worried."

Yes, that I didn't bring the appropriate sleepwear to seduce you. I laughed awkwardly. "Yeah. She was. It's all good now though."

"Listen. I found a cleaning company to go over to your studio in the morning."

The side of my mouth hitched. I wasn't surprised. I'd heard him on the phone while I'd been coloring a field of one-dimensional daisies. It was still crazy sweet that he'd taken the initiative to help me. The sewage in my studio was far from my biggest concern, but I liked that someone cared.

No. Strike that. I liked that *Caven* cared.

"Thank you."

He slid his arm behind his daughter and across the back of the couch, capturing a lock of my hair. He rolled it between his thumb and his forefinger. "I also found a restoration company that will cut the mural out and seal it so they can reinstall it when the cleaning and repairs are finished. If you give me the keys, I'll go over there in the morning and let them in."

First, he'd saved my life. Then I'd lied to him for months. And *now*, he was letting me stay in his home, with his daughter, and sending cleaners and a restoration company out to my house. I did not deserve that man.

Though I didn't exactly have him, either.

There were over six thousand languages, and while I only spoke English and broken Spanish, I could have known them all and still not have been able to find the words to adequately express my gratitude. So, as the guilt crashed down over me, I took a play from Caven's playbook. "I'm so sorry."

The muscles at his jaw twitched. "Don't do that. Not tonight."

I had no idea what else to say, so I said nothing.

The hum in my veins sang as I stared at him, remembering the boy and then the man who had once given me his body. First with a shared bullet. And then years later with a night wrapped in each other's arms.

But he wasn't mine.

Even if I had always been his.

"Awww, why doesn't she want a hug?" Rosalee asked.

I glanced up in time to see a lioness fighting with a lion attempting to mount her.

"Because that is how you should act any time a boy tries to hug you," Caven replied.

"What about Jacob?"

"Especially Jacob."

I giggled, and while he didn't look at me, I saw his lips twitch.

He clicked the remote just before the lion was successful. "I think we should pass on TV tonight. It's been a long day. Maybe we should all hit the hay."

"You got hay?" Rosalee asked.

"No, baby. It's a saying. It means go to bed for the night."

She tilted her head to the side. "In the hay?"

"No hay. Forget I said anything about hay. Let's just go to bed."

She sighed, scrambled off the couch, and tugged on my arm. "Come on, Willow. You can sleep on my tremble."

Caven stood up with her. "Nope. Willow isn't sleeping on your *trundle*. She's staying in the guestroom, like I already told you."

"Whyyyyyy?" Rosalee whined.

"Because I said so. Now, go brush your teeth and I'll be up to read you a book in a minute."

My heart could not take the cuteness as she crossed her arms over her chest and glared at her father. "I want Willow to read me a book."

"Then I suggest you drop the attitude and *ask* Willow to read you a book."

My gaze jumped to his, emotion swirling in my chest. He was going to let me read her a book. It was something so small, but to me, it meant so much.

"Will you read—"

"Yes," I replied immediately. "Absolutely. Whatever book you want. I'm there."

"Good, I'm going to pick a really, *really* long one so maybe you'll fall asleep like Daddy does and then you won't have to sleep in the stinking guestroom."

I gasped and clutched my chest. "The guestroom is stinky? What's it smell like?"

"Like brown. It's all brown."

Caven chuckled. "We've established you aren't a fan of my decorating, but not everything can be pink. As far as I know, Willow isn't allergic to brown, right?"

"Nope. Not at all." I looked back at Rosalee and waved my hand front of my nose, making her giggle.

"Traitor," Caven mumbled.

I shot him a megawatt smile and let Rosalee pull me to my feet and then straight up the stairs.

We read six books. Six *long* books. Rosalee only heard five and a half of them though because she fell asleep while the princess was still stuck in the tower. With her curled into my side, I was in no rush to move, so I finished reading. And even after that, I remained in her bed, watching her sleep until my lids got heavy. As I drifted off beside her, I decided she was right. The brown guestroom really did stink.

I didn't know how long I'd been out when I was startled awake by a man standing over me.

"Shhh," he whispered, scooping me into his arms.

It took several heartbeats for my mind to make sense of the fact that it was Caven and he was carrying me out of Rosalee's room, the day coming back to me with a crash.

It was embarrassing, given our situation, but a pang of disappointment hit me hard as he bypassed his bedroom door and carried me straight into the guestroom.

He set me on my bed then walked around to move my bag to the floor.

"You could have left me. I didn't mind sleeping with her."

"She kicks," he said without looking at me.

And it was done without looking at me because he was grabbing the back of his shirt with one hand and tugging it over his head.

My mouth dried as I watched the muscles on his back and his shoulders ripple when he closed the bedroom door. And then I lost him completely when he turned out the lights.

"Caven," I breathed.

"Lay down."

My heart was in my throat, but I obeyed, eager for anything and everything he was about to give me. The bed dipped along with my stomach as he crawled in beside me.

Like a juggling routine, he turned me, facing away from him, and scooted in close, his front becoming flush with my back and his face nuzzling into my hair at the curve of my neck.

I struggled to breathe as his every exhale danced across my skin, but it was his hand that ever so slowly inched under the hem of my shirt that stole the air from my lungs.

Only it didn't drift up to my breasts or down into my panties.

It moved only far enough to rest directly over my scar.

My chest ached as he let out an agonizing groan, his finger curling into my skin as if the marred flesh were burning his palm. He'd seen it the day at my house when he'd found out who I truly was, but this was different. This was tangible.

This was the brutal past crawling into bed with us.

"Caven," I whispered, trying to roll toward him, but he had me anchored to his front.

"Please," he murmured into my hair. "Just let me have this."

I would have let him have anything. But why that? Why did he need that?

"Oh, God, Willow," he rumbled like the words had been torn from his throat. His shoulders shook as his hold on me became tighter.

I screwed my eyes shut, hating the thought of the memories ricocheting in his head far worse than I'd ever hated the scar. Unable to take it any longer, I covered his hand in an attempt to move it, but he laced our fingers instead.

"I don't want to be the girl from the shooting," I confessed into the darkness. "In your head, I want to be the woman you were falling in love with, not a reminder of that horrible, horrible day. And I know that might not be a possibility anymore because of what I did, and you now have an even worse reminder of me from when I lied to you. But if I could wish anything, it would be that we were strangers so we could have something real that wasn't tainted."

His hand flinched, and his body went solid. "If we were strangers, Willow, I'd be dead."

"No, you wouldn't," I croaked, unable to keep the devastation out of my voice. "The paramedics weren't going to let you die that day."

Suddenly, his hand was gone and I was flipped over, first to my back and then to my side, facing him. My eyes had adjusted to the darkness, and as his head came down, sharing a pillow with mine, his face was the picture of desolation.

"You didn't save my life that day because you made me get medical help. You saved my life because you forgave me."

Chills exploded across my skin. "W-what?"

"It's taken years, but I do realize that I'm not responsible for what he did. But that doesn't mean I'll ever be able to stop blaming myself for what happened. It's haunted me since the first shot was fired. I was the only reason he came to the mall that day. But then there was this little girl who, at the very least, had lost her mother and was bleeding out of her stomach, with no idea at the time if she was going to survive or not. And she forgave me. Truly *forgave* me. Knowing that someone was out there who didn't blame me was the only way I got through a lot of really dark times."

I rested my palm on the side of his face. "There was nothing to forgive you for. I was *eight* and I knew that."

His hand slid around my back to my side, holding me where the exit wound should have been.

But that bullet hadn't left my body at the mall.

It'd ravaged me from the inside out before the doctors had removed it.

"You can't have kids, Willow. There's still a lot to forgive me for."

God, how could he be so smart and still so wrong?

"Okay, fine," I said. "Let's for a minute say that the bullet that *you did not fire* damaged one of my ovaries and destroyed the other along with the majority of my uterus and it's all your fault. But we also have to factor in that if it weren't for you, I more than likely wouldn't have made it out of that mall at all. I was going to run or scream or… I don't know. My parents were gone and I was freaking out. You calmed me down and gave me hope in a hopeless situation." I paused, waiting for the lump to clear from my throat.

He inched impossibly closer. "You don't have to say anything else. We don't need to talk about this. Not now. Not ever."

"Yeah, we do, Caven. Because no matter what happens between us, you will always be the boy I owe my life to. You don't get to claim that I *figuratively* saved your life by forgiving you and then negate the fact that you *literally* saved my life when you chose to help a stranger, a terrified little girl, escape a madman. Last I checked, dead women can't have babies, either." My hands were shaking by the time I finished.

He didn't understand what he meant to me. But how could he when I'd spent the first four months lying to him about who I was?

"Jesus," he breathed, tipping his forehead to mine.

The tears finally escaped my eyes. "I have loved you since I was kid, but back then, it was something different. You were almost this fictional character in my head—a white knight who saved me. And there were so many times I leaned on the memories of this hero—"

"I'm not a—"

I kissed him. I didn't think or consider the implications of what it would mean. I just did it because in my heart it would always be right.

His strong body sagged as he let out a long exhale, as if he'd been holding his breath for the last eighteen years. And maybe he had.

Because, while I'd kissed Caven numerous times, that was the first time he'd ever kissed Willow.

His head didn't slant. Our mouths didn't open. But there was a soulful exchange all the same.

He drew me in close, holding me against his lips and speaking silent apologies that didn't need to be issued.

I took them.

Accepted them.

And lived inside them for every single one of those seconds.

When he finally broke the kiss, he didn't move far before coming back in for one more lip touch.

"The elephants are suffocating us," he whispered.

"I know. But I still love you. And not because you were that boy at the mall. You have no idea how many times I've wished you *weren't* Caven Lowe. Because then you could be mine."

He closed his eyes and came back for another lingering kiss capped off by another exhale ripped from his soul. "It's a little different for me. Because if you *weren't* Willow, you wouldn't be sitting here at all. I'm so conflicted when it comes to you and all the lies because I'm so damn mad at you, but it makes me the biggest hypocrite in the world. You forgave me for the unimaginable and I can't seem to let this go."

"It's because of all the boxes."

"What the hell are these boxes you keep talking about?"

"Ian said you compartmentalize everything. And, now, you have me in three different boxes and you can't decide who I am. Sometimes you hate me because of what I told you. Sometimes you feel guilty because I'm the little girl from the mall. And sometimes you miss me because I was the woman you were..." I paused, not wanting to say the words.

He laughed, sad and resigned. Rolling to his back, he took me with him, my head resting on his shoulder. "For the record, I currently only hate Ian."

"Don't be mad at him. We ran into each other at the grocery store. He was trying to help."

He stared up at the ceiling with one arm wrapped around my shoulders, his other hand resting in the center of my chest. "I'm not mad at him. He knows me better than anyone else. And he's right. I'm all fucked up over this. But I don't for a second wish you weren't Willow."

"I'm sorry," I told him, peering up at the underside of his jaw. "Really and truly sorry."

"I believe you. And that's one more reason why I'm so messed up about all this."

I waited for him to say something else.

I waited for him to tell me that it was going to be okay.

I waited for him to leave.

But after what had to have been close to twenty minutes, all I got was his heartbeat in my ear as his breathing evened out.

Nothing had been solved.

Nothing had changed.

But we were there together.

Caven and Willow.

And that was enough to make me fall asleep too.

FIFTEEN

CAVEN

I snuck out of the guestroom around four in the morning. I didn't want to go, but I also didn't want Rosalee to wake up and find me in Willow's bed.

The only heroic task I'd ever performed was forcing myself out of that bed. It'd felt right, being there with her. Like it was the way it was supposed to be.

Our cruise ship's worth of baggage aside, Willow would have been the perfect woman for me.

Smart, beautiful, funny, and incredible with my daughter were the obvious things.

But she was also a soothing warmth to my cold, guilt-ridden soul.

She understood me on levels no one else could.

And most of all, I had faith that if I'd just let her in, she could teach me to forgive myself too. That could be her heroic task.

Ian wasn't wrong about my confusion. I'd yet to be able to land on any kind of solid emotion I felt for her; that pendulum inside me swung hard and fast.

But there was one common thread that ran through all the boxes I kept this woman in.

I loved her.

I loved her as Willow, the girl from the mall.

I loved her as Hadley, the woman who'd traced her fingers over my tattoo and cried in my arms.

I loved her as Rosalee's family—the one who'd cared enough to give up everything she had to be a part of my daughter's life.

The mountain to any kind of future together was tall and the terrain grueling. But I wanted to try.

However, Willow wasn't the only one who had secrets. And if there was any hope of starting over with her, of building a foundation that didn't revolve around my father or her sister, we needed to start fresh.

But before we could be strangers, she needed to know the real Caven Lowe.

Eighteen years earlier...

"Get in the fucking car!" Trent yelled as he skidded to a stop on the gravel outside the trailer we shared with our father.

I dove through the window when I heard Malcom behind me, yelling, "You are dead! Do you fucking hear me? *Dead.*"

My legs were still dangling out the window as Trent peeled out.

"Jesus, Cav," he rumbled, grabbing the back of my shirt and dragging me the rest of the way in.

My face was covered in dirt, and my ribs ached from rolling around on the floor and fighting with my father.

He'd caught me in his room. I'd needed a fucking clean undershirt to wear to work, but what I'd found was a soft spot on the linoleum in the back of his closet.

One that turned out to be a secret compartment containing a stack of Polaroids.

All pictures of dead bodies.

Watersedge was a relatively small town depending on what socioeconomic clique you ran in. Ours was the bottom of the barrel, a rather large sect, but struggling people tended to know the names of who else was struggling too.

Derrick Grath had struggled a lot before he'd been found dead on his back porch, a needle on the floor beside him.

Sara Winters was another one who'd had a rough go at things. She'd been found at the base of Manner Rock, her death ruled a suicide.

Travis Glenn was a friend of mine's dad. He was a dick. A lot like my dad. So, whether he'd been struggling or not, no one cared. That is until he'd gotten so drunk that he'd drowned in his own damn bathtub.

Shit happened in our community. People were idiots, using the little money they did have to buy drugs or booze. I could have listed at least a dozen other people who had met their untimely demise over the last ten years.

But none of that would explain why my father had a Polaroid of each and every one of their dead bodies.

Derrick facedown on his porch.

Sara's limbs bent at stomach-revolting angles.

Travis underwater, his dead eyes wide open.

And those were just the people or places I'd recognized in the stack of photos.

No one should have had pictures of that shit. Derrick had been found by his mother, Sara by the police, and Travis by his son.

No one should have had pictures of those people. Especially not beneath the linoleum in their closet, literal skeletons hidden from the world.

But my father did.

He was crazy, abusive, and narcissistic to the point of delusions. I was fifteen and working, saving up every penny I made at the Pizza Crust, and biding my time until I could get out on my own. Trent was going to school and only came home when he couldn't find a girl with an apartment he could shack up with for the night. We hated our father, but I'd never thought he was capable of what I'd seen in those pictures.

However, his reaction when he'd walked into the room and seen what I was holding said otherwise.

No words were spoken before he tackled me to the floor, my side hitting his dresser on the way down. Trent was there, and he attempted to wade into the melee, but my dad shoved him out of the way as I took off toward the front of the house. He caught me as I pulled the front door open, taking me back down to the ground, half in, half out of our piece-of-shit trailer. He was a fucking rabid dog, taking every kick and punch I threw at him. He finally got his hands around my neck, trying to choke the life out of me, but through it all, I clung to those pictures.

I wasn't going to be another photo to add to his stack.

Adrenaline had thundered inside me, and with a hard buck, I'd been able to knock him off me, just long enough to jump off the front steps and dive directly into Trent's waiting car.

"He killed them," I panted, throwing the pictures into his lap as he pulled onto the main road. "I know he did. Why else would he have pictures of people who supposedly committed suicide?"

He looked down at them, lifting one into his line of sight, and let out a boomed curse as he hit the accelerator.

"He's a fucking psychopath," I panted. "We need to go the police. Lock his ass away forever."

"Okay, okay," Trent whispered, raking a shaking hand through the top of his hair. "Let's think about this for a second. We gotta be smart here. This is some heavy shit."

"There's nothing to fucking think about! We gotta go to the cops."

He banged his hand down on the steering wheel. "There's a shit-ton of stuff to think about! You're fucking fifteen. They'll send you to foster care."

I stared at him with my mouth gaping open. "You think I give a fuck if they send me to some group home? It'd be a damn vacation."

He shook his head. "No. I won't let that happen. We need to buy some time. I've got a friend we can stay with tonight. How much money do you have?"

"I don't know. Maybe five hundred bucks."

"Okay. Okay. We'll do this right. We can pack our stuff and leave."

I leaned against the door, my body twisted to face him. "What the hell are you talking about?"

"Our father is a murderer! Who do you think is going to help us in this town once they learn this shit? No one. Fucking *no one*." His wild gaze flicked to me for only a second. "Here's what we're going to do. I'm going to take you to work. Finish your shift and then see if you can get your last paycheck. If they say no, take that shit out of the register. I'll do the same, and then tonight, we'll go to the police. But I'm telling you, we gotta be ready to go as soon as this shit hits the news." He reached over and grabbed my neck. "He's done. We'll make sure of that. But I'm going to take care of you. That's what Mom would have wanted, right?" When I didn't reply, he repeated, "*Right*?"

I swallowed hard and then ruined the lives of forty-eight people and their families. "Right."

SIXTEEN

WILLOW

I don't remember stirring the entire night. At some point, Caven had left, because when I woke, I was alone in a dark room, the two chocolate-brown curtains excelling at their job.

I rolled over and grabbed my phone off the nightstand to see what time it was.

Ten. Shit, how had I slept so long? I wasn't exactly an early riser, but my internal clock had been set at eight thirty for years.

A text notification on my home screen caught my attention, and when I opened his thread, I had to scroll up through a series of messages I'd missed while sleeping.

Caven: Maybe you were right.

It was followed by a GIF of elephants running free in the wild. My heart lurched as I bolted upright in bed, praying that meant what I thought it did.

Caven: Hi, my name is Caven. Pronounced like Gavin, but with a C. Not like Kevin. Or the cave bats live in. Anyway. This might sound strange, but I saw you the other day, dragging a massive recycling bin to the curb. And I honestly thought you

153

were the most beautiful woman I had ever seen—and obviously ecologically conscious too. I was wondering if you would consider letting me take you to dinner on Sunday night?

My lungs burned as I stared down at my phone, the smile on my face so wide I probably looked like a maniac. But I didn't care one bit. He was giving me the second chance I never thought I'd have. My vision swam as I typed out a reply.

Me: Wow. This is strange. Who gave you my number?

His reply was almost immediate.

Caven: I bribed it out of a contractor who was in your backyard ripping out the majority of your studio. He looked scared, like someone had threatened to sue him for doing a botch job on your plumbing.

My already huge smile stretched wider.

Me: First screwing up my studio then doling out my personal information. It's possible that he is the worst contractor in history.

Caven: Well, according to a complaint filed at the Better Business Bureau this morning, he is the worst contractor in history. But what do you say to dinner tomorrow night?

Me: Oh, I don't know. You seem to have me at a disadvantage, Caven. I'll need to know a little more about you before I can decide.

Caven: Okay. Let's see. I'm 33. Never married. I have a

4-year-old daughter who is my entire world. I used to work in technology, but now, I own a private investing firm with my best friend. Though I've taken some time off recently to spend time with my daughter. My favorite color is currently red. I have one tattoo. I'm obsessed with R.K. Banks art. Oh, and you know that actor Ryan Reynolds?

Me: Oh my God, yes! Please tell me you look like him.

Caven: No, but we have the same color hair.

I burst into laughter, my heart swelling beyond anything I could have imagined.

Me: You sound like a real catch.

Caven: I am. And you want to know the best part? I come with exactly zero baggage. What about you? Any baggage I should know about?

Me: Nope. No baggage. I'm an unemployed mule.

Caven: How do you feel about elephants?

Me: That they belong in the wild.

Caven: Great. No baggage. No elephants in the room. Just two strangers. Meeting for the very first time over dinner. Sound good?

I stared at my phone, reading and rereading his message. It didn't sound good. It sounded like everything I'd ever dreamed of.

Me: That sounds incredible.

I rested the phone on my chest and closed my eyes. My

life had been one long series of heartbreak. I could never forget the pain, fear, or sadness. I lived in the seconds because they were all I could manage. But right then, with the prospect of a future with Caven—and thus Rosalee—on the horizon, I wanted the whole hundred years at once.

I threw the covers back, and after a stop at the bathroom, I headed downstairs, my steps lighter than they had been in eighteen years.

"Willow!" Rosalee called, jumping up from the couch.

"Morning, beautiful," I purred, picking her up for a quick snuggle.

She ran right back to the couch, peering up at the cartoons playing on the TV, while I walked to the barstools overlooking the kitchen. Caven was standing over a pan at the stove. I smiled at his back, relishing in the hum only he could give me.

"Morning, Caven."

He didn't bother turning to look at me before replying, "Good morning."

"How'd you sleep?"

He finally turned around, and while I was a grinning fool, his face was stoic as ever. "I slept great for the half of the night. After that, I tossed and turned. You?"

I raked my teeth over my bottom lip. "Same."

His gaze dropped to my mouth, but I had to give him credit. He didn't let it linger. "So, Rosalee and I already ate, but we saved you some bacon."

"Thanks. But I'm a vegetarian, remember?"

He pointed at me with the spatula. "Right. Which is why I was going to eat the rest of the bacon and offer you some..."

He opened the door to the fridge and leaned in searching for a moment before finishing with, "Grapes and yogurt?"

I laughed. "Perfect."

He slid the yogurt across the bar with a spoon on top and then got busy washing the grapes. "So, listen, I got in touch with your contractor today. He's tearing out all your flooring and will be refunding you for clean-up. I sent my guy over to handle the mural. I didn't trust this asshole with that task. But hopefully you should be back in business next week."

"Someone should really report him to the Better Business Bureau."

"I did that too." He pushed a bowl of grapes my way, not even a hint of a lip twitch.

Wow. He was really sticking to this strangers thing.

I glanced back at Rosalee who was currently enthralled by a cartoon pup riding a fire engine and decided to push my luck. "We're friends, right, Caven?"

He handed me a cup of coffee before replying. "We are."

"Okay, well, it might be weird to tell you this, given our history and all, but I'm so damn excited that I need to tell someone."

He canted his head. "I'm listening."

I leaned forward on my elbows and whispered, "I got a text from a guy who asked me on a date and he says he looks like Ryan Reynolds."

His eyebrows shot up, but this time, there was no hiding that damn lip twitch. "A date? With a Ryan Reynolds look-alike?"

"Yep."

"But you've never seen him before. What if he's catfishing

you and he doesn't look like Ryan Reynolds at all? What if they only have the same color hair?"

"He sounds incredible, so I'm willing to chance it."

No matter how much he'd tried to play it off, he'd been joking around before. But suddenly, a dark shadow passed over his face, stealing all humor—hidden or not. "I hope he's incredible for you. I truly do, Willow. But maybe you could spend the day with me today first? I have something I need to talk to you about."

My stomach twisted. "Yeah. Of course. What's up?"

He flicked his gaze to Rosalee. "Not now. We'll talk when Alejandra gets here. We'll go for a ride."

I wasn't quite sure what was going on or how he had flipped from fun and flirty to broken and mysterious so fluidly, but then again, there was a lot I didn't understand about Caven Hunt.

Whatever it was he wanted to talk about, he was worried.

And even though I had a date with Mr. Reynolds the following night, thick concern crawled up the back of my throat.

SEVENTEEN

WILLOW

I knew where we were going the minute he took the ramp toward Bellton. A southern suburb in New Jersey, it was even quieter and sleepier than Watersedge. It was over an hour from Caven's house, and despite the way he drove with his hand locked on my thigh, there was a heavy weight blanketing the air.

My heart sank as he took all the familiar turns.

And then it crumbled when I realized just how familiar they were to him too.

As far as I knew, Caven hadn't had any interaction with the survivors of the shooting, but then again, Truett West was no ordinary survivor. He was the tattooed man who had rushed in, helped Caven wrestle his father to the ground, and then fired the bullet that ended Malcom Lowe's life.

Caven put the car into park in front of Truett's small brick home in the downtown district of Bellton. Well, *downtown* was a stretch. There was a coffee shop on one end of the street and a diner on the other. Two blocks up, there was a row of mom-and-pop storefronts, but that was about it as far as shopping went. There wasn't a chain or franchise in a fifteen-mile radius.

Just the way Truett liked it.

I'd shared a meal with Truett multiple times over the years.

It had taken a while for me to break down his walls, but I could be persistent when I wanted to be. I wouldn't say he was exactly fond of me, but he'd put up with me—grumbling the entire time.

Truth be told, he'd needed those visits just as much as I had.

Truett was a military veteran who suffered from severe PTSD after an incident overseas. After his return, he'd left the Army and become something of a recluse. The day of the mall shooting, he'd been out with his therapist on an exercise to help him reintegrate into society. His therapist had died beside him while he'd sat paralyzed with fear. Ultimately, he'd found himself again long enough to take down Malcom, but he was destroyed in the process.

He was now in his early forties. No wife. No family. No friends. Just Truett, alone in his house. He forced himself to the diner one day every week for dinner. After I'd witnessed the sheer terror on his face as his hands trembled while eating a club sandwich, it was all too clear that the venture out of his safe space was more of a punishment than it was therapeutic.

I rested my hand on top of Caven's. "What are we doing here?"

He was sitting with all the comfort of a man on death row as he drew in a deep breath and turned to look at me. "I want this with you, Willow. Even after everything. Maybe especially after everything."

My breath hitched. It felt like I'd been waiting my entire life to hear him say those words. He wanted this. With me. *Willow.*

"I want it too. So bad, Caven."

"But we can't start over and be strangers as long as there

are still secrets lurking in the background. I just want you to know, whatever happens here today, Rosalee is still your niece. I promised you Mondays and Thursdays. You will always have that with her. You have my word. If you don't want me around, Alejandra or Ian can bring her to you. But you don't have to worry about losing her. Okay?"

My concern caught fire. "What are you talking about?"

"Tell me you understand. Whatever you feel or think about me after today, it will have no bearing on your relationship with her."

"Caven, stop. You're scaring me."

He intertwined our fingers and brought them up to his mouth, where he kissed the backs of my knuckles. "Please, Willow. Just say you understand."

"I understand. But there's nothing that could—"

"My father killed twelve people before the day at the mall."

"What?" My whole body jerked, and he was quick to release my hand, as if he thought my reaction was repulsion rather than shock.

He cleared his throat, but it still sounded like he'd swallowed broken glass. "I found pictures of his victims the morning of the shooting. They were the reason we got into that huge fight." Disgust lined his forehead as he drew in a shuddering breath and then continued to confess his darkest demons. "He'd been doing it for years. Making it look like an accident or suicide. The town didn't even realize there was a serial killer right under their noses. Trent and I had big plans to go to the police after we collected our final paychecks." His hand inched toward mine before he stopped it. "We desperately needed the money if we were going to take off and start a new life. But

Malcom had other plans. The truth was out and there would be no escaping for him. The only thing he could do was take me down with him. If I'd gone to the police first, the mall never would have happened. It's my fault, Willow. It's all my fault."

"Stop," I begged. "Don't say that."

"It's true. I had all the evidence I needed to stop Malcom. But instead of turning him in right away, I gave him time to gather his weapons, create a plan, and kill forty-eight innocent people."

"Caven," I breathed, his palpable anguish slashing through me.

Like the rest of the world, I'd learned a lot about Malcom Lowe after the shooting. I was a kid when it happened, but as I got older, my curiosity about that day grew to unhealthy peaks. The computers at the library had become my best friend and greatest enemy. The world was at my fingertips, but I didn't need to focus on the world. I needed to focus on Willow Anne Banks—a child who was quickly falling down the rabbit hole of guilt and blame.

But in all of my years spent at those computers, I'd never, not once, seen anything about Malcom having committed any crimes before that day at the mall. Which meant…

All at once, my stomach rolled as understanding dawned on me. Nothing would surprise me when it came to Malcom Lowe.

But I shattered for Caven.

"You never told anybody?" I whispered.

He rubbed his eyes with his thumb and his forefinger. "He'd already left us in Hell. He couldn't hurt anyone else, but Trent and I were two scared kids, worried that the world was about to crucify us for the sins of our father. Neither of us wanted to add to the list of his victims. Trent made the decision and burned the pictures. After multiple surgeries on my abdomen, I was out of it for several days. I almost died twice. When I finally came to, he'd told the police all about the fight that morning but decided not to mention the pictures. What was I supposed to say? 'No, officer, the only person I have left is lying'?"

He rumbled deep in the back of his throat, his frustration thick as if it had happened yesterday. "Then when he showed me the devastation of the families from the mall as they spoke to the news on TV, I truly thought he'd made the right call. The families of Malcom's original victims had already come to terms with the fact that their loved ones had died by accident or suicide. Imagine the agony of finding out that the man who had killed your loved one lived just down the street for almost a decade. He'd even been over to some of their houses and attended their children's birthday parties."

I covered my mouth, bile burning a fiery path up the back of my throat. "Oh my God."

He hung his head. "I could have stopped him, Willow. I could have stopped him, but instead, I've spent the last eighteen years covering for him. You call me a hero. But I'm not. I helped one little girl and killed forty-eight others." He tipped his chin to the brick house outside my window. "If you want a hero, he's in there. But it's not me. And you deserve to know that it will *never* be me. I'm not just a hypocrite because you forgave me for the unimaginable. I'm a hypocrite because I've lived the last four years of my life trying to protect Rosalee from the monsters in this world, all the while carrying the secrets of my father, the biggest monster of them all."

His breathing was ragged by the time he fell silent. His blue gaze boring into me almost begged me to berate him the way he so thoroughly believed he deserved. But all I could think was how maybe those forty-nine feathers tattooed on his arm were the right number of victims after all. Because, even eighteen years later, Malcom Lowe was still killing his son.

"Okay," I croaked out before clearing the lump from my throat. It wasn't the time for me to break down.

He'd just confessed his deepest and darkest secret; the last thing he needed was pity.

He did, however, need a good, long reality check.

I reached for his hand and he tried to dodge me, but in the confines of an SUV, he had nowhere to go. Curling my fingers around his, I kissed his palm. "I'm glad you told me this."

"I'm not," he replied, looking very much like he wanted to peel out of that car and never look back. "What do I do, Willow? Please just tell me how to make this right. Please tell me what I can possibly do that will *ever* make this right to all those people and all those families."

I didn't have to think about it long. It was what I'd been trying to do since I'd become Hadley Banks.

"You live."

He blinked at me. "What?"

"Personally, I don't think it would be a bad idea for you to go to the police and tell them the truth about your father. Give yourself and those families some closure once and for all. But that's something you and Trent are going to have to decide to do in your own time. I don't get an opinion on that. But just know your secrets are safe with me. Now and forever."

"You *do* get an opinion. The choices I made that day ruined your life."

I leaned back in my seat and stared at him. "Caven, my life isn't ruined."

"You know what I mean. I failed so many people that day. I've spent my life trying to make up for it. When I first started Kaleidoscope, I thought if I could just help one person, I'd feel better. We managed to put hundreds of criminals like my father behind bars, but it wasn't enough. Nothing is ever enough. I just need someone to tell me what to do to make this right."

"Okay. Well, first off, you have to stop assuming that you could have changed what happened. It's an illusion that has kept you locked in a prison of guilt. There is no magical key to escape. The truth is the door has always been open. You can't change anything. There is no right to be found in tragedy."

"There has to be something."

"Okay, step two: Stop assuming it's your something to give. Why didn't Trent tell the police about the pictures while you were still in surgery?"

His back snapped straight. "Don't pin this on him. It's not his—"

I quirked an eyebrow. "Fault? Exactly. That's because it's nobody's fault but Malcom's. Let me ask you an honest question, and I want you to really think about it before you give me an answer. Did you have any reason to believe that he was going to show up at the mall with an arsenal of guns?"

"I saw the pictures. I knew what he was capable of."

"I'm not talking about hindsight. I'm talking about in that second. That one second when you made the decision to go to work. Did you ever once think it was a possibility?"

He groaned and dropped his head back against the head-rest. "No."

"I didn't, either."

His head swung my way. "What? You couldn't have known."

"No. I couldn't. But I was the only reason my family was at the mall that day. We'd gone to get my film developed. Hadley was pissed. After a morning at the park, she wanted to go home. My mom even tried to talk me out of it, saying she'd take me later in the week. But I wanted those pictures. I begged my parents on my hands and knees, promising to do extra chores, whatever it took. My dad finally relented. They were dead an hour later."

"Jesus," he breathed, catching me at the back of the neck and dragging me toward him.

I didn't need a hug, but I thought maybe Caven did, so I remained silent and got lost in his scent.

He smoothed the back of my hair down and kissed the top of my head. "There is not a day that will ever pass where I won't regret going to that mall."

"And yet every day you thank God for your daughter."

His hand at my neck spasmed, and his body turned to stone. "That's…"

"The truth." I righted myself in my seat.

Just as I'd suspected, he was inching toward the edge of panic. "Don't give me that 'everything happens for a reason' bullshit."

"Don't worry. I don't believe there is a reason for anything that happens. There are only actions, consequences, and unorchestrated coincidence. But every now and then, after the pain and heartache settle, beauty can be found in the consequences. There will never be a moment that I don't also wish Malcom had never gone to the mall that day." I lifted a shoulder in a noncommittal shrug. "But I can't change it. And punishing myself for choices I made in the seconds of the past was ruining the seconds I had in the present. So I let go. I let time march on and I joined it for the ride." I curled my hand around the feathers on his arm. "It's okay to live *with* regret, Caven. But it's something totally different to live *in* regret."

He stared at me for a long time, his eyes searching my face, disbelief shining through unshed tears. "Letting go. That's easier said than done."

"Absolutely. But when was the last time life handed either of us something easy?"

The side of his mouth lifted in a boyish smirk. "Falling in love with you was easy."

"Wow, you're a bigger liar than I ever was."

He chuckled, sad and distant. "I've never had anyone I can talk to about stuff like this. Not even Ian knows about the pictures."

"Well, now, you have me. And I'm good at all kinds of things—bath bombs, tie dying, *listening*."

He rested his hand against the side of my face, his thumb stroking back and forth across my cheek. "I know you want to be strangers. But I want this. Right here. Me and you. Willow and Caven. Two fucked-up people trying to make sense of the world."

My heart soared, and I covered his hand with my own. "I'd like that. I really would. But I have a date with a Ryan Reynolds look-alike tomorrow."

With a smile, he pulled me toward him, meeting me

halfway. Ghosting his lips over mine, he whispered, "Fuck him. I'll treat you better than that asshole ever could."

I nipped at his bottom lip. "I don't know. He's taking me on a real date. You just brought me to Truett's house."

His smile fell along with his lids, and his nose brushed with mine, our exhales mingling. "I'll take you on any date you want. Any time of day. Anywhere in the world. I'll give you absolutely anything, Willow. Just as long as you stay with me."

My chest filled with more warmth than I knew possible. And after spending five months with Caven and Rosalee Hunt, that was saying a lot.

"Anywhere?" I croaked out, teasing the tip of my finger up his forearm.

"You name it. Paris. Rome. Hawaii. *Anywhere.*"

"And on this date, we can do whatever I want?"

"Anything."

"Okay. Then I want to go to your house and play in the backyard with Rosalee until she's exhausted. Then I want to cook dinner and force you both to eat lots of vegetables. Then I want to curl up on the couch and watch the Animal Channel until she passes out. And then I want you to take me to your bed and whisper my name. *My* name, Caven. Not Hadley's. Not the woman who came back. Not even the little girl from the mall. Just *me.*"

He smiled. "That was very specific."

"I may have given it some thought before now."

He touched his lips to mine. "Fine. If I give you all that, you'll blow off the stranger and stay with *me*? Not the kid from the mall. Or Rosalee's dad. Just *me.*"

It was a worthless promise. He would always be the boy from the mall to me. Just like I'd always be the girl at the mall to him. But we could grow into more.

More than the love we already shared.

Maybe we'd even grow into the permanent kind.

My nose began to sting, but I blinked the emotion back. It wasn't a time for tears.

"Ryan Reynolds is going to be devastated. But yeah, I'll do it for you."

He was still smiling when his mouth came down on mine. It started as a lip touch—a shared sentiment of happiness and hope—before slipping into something slow and reverent. Tasting and memorizing. Life-altering and undefinable.

And I kissed him back, returning his worship stroke for stroke.

We'd said a lot of words in that car. More elephants had slid into the backseat, while a few had managed to break free into the wild.

But it finally felt like something had gone our way.

That kiss became a promise to work together.

A promise to heal.

A promise to step out of the prison of regrets and live in the seconds of the present.

We were a long way from forever, but just like the day at the mall when he'd appeared next to me, seemingly out of nowhere, I had hope that we could find a way out of this mess.

We were going to be okay. We were *all* going to be okay.

"It's Saturday," I whispered against his mouth. "Can we wait here for another twenty minutes or so? I'd like to see Truett."

He backed away so fast that it felt like a Band-Aid being ripped from my lips. "Willow, I—"

"Relax. We aren't going to talk to him. He's not much of a conversationalist anyway. Have you ever met him?"

"No. Have *you*?"

"Yep. He might be the only person in the world holding more guilt than you."

His forehead crinkled. "What the hell does he have to feel guilty about?"

"I don't know. Apparently, it's what good and decent men do when they come face-to-face with the stark reality that they aren't superheroes who can save the world." I winked. "Anyway. He's not a talker. But if we stay a little while, he'll see us and know someone cares. Sometimes, that's the hardest part of being alone."

His face got soft as he stared at me with rapt adoration, but he said nothing else.

I heard the *I love you* all the same.

We sat in the car for twenty minutes, and like clockwork, Truett's front door opened and the tall, dark, and ominous man appeared. It had been at least a year since I'd last paid him a visit. But he looked the same: handsome, lonely, and terrified.

His brown eyes collided with mine through the window and a deep frown curved his lips. That was as happy as Truett ever looked.

His heavy gaze flicked to Caven, who I swear nearly broke my hand, squeezing it as he desperately tried to disappear into a crack in the seat.

Yeah. He wasn't ready to talk to Truett.

And Truett was more than likely beyond relieved.

Lifting two fingers into the air, our tattooed hero started down the street toward the diner. Holding hands like we were slipping off the edge of the Earth, Caven and I watched his every forced and calculated step until he disappeared.

EIGHTEEN

CAVEN

Fuck.

This was going to hurt. After the day we'd had, delivering more pain was not what I wanted to do. What I wanted to do was get my daughter to sleep and then take Willow to bed, bury myself inside her, and forget about everything and everyone that was not inside the four walls of my house.

But after the news Leary PD had just delivered, I doubted that was going to be possible. Thanks to Aaron White, the asshole they had identified as the guy who had assaulted Willow outside the grocery store, breaking her heart had been carved into the top of the night's agenda.

"Yes, sir, I'll let her know." I looked at Willow, who was rolling little bits of paper towel while watching me from across the kitchen. "Right. We'll be there. Thank you. I appreciate all your hard work. Okay. See you then." I hit the end button and set my phone on the counter.

She swallowed hard. "I'm going to pretend not to notice how sexist it is that they called you instead of me."

I grinned. "They called you twice and were sent to voicemail both times. Rosalee still have your phone?"

"Yeah. She wanted to take pictures of her stuffed animals before bed."

"Right," I murmured, closing the distance between us. She looked as nervous as I felt, so I wrapped her in a hug. "They got him, babe."

"That's good, right?"

"Very good. His name was Aaron White and they found him OD'd on a park bench about two hours ago. He still had your ID in his pocket."

"Damn," she mumbled.

I tightened my grip. "But it appears he hit your house first."

Just as I suspected, her whole body tensed. Craning her head back, she put her chin on my chest and peered up at me. "What does that mean? Hit my house?"

"It means, at some point after the patrol car drove past this morning, he broke into your house and trashed a lot of stuff."

She shoved at my chest, but I refused to let her go. "What kind of stuff?"

"Mainly the boxes in your garage. And your bedroom." I stared down into her green eyes, my chest aching for what I was about to tell her. "But also all the paintings in your downstairs studio."

She stared up at me, her face unreadable. I'd seen that makeshift studio; there had to have been fifty paintings lined against the wall. Some of them had been moved out to the backyard studio, but after it'd flooded with sewage, they'd been moved right back. For what an R.K. Banks original went for, that could have been as much as several million dollars in loss. Willow wasn't hurting for money, but that kind of loss could be paralyzing for a business. Especially for an artist who had dedicated months of her life creating them.

Her breathing sped. "Wh-what about the ones in my living room? The ones on the wall?"

"He didn't mention them. But he said the damages were pretty isolated to the garage, your bedroom, and the guestroom. So, I'm assuming they're okay."

"Oh, thank God," she rushed out, her entire body sagging in my arms. Laughing, she patted me on the chest. "Jesus Christ, Caven. You scared me for a minute."

I quirked an eyebrow, thinking maybe she was in some kind of shock. "Willow, baby, you heard what I said about all the paintings in your studio, right?"

Her lips flapped as she blew out a relieved breath and stepped out of my arms. I reluctantly released her that time.

"Yeah, but those were all junk. I painted them."

I twisted my lips. "I've seen your work. They weren't junk."

"Maybe not total junk, but Hadley was the painter in R.K. Banks. I've been fooling myself that I could ever fill her shoes. We were a team. That was what made us work. I've been trying for months to replicate her strokes. Maybe this was the sign that I shouldn't."

"This guy being an asshole isn't a sign. You spent a lot of time on those paintings."

"I did. But they'll never be the same without her. The ones hanging in my house were hers. That's all I care about. He could have created a bonfire in the backyard with my stuff and it wouldn't have mattered."

"What about the stuff in your garage and your bedroom?"

She shrugged. "The boxes were mainly her clothes and a few other things she'd shipped to me in Puerto Rico when she was supposed to be moving there. I haven't had the heart to go through them yet. I had a few of my mother's things in my bedroom, but unless he had a fetish for silk scarves, they can probably be salvaged."

I eyed her skeptically as she swept the paper towel balls into her hand and carried them to the trash. "I told them we'd come by tomorrow morning around ten so they could take a report of what, if anything, was stolen."

"Okay."

"Okay? You sure. Having someone break into your house and destroy your property is hard, babe. You don't have to pretend for my sake. It's okay to be upset."

Her deep-red hair brushed her back as she turned to look at me, a peace I never could have imagined only minutes ago gracing her face. "Well, I'm not thrilled about it. But it's hardly a reason to ruin the night. We're all safe. He's gone. And well, the rest was just...*stuff*." She stopped in front of me and looped her arms around my hips. "And just think: Now that the coast is clear, you can finally be rid of me."

This woman. This strong, beautiful, incredible woman. She'd spent the day talking me off the ledge of guilt only to find out her house had been vandalized. And she didn't care because we were all okay and stuff was just stuff.

I trailed my fingers over the curve of her jaw. "Maybe I don't want to get rid of you."

"That's good considering we haven't finished our date yet."

I dipped low and pressed a soft kiss over the bruise on her cheek. "Oh, yeah? How's that going for you?"

"So far? Five stars." I grinned until she finished with, "Out of ten."

"Hey!" I objected.

"I'm not sure if you're a closer in the boardroom. But there's still time for you to pick up a few more stars."

I slid my hands down to her ass. "Oh, I'm a closer."

She sucked in a sharp breath. "You totally just went up a half star."

After nipping at her bottom lip, I mumbled, "A half star for that? Really? We should have no problems getting you to a ten." I went in for a kiss, opening my mouth, and as if on cue, Rosalee yelled down the stairs.

"Daddy! Can I have my iPad?"

Willow giggled and shook her head.

I loved my daughter. Truly, I did. But it was times like those where I wished she had an off switch.

"No," I called back, staring into Willow's eyes. "It's bedtime. I'll be right up to tuck you in."

"Willow too?"

"Yes, ma'am!" she replied.

And in a demonstration of the utmost maturity, I didn't even stare at her ass as I followed her up the stairs.

Just kidding. I absolutely did.

———◆———

"It was so gross," Rosalee whined as I tucked her in and settled on the edge of her bed.

"Don't say that. You're going to hurt her feelings."

Willow propped her shoulder up on the doorjamb. "Oh, I already gathered that she thought it was gross when she hid it under the couch."

She had done that, but if it had hurt Willow's feelings, she hadn't let on at all. Sans the phone call from the police, she hadn't actually stopped smiling all day.

True to my word, I'd taken her on the date of her dreams— back to my place. We played hide-and-seek in the backyard, and I'm not too proud to admit that this included me sitting on the front steps of the house and drinking a beer while they searched the backyard for over twenty minutes. However, I am proud enough to brag that, once they did find me, I was still able to beat both of them back to base before they tagged me.

Willow claimed I cheated.

Rosalee told her I *always* cheated.

And while they were fuming and pissed off, I grinned like I was the luckiest man on the planet.

After that, Willow cooked an incredible "family friendly" dinner of white bean quesadillas with spinach and sun-dried tomato orzo. Clearly, she had not eaten a lot of meals with Rosalee though. The moment she said "beans and spinach," she lost her. This led to Rosalee shoving a quesadilla into the pocket of her shorts, asking to be excused, and then hiding it under the couch. Two hours later, while I was on my hands and knees, cleaning up Willow's water that had been spilled, I found the hidden meal.

Why was Willow's water spilled all over the floor?

Well, because Rosalee had asked why the baby zebra came out of the mommy's butt instead of the tummy while it was giving birth on the Animal Channel and then quickly followed that jarring question by asking if she had come out of Hadley's butt when she was born. That was followed by me accidentally-on-purpose knocking the water over to escape that discussion.

After the quesadilla was found, I declared that it was time to call it a night.

And that had absolutely nothing to do with the way Willow had been looking at me all night.

Or the way my hands itched to touch her.

Or that, after our day of confessions, for the first time in my entire goddamn life, I didn't feel like I was being suffocated by gravity.

Or the fact that she'd told me she wanted to end her date in my bed with me whispering her name.

Nope. Those were all just purely coincidental—*ish*.

"It's okay, Rosie," Willow said. "I didn't like spinach when I was a kid, either. Tomorrow, I'll make you some avocado toast for breakfast. It was my favorite."

It was a damn good thing Willow drew a good unicorn butt because, for the look on my daughter's face at the idea of eating avocado anything, she was about to be asked to leave.

"Daddy, no," she whispered.

I shot her a wink and mouthed, "I'll make pancakes," before kissing her on the forehead. "Goodnight, baby."

"Night, Daddy. Night, Willow."

Willow's eyes lit. "I love you, Rosie girl."

She spoke through a yawn as she replied, "Love you too."

"Hey, what about me?" I teased.

Rosalee giggled. "Love you too, Daddy."

I grazed my fingertips across Willow's stomach as we walked out of Rosalee's room, leaving the door slightly ajar.

She started toward the guestroom, but I caught her arm and pulled her into my chest.

"Where are you going?"

Her cheeks pinked as she pointedly flicked her gaze to Rosalee's door. "She's not asleep yet. I figured I could read or something for a few minutes until she is."

I slid my hands down to her ass. She was wearing my favorite little shorts and a tank top, but she'd ruined it with a bra. "She's not going to be asleep for like half an hour. You lucked out last night because she fell asleep while you were reading. That right there was just step one in the bedtime parade. We have time to kill and you aren't going to do it sitting in the guestroom, reading."

As if on cue, Rosalee yelled out, "Daddy! Can I have some water?"

I winked at Willow and replied, "Left a bottle on your dresser, sweetheart."

Willow and I listened, nose to nose, sharing the same oxygen as Rosalee padded across the floor, fumbled with the bottle before putting it back on her dresser, and padded back. The creak of her bed announced her return.

Less than a second later, she asked, "Can I have a snack?"

"Sorry, Charlie. You should have eaten your dinner."

Willow leaned into me, sagging in my arms, and whispered, "Dinner was gross, remember?"

"Dinner was amazing. And if I give her a snack now, it will be a whole production and she won't be asleep for *two* hours." I gave her ass a firm squeeze. "I don't have two hours to wait."

Her breath hitched, and she inched deeper into my curve, resting her hands on my pecs. "Good call."

"Daddy! How long is Willow going to be sleeping here?"

"I don't know. Go to sleep, Rosie Posie."

"Will she still be here at Christmas? Can we get her a guinea pig?"

I shook my head as Willow let out a soft giggle. "It's the summer, Rosie. We have plenty of time to worry about Christmas shopping. Now, go to sleep."

"Will Miss Gallis be my teacher next year?"

Willow dropped her forehead to my chest and looped her arms around my waist, her breasts pillowing between us, and I felt every single curve.

I'd been performing this nighttime Q and A since Rosalee had learned to string together a sentence. I usually stood in the hall, scrolling through my phone and catching up on emails.

But this…

Holding her.

Listening to her giggle.

Knowing she was Willow and knowing she was mine.

Fuck. It was better. *So much better.*

"I don't know, Rosie. But you need to go to sleep. I'm going to bed now. You do the same. Okay?"

"Okay," she grumbled.

I released Willow and lifted a single finger in the air. "Wait for it."

"Daddy, wait! I need one more hug."

"Of course, you do." I tipped my head, signaling for Willow to go to my room, and then went to hug my daughter one last time for the night.

This naturally turned into a hug *and* a kiss. Then turning on her bathroom light, which she declared was too bright as though I'd changed the bulbs since we'd tried it almost every night for the last two years.

Turning off her bathroom light.

Turning on her nightlight.

Another sip of water.

Finding her favorite stuffed animal, but not the one that was her favorite the last time I'd put her to bed. Her *new* favorite stuffed animal.

And then, finally, another hug, another kiss, and another I-love-you before I was able to leave again.

Willow was standing in the hall, a huge smile on her face. "She does that every night?"

"Pretty much." I put a hand at her stomach, guiding her backward into my room.

I followed her step for step until she reached the edge of my bed. Rosalee was still awake and would be for some time, so there was little we could do in that bed.

But I still wanted her there.

Talking. Laughing. Freezing the guilt coursing through my veins as only she could do.

"Lay down," I ordered.

"What if she comes in here?"

"Then she's going to see us hanging out on my bed."

"And you're okay with that?"

I peeled my shirt off before climbing onto my side. "We're going to have to tell her about us eventually. This will soften the blow."

Her eyes grew wide. "Oh, God, do you think she's going to be upset?"

"No, I think she'll be stoked. The blow will be to my wallet when she insists we throw a party to celebrate." I pulled the covers back. "Get in bed."

She grinned without moving. Just standing there, devastatingly beautiful and completely out of my reach. "I like parties."

"Good. I'll get the Daddy-has-a-girlfriend balloons ready. Now, get in my damn bed."

She giggled, biting her bottom lip, but she finally made her way around and crawled under the covers. The only problem being that the bed was a king and she was hugging the edge like I'd just developed a case of leprosy.

She squeaked as I hooked her around the waist and dragged her toward me.

"Caven, this isn't hanging out. Your door is wide open. She could walk in at any second."

"Okay, so she sees us cuddling. The balloons have already been ordered, Willow. You're stuck."

She turned, rolling into me and tangling our legs like it was the most natural thing in the world while continuing to argue. "You haven't ordered any balloons. We've been together for approximately twelve seconds. This time last week, you hated my guts."

I bent my arm between us so my hand was under my head, and I rested the other on the curve of her hip. "I didn't hate your guts."

"Oh, sorry, my mistake. You only hated that you *didn't* hate my guts."

"True. But I still loved you."

Her eyes lit, and whatever fight she was holding on to left her in the next heartbeat. Her whole body relaxed into mine. "Caven," she breathed.

I loved the way she said my name. It was only two syllables, but she made it sound like a symphony.

"I could get used to this with you, ya know?"

Her green eyes twinkled. "I want that."

Teasing at the hem of her shirt, I slipped two fingers beneath it and traced the scar on her side. Every raised seam caused an ache in my chest. But it soothed me as well.

She was Willow.

My Willow.

Well, almost.

Giving her a tight squeeze, I murmured, "I want you to be Willow again."

Her brows drew together. "I am Willow."

I trailed my fingers up her side and then moved in to dance across her collarbone. I'd never forget how many times I'd imagined tracing my tongue over the delicate curve of her neck while she was sitting at my dining room table, doing some silly craft with Rosalee. Given who she was, or who I'd thought she was, it had been wrong on more levels than I could count.

But it'd never *felt* wrong.

I'd had no idea she wasn't Hadley at the time. Though, deep down, some part of me recognized her. She was all grown up, but my draw to that woman was just as strong as it had been from the start.

It was like I had known she would be my salvation.

There had been dozens of people in that mall that day.

People closer to me.

People farther away from Malcom as he'd paced his path of destruction.

And then there'd been *her*.

I remembered cussing to myself as I made my way over to her, crawling on my stomach, my hat pulled low as if I honestly thought my father wouldn't recognize his own son because I was wearing it.

But even at fifteen years old, nothing could have stopped me from getting to her.

That didn't change when she came back.

It didn't matter that it had been eighteen years. Or that she had a different name. Something inside me recognized her. And it was that same something that overrode all logic and reason the first time I kissed her.

My need to be with that woman was inexplicable. And while daydreaming of tracing my tongue across her collarbone was how it had manifested in the beginning, I could have lived the rest of my life having her safe, smiling, and breathing my name like a prayer.

"No. I want you to *be* Willow again. The real Willow. You're not Hadley when you're inside this house. But the minute you walk out that door, that's exactly who you become. And it's dangerous, babe. I hope your sister rests in peace—genuinely, I do. But she left a shitshow behind and I don't want you getting wrapped up in that any more than you already are."

It was an innocent request not intended to upset her in the least. However, in the very next second, it was as if a fire had been lit between us.

She suddenly sat up, crisscrossing her legs like a physical barrier. "She was my *sister*. My name being Hadley isn't going to wrap or unwrap me from her."

I sat up too, propping my back against the headboard. "I don't mean it like that. I just mean you could finally be free from her chaos."

Clearly, it was the wrong thing to say.

Her eyes narrowed, and her mouth fell open "Free from her *chaos*? Seriously?"

I tipped my head to the side, confused and incredulous. "Yeah, seriously. You're currently staying at my house after a man attacked you because he thought you were Hadley. That's chaos. And if word got out that you were not your sister, that chaos would disappear."

She scrambled from the bed, rising to her feet and crossing her arms over her chest. "Maybe I don't want it to disappear."

"What the hell are you talking about? That makes no sense. You could finally be yourself again."

Like a bomb had been detonated, her eyes flashed wide before the explosion flew from her mouth. "I don't want to be myself! If Willow is alive, that means Hadley is gone forever."

Oh, fuck.

How had I not seen that coming?

She was her sister. Her *twin* sister. One she had loved so completely that she'd given up her entire life to be close to the daughter Hadley had abandoned. And knowing Willow, I'd have bet my bank account that during that time she'd spent hatching a plan to reclaim the only remaining member of her family, she'd never taken the time to grieve the sister she'd lost.

Only hours earlier, as I'd poured my heart out to her over all the things she should rightly hate me for, she'd been nothing but patient and understanding, And there I was, in a roundabout way suggesting she bury Hadley all over again. Something that wasn't my call to make.

"Willow, come here."

She shook her head. "She always wanted to be me, ya know?"

185

"Willow. Come *here*."

"She always thought I had it so easy. And, compared to what she went through, I'm not sure she was wrong. I get to live. Maybe if she's finally Willow, she won't resent me so damn much anymore."

Throwing the covers back, I stood up and walked straight for the bedroom door. I quietly shut it and twisted the knob to lock it before turning back to face her.

For such a terrible day filled with confessions and ghosts from the past, it'd been amazing.

But only because *she* had made it amazing. The way she'd lightened my guilt just by holding my hand as we'd driven the hour home. The way she didn't look at me with contempt and blame the way I did so often in the mirror. She might not have said the words that day, but just as it'd been when she'd been a girl, her forgiveness was a comfort I'd never felt with anyone else.

Willow was a warrior on levels neither I nor Truett West would ever understand.

And, now, she was standing in my bedroom, her shattered heart all but on display because I'd unwittingly found the chink in her armor.

The vulnerability that had been right in front of me all along.

The one that had brought us together.

And the one that had the ability to ruin us both.

And she wasn't even alive anymore

Hadley.

NINETEEN

WILLOW

I watched as he walked toward me. His steps were calculated, as though I might spook at any minute.

"I didn't know Hadley well, so you're going to have to help me out here. Okay?"

I shook my head and backed away. I didn't know what he was about to ask, but I knew with an absolute certainty that I didn't want to help him out. I didn't want to talk about her at all. This was our night—our date.

She had no part in that.

But she did.

And because of the little girl fighting sleep just down the hall, she always would.

However, talking about Hadley meant thinking about Hadley. And, with Caven, it meant thinking about her in past tense. That was not a task I was ready to tackle.

For the majority of my adult life, I'd only seen Hadley in sporadic bursts. She'd wandered in and out of my life based on what she'd needed at the moment. I'd just wanted a family. So, when she'd come knocking on my door at three in the morning, I'd let her in. Sometimes, she stayed for a few days. Sometimes, a few hours. Occasionally, a month or two under the promise that she was getting clean and back on her feet. But it never lasted.

At Beth's urging, I moved to Puerto Rico to escape the constant need to stress about where she was or who she was with. It was killing me. I wasn't sure what, if anything, an ocean between us could solve, but it did wonders for my mental health. And, for Hadley, finally knowing there was no one she could fall back on seemed to serve as a reality check.

For two years, Hadley settled down. We started R.K. Banks. I emailed her photographs. She printed them and then painted over them. Most, she'd mail back to me, and some, she'd ship to the customer herself. What she did at night or on the weekends, I didn't know. But when I called with a question or a custom piece for a client, she'd always answer the phone. And we'd talk. Without fighting. Without name calling. Without…all the other bullshit that seemed to get in the way. It was one of the best periods in my life, and even though I only saw her a few times during those years, I was genuinely happy to have my sister back.

However, as the old adage states, all good things must come to an end. At some point, Hadley got back into drugs. And stealing. And obsessing over the woman in the picture from the mall. She stopped answering my calls. She stopped laughing. Ultimately, she stopped painting.

I sold off whatever inventory we had left, except for a few I kept for my personal collection. And then Beth and I did what we could to just keep her alive. The longest I'd ever gone without seeing Hadley was six months.

It had been over eight now, and the time had been weighing on me. I missed her fiercely. But it was easy to pretend she was still alive. To imagine she had a new boyfriend and was out wreaking havoc with him. Maybe she was high and happy, bouncing from house to house, and I was letting her go, tough-love style. Maybe she was pissed at me again for something completely out of my control. But in the back of my head, even as I was pretending to be her and cleaning up the mess she'd left behind, she was always somewhere living, breathing, and not gone from the Earth forever.

"I don't want to talk about this anymore."

Caven's large hands landed on my hips. Pained as I was, the way my pulse immediately slowed was almost laughable.

A chill prickled my skin as his mouth came down to my ear, his warm breath fluttering over my neck. "I think we have to talk about her, babe. She might be the only elephant we haven't set free yet."

"I thought we were trying to set *me* free. Get me back to Willow. Erase Hadley from our lives once and for all."

He moved closer until my only choice was to look up or face-plant into his chest.

Reluctantly, I gave him my eyes. "Just drop it."

"I'm not trying to erase her. This shit with us... It's *difficult*. It's going to take a lot of work and tiptoeing through the hard stuff on both of our parts to start a relationship with a solid foundation. But hear me when I say this: We are going *through* this. Not *around* it. Yes. I want you to be Willow. But that's not completely selfish. A man put his hands on you because he thought you were Hadley. The type of man I am, I expect the worst to happen at all times, and thus far, life has not let me down. When that asshole attacked you, it didn't matter that we'd been having problems. It didn't matter that I was supposed to be trying to perform the impossible and forget everything I'd ever felt for you. All that mattered was that you were safe. And I'd really like to keep you that way. It's not about forgetting Hadley. It's not about erasing her. It's about solving a problem head on. And our current problem is I don't think you're ready to say goodbye to her."

I opened my mouth to argue, but that had been eerily accurate, and I both loved and hated that he recognized it.

Loved because I loved him and it meant a lot that he noticed and understood things about me long before I was willing to admit them.

Hated because it meant that it had been over eight months and I was failing at pretending, which meant accepting that Hadley was gone forever was just around the corner and I was seriously not ready to lose her yet.

Tears hit my eyes at the same time I face-planted into his chest and blurted, "It's easier to see Willow on her headstone. I'm Willow. So it seems like a silly mistake. But then I remember that she's in there. And then I want her to be happy. She always wanted to be me. So I keep thinking that maybe I can live the easy life for her. There can be a world where Hadley loves her daughter and teaches her to paint and they do all the things she used to love. They can laugh about animals and she can sleep in the arms of a man who truly loves her and she won't hurt anymore. I can't fix the past for her. But I can fix the future."

His strong arms folded around me, pinning me to his chest as the sobs devoured me.

"You read her journals, Caven. They were all so dark and depressing. I want her to finally have something good to write about."

"But I want to write that future with you, Willow," he breathed into the top of my hair, holding me so tight it was as if he thought he could keep me from falling apart. And let's be honest. It was Caven. He probably could. But if he couldn't, I knew he would stand there for however long I needed him to, fighting a losing battle and trying anyway. "We don't have to talk about this now. We actually don't have to talk about it ever again. But just know you will always be Willow to me."

My heart simultaneously ached and soared. I wanted to write that future with him too. I didn't know how long we stayed there. Standing in the middle of his room, his bed only a few feet away. He didn't ask any questions, nor did he try to give me any sage advice.

There was nothing left to say.

The fact was Hadley was dead. My using her identity wasn't going to change that.

There would be no painting with her daughter.

No laughing over animals.

No journal entries decorated with hearts and smiley faces.

That wasn't Hadley's life.

But it could be mine.

With Caven.

I had a successful career as an artist. An incredible man who would hold me until his arms fell off. A beautiful little girl who looked like my mother, laughed like my father, and had every bit of my sister's attitude.

And, in one way or another, Hadley had given them all to me.

Maybe the answer wasn't rewriting her life.

Maybe he was right and it was all about embracing my own.

Or maybe it was just about putting off the inevitable and forgetting if only for a few more hours.

"Caven," I whispered, raking my nails down his back.

He turned to stone as I slipped my hand down the back of his sweats. "Fuck," he rumbled.

Pressing up onto my toes, I kissed the base of his neck and murmured, "Go see if she's asleep."

He took my mouth in a needy kiss, but as I was getting lost in a taste that would forever be engrained in my memory as Caven Hunt, he was removing my hands.

Palming either side of my face, he stepped away. "Stop."

"No, don't stop. Stopping is bad." I tried to capture his mouth again, but he held me out of reach.

"Jesus, Willow. Your cheeks aren't even dry yet."

I tugged at his waistband. "So dry them while you get me naked."

Releasing my face, he took a giant stride back. It was only a few feet, but for as deflated as I felt, it might as well have been a mile.

"We're not doing this. Not after that."

Without a care in the world and a desperation to forget, I peeled my shirt over my head, leaving me in a simple, but sexy, white bra.

His gaze jumped to my breasts, but it was the way it flicked to my scar that sent the chill down my spine.

"Willow," he breathed. After one last perusal, he bit his bottom lip and looked toward the door. "Don't do this to me. Don't make me tell you no. I don't have it in me."

I prowled closer and peppered kisses across his defined

chest. "If you tell me no, I'm going to have to start deleting stars on your date review."

He let out a growl when I grazed the tips of my fingers across the fabric covering his hard length. And no sooner than I slipped a hand into the front of his pants was I up off my feet, being carried to the bed.

I grinned in victory, eager to shut the world down and lose myself in Caven the way it was always supposed to be.

He dropped me to the bed and followed me down with his upper body, his hands landing on either side of my head. His kiss was deep and greedy, igniting everything from my nipples to my clit. Fighting with his pants, I shoved at them with my hands and my feet.

I needed to feel him.

To close my eyes and block out the rest of the world.

I just needed a few minutes to shut down the side of my brain that haunted me with all the ways I'd failed my sister.

That wasn't what I was going to get though, because in the next second, Caven flipped me to my side and crawled into the bed behind me, his chest coming flush with my back and his arm going over my hips.

"We're not doing it like this," he rasped.

I rolled my hips, finding his cock, thick and straining. "Caven, please."

"Fuck," he hissed, clamping down with his arm to stop my movement. "Stop. The last time I was inside you, I thought you were her. I'll be damned if we are bringing her to bed with us again. You're hurting, and I get that. I'd give anything to be able to make that stop, but not at the risk of damaging what we have."

"It's not going to damage anything," I argued.

"I know—because it's not going to happen." He blew out a long exhale and rested his chin on my shoulder. "I love you. I want a future with you. I want a family and maybe even a fucking dog. But, most of all, I want a bedroom where there isn't a ghost sitting in the corner. So get some sleep and hopefully some separation. Hadley will always be a part of our lives, but not here. Not in this bed. Not when I'm inside you. And especially not when I'm making love to you for the first time knowing you are my Willow."

God. This man.

My chest ached. "What if she's always here?"

"She won't be."

"But Rosalee—"

He shifted closer, sliding an arm under my head so we were touching at every possible point, head to foot. "She's not in here, either. When that door closes, Willow, it's me and you. Only ever me and you. And that's not because of Hadley. If by some miracle we have kids sometime down the road, they won't be in here, either."

I screwed my eyes shut. "Caven, I can't…"

He kissed my shoulder. "There are other ways, Willow. You're twenty-seven and the world changes more every day. You said you have one ovary left. I looked it up. There are fertility treatments and surrogacy. Adoption. Foster care. The options to start a family are endless. Though I'm not suggesting we start trying any time soon. I'd kind of like to have sex with you more than once first. Maybe take you out on a date that doesn't involve zebras giving birth and quesadillas hidden under the couch."

I let out a choked laugh. "I'd like that too."

"What part? Sex, kids, or quesadillas?"

"I don't know. Maybe all three."

"Okay. Then go to sleep. Get some distance from the things we talked about tonight, and we can start working on some of those hopefully sooner rather than later."

I smiled and snuggled in, tangling my legs with his.

My heart was overflowing.

He loved me.

He wanted a future with me—a *family* even.

And a life that didn't involve the ghosts of our past.

And God, I wanted all of that more than I wanted my next breath.

He rolled to the side, hitting something on his nightstand and plunging the room into darkness. Then, when he came back to me, he reached over with his cell phone in his hand. On the screen was a live video of Rosalee, fast asleep in her bed, a unicorn stuffed animal tucked to her chest.

Smiling, I took the phone from his hand to get a better look at her. "Wow, you are such a creeper."

"I'm her father. It's my job to creep. Just wait until she's a teenager."

I put my chin to my shoulder to catch his gaze. "Are you going to be the dad hiding in the bushes when she goes on her first date?"

"Nope." He plucked the phone away and gave it one last glance before setting it aside. He used his arm around my hips to drag me deeper into his curve. Caven clearly took his job as the big spoon very seriously.

I intertwined our fingers. "And is that because she's never going on a date?"

"You got it."

I giggled until he inched our joined hands down to my scar. It didn't quite line up with his given our height difference at the time. But it was a solid line, a thread that connected us in ways that could never be altered.

Our relationship was born in a tragedy, but I had faith we could flourish in the fortune of the seconds on the other side.

The baggage we both carried was daunting. And it was the permanent kind that wasn't going to disappear into nothingness. But maybe it would fade. With time. With happiness. When the good times we'd create together finally outweighed the bad. We were going to have to fight for every moment of peace from now until eternity. But there was no one in the world I would rather have on my side.

Life was crazy and confusing, filled with twists and turns, change and the unexpected being the only constant. Though, in that second, that *one second* with his arms wound around me, linking us as one rather than two individuals, life finally felt beautiful again.

"Hey, Caven," I whispered.

"Right here, babe."

"She's asleep. Does that mean we can finish our date now?"

He chuckled. "No. Go to sleep, Willow."

I waited a few seconds and pressed my ass into him. "What about now?"

"Sleep," he grumbled, but the way his cock began to thicken between us wasn't fooling me.

I guided his hand up to my breast, dipping his fingers beneath the fabric of my bra. "What about now?"

He roughly plucked my nipple. "Go to sleep. Space and separation, remember?"

"Right. Of course. Sorry," I replied. Though I suspected the apology didn't hold much repentance as I'd said it while circling my ass over his cock.

"Jesus Christ," he cursed.

"What about now?"

"No."

Another circle. "Now?"

"Woman."

"Man," I parroted. Yes, with another torturous circle of my hips.

The whiskers on his chin brushed my shoulder as he shook his head. "Willow, stop. Seriously, babe. Not now."

The rejection didn't sting as much as the ache between my legs throbbed.

I knew he wanted me. The proof was all but stabbing me in the back.

He was just trying to do what was right.

It was commendable. Truly. Even if it did suck. *A lot.*

"Fiiiiiine," I huffed, kicking one leg free of the blanket, trying and failing to get comfortable with the heat still licking across my skin. I must have adjusted my pillow a dozen times, flipping it from one side to the other, searching for the coolness. My hair slapped him in the face numerous times, but he didn't move or voice any objections.

It took a while, but I finally settled. The drama and emotion from the day overtook my wanton body. Sleeping in the bed with Caven wasn't exactly torture. Well, I mean, it was. But it was also a nice change of pace from years of sleeping alone.

Consciousness had just started to leave me, carrying me to the blissful twilight halfway between sleep and cognizance, when I heard him. He was counting so softly that I couldn't be sure if he was saying numbers or just ticking off the seconds.

There was a distinct *ten* before I felt him stand up.

Without him there to support me, I rolled to my back. "Caven?"

He didn't answer. At least not with words. I heard the rustling of fabric, and before I had the chance to open my eyes, my shorts and panties were stripped down my legs.

I smiled, victorious. It fell in the next heartbeat when his finger blazed a path through my wetness, going directly to my clit.

"Oh, God," I cried.

He tugged the front of my bra down, popping my breast free, and in the same fluid movement as two of his fingers entered me, his warm mouth sealed over my nipple.

I arched off the bed, and desire came roaring back into my system like a thunderstorm. My every nerve ending fired off bolts of lightning while the waves of my impending release surged just short of the shore.

I threaded my fingers into the top of his hair, moving with him as he shifted his attention from one breast to the other.

"Caven," I breathed, the sound so erotic for no other reason than it was *his* name.

His head suddenly popped up. "Fuck. I need you, Willow. So much."

"Yes," I breathed, wrapping my arms around his neck to drag him down.

He captured my mouth, his tongue snaking out to duel

with mine in an ebb and flow of a breathless urgency. His hand disappeared between my legs again, the backs of his knuckles igniting more sparks as he guided himself to my opening.

He paused for a second and I swear the wait was agonizing.

"Willow," he asked, the question clear.

I couldn't have kids, but there was more to unprotected sex with someone than the chance of pregnancy. "I trust you. I've always trusted you, Caven."

A masculine rumble vibrated his chest and his blue eyes lit in the moonlight as he sank in deep. Stretching and claiming, he seated himself, giving my body time to adjust. Time I did not want.

I rolled my hips, urging him forward in a plea he did not miss or deny.

It was Caven. Almost everything about him was gentle, from the way his lips trailed up my neck to how his hands roamed my breasts.

But there was nothing gentle or controlled about the way his every thrust sped up. Heat and power radiated through him. The muscles on his back rippled beneath my fingers, and every so often, I'd glance down at that one misshapen ab that was all him and beautiful because of it.

"Fuck, you are incredible," he murmured when he momentarily stilled and I rode him from the bottom. His hand went to my scar, not covering it because it was an ugly reminder, but holding it as though he could absorb it as his own.

It wasn't long before I was crumbling into the ocean of climax, writhing beneath him.

And he wasn't far behind me, his strokes becoming unpredictable and intoxicating as he hunted for his own release.

It became a frenzied race to who could fall off the edge of oblivion first.

I won.

Though I had a sneaking suspicion that he'd let me.

Only seconds later, he cursed and buried his face in my neck. I could feel the syllables of my name against my neck. I didn't hear my name, but the breath of the W breezing over my skin was followed by the touch of his tongue at the double L.

Panting and thoroughly wrung out, he collapsed on top of me, shifting his upper body a fraction to the side so we could both breathe without him breaking our connection.

Sated and with a smile, I closed my eyes and burned that second into my memory. I had no idea where life was going to lead us. In some ways, this felt like the beginning of a new day. In other ways, that beginning had happened eighteen years earlier when I had been a child and he had been a broken boy and this was the culmination.

But as he lay on top of me, his body joined with mine, it felt like an end.

An end to the struggle.

An end to the uncertainty.

And, hopefully, if wishes and prayers actually worked, it would be an end to a lifetime of pain that had been cursing us both.

"I forgive you," I whispered.

His head came up so fast that I was worried for his neck. "For what?"

"For being mean and making me wait."

His lips tipped up into a smile, and he was still wearing

it as he brought his mouth down for an all-too-brief kiss. "I wasn't making you wait. I was making you go to sleep. I wanted separation."

I brushed his hair off his forehead. "That makes no sense."

"It makes perfect sense. Sleep is a clear split. You fall asleep, you wake up, it's a different day."

"What about naps? That's not a different day."

"Yeah, it is. Maybe not on the calendar. But if you lie down after being pissed or upset, you sleep a few hours, you wake up confused as shit but probably not pissed anymore. There is a clear splice in your emotions when you fall asleep and wake up. I wanted to fuck you. I also wanted separation from all that other stuff. So I waited for the splice."

I barked a laugh. "I didn't even fall asleep."

His lips tipped into a crooked smile. "Yeah, you did. Snoring and drooling and everything."

"I did not. I was barely twilighted. I heard you counting to ten."

"But did you hear me count to a thousand first?" His smile grew wide and toothy. Probably not the most attractive grin in his repertoire, but it was playful and he was still inside me, his heavy weight on top of me. And his eyes were locked on mine as if he never wanted to look away.

Therefore, it was officially my favorite smile of all.

I traced my finger over his bottom lip and then sat up a fraction to kiss him. "I love you."

His face was warm, not a hint of guilt showing in his handsome features. "I love you too."

"We're going to make this work, right? We're going to do this together."

"Yeah, Willow. From here on out, whatever comes our way, whatever happens. We're going to do this."

I needed to go to the bathroom and clean up, but I was in no rush. So, when he dipped to kiss me again, his mouth opening as his tongue rolled with mine, I lived in those seconds for everything they were worth.

TWENTY

CAVEN

My steps were light as I made my way down the stairs. My bed had been empty when I'd woken up, and a cursory stop at Rosalee's room showed that it was empty as well, but the scent of pancakes infused my nose.

I stopped at the bottom step and quietly sat down, enjoying the show that was my girls.

"Four plus one," Rosalee quizzed.

"Five."

"Six plus one."

"Seven."

"Twenty-nine plus seventy-three."

Willow swayed her from side to side. "Umm…"

Rosalee's legs dangled, kicking back and forth as she sat on a barstool at the counter, still wearing her favorite Minnie Mouse nightgown. Willow was at the stove with her back to the stairs and wearing the same sleep shorts I'd all but torn off her the night before. It was a different tank top, but I could see the outline of her bra. Considering I hadn't seen it on the floor in my bedroom, I assumed it was the same one I'd removed a few hours later—after the second time I'd taken her body but before the shower just as the sun had peaked over the horizon when she'd come on my fingers.

As I stared at her ass as she flipped pancakes, I decided that had it not been for my daughter, we'd have started that morning with coffee, pancakes, and her bent her over the counter as I took her from behind.

But we always had later that night.

And the night after that.

And the night after that.

And the night after…

"One hundred and two," Willow answered.

"Ten plus one thousand."

Her face was warm as she turned, a spatula poised in her hand. "One thousand and ten."

"Whoa," Rosalee breathed. "You're good."

It was hard not to chuckle when Willow curtsied and then picked up a piece of bread that I was positive was avocado toast. And that was based on little more than the disgust on Rosalee's face as Willow took a bite out of it.

Reclining back, I rested my elbow on the step above me and just watched the beauty of it all.

Willow wasn't her mother, but that was what a family looked like. A happy family. A healthy family. The forever kind of family.

I'd never considered that I'd have something like that, much less be able to give it to Rosalee. Dating as a single dad was a nightmare. Between work and trying to be both a mother and a father for my daughter, I didn't have a lot of time to build trust or a relationship. The idea of introducing a woman to my daughter who may or may not stick around was terrifying. Rosalee had a huge heart; she would have gotten attached. Basically like she had with Willow.

But strange as our situation might have been, it was quite possibly the only road that would have led me to a point where I was filled to the brim with happiness while watching my woman standing in the kitchen, making pancakes with my daughter.

Willow had lied to me. A lot.

But forgiveness had been a part of our bond from day one. This would be no different.

"Eighty-seven plus twelve," Rosalee asked.

Willow replied, but not with an answer. "Caven? You got this one?"

Busted!

Grinning like the damn fool I was, I stood up and ambled their way. "How'd you know I was there?"

She batted her eyelashes and dreamily stared off into the distance while patting her chest. "Because my heart was aflutter." She shot a wink at Rosalee. "Nah, I'm kidding. I heard you come down."

"Hey, Daddy!"

I went to my daughter first, kissing the top of her head. "How'd ya sleep, baby?"

"Good. Until a zebra attacked me."

"What?" I turned her on the stool and tilted her head back to inspect her face.

"Willow said it was just a dream."

"Why didn't you wake me up, crazy? I'm the world's best zebra defender."

Willow cleared her throat. "She, um, woke *me* up. When she came into your room this morning. And found me... um, *sleeping* in your bed. I told her you would explain when you woke up. Her theory is I also had a bad dream and crawled into your bed." She flashed her eyes wide. "Though there has been some conversation about us getting married because Jacob's mom and dad sleep in the same bed and have babies, because Jacob says that babies are made when moms and dads sleep in the same bed. Sometimes from kissing but also from wrestling." She flashed me a pair of wide eyes. "Care to explain?"

"Ohhhh," I drawled, flicking my gaze back to Rosalee.

I'd known that her walking in was a possibility when I'd unlocked the door after the shower. It wasn't often she came into my room anymore, but she'd occasionally pop in, such as in the case of when zebras attack. Willow had argued that she should sleep in the guestroom until we became a little more established and felt comfortable telling Rosalee about our relationship. But no fucking way after the last few days, weeks—hell, months—we'd had was I letting her sneak out of my bed. Besides, Rosalee had already been onto us when she'd thought her name was Hadley. She'd been the one to originally ask if I loved her and that was before I actually did love Willow. Or at least before I had admitted it to myself, anyway.

Now though...

There was no use in keeping secrets.

I sucked in a deep breath, looked my daughter right in the eye, and said, "So, I think I'm in love with Willow."

"Caven," Willow hissed, but I didn't tear my eyes off my Rosie Posie.

Her face remained blank. "Is that why she was sleeping in your bed?"

"Yes."

"So, you got married?"

I laughed. "No. For now, she's just my girlfriend."

"Like me and Jacob."

"No," I stated firmly. "You are not old enough to have a boyfriend. Much less a love expert like Jacob."

Her eyes narrowed. "Did you kiss her?"

"Yep."

"*Caven*," Willow scolded.

"On the mouth?"

Among other places. "Yes."

She shrugged. "So just like me and Jacob."

I rolled my eyes. That was a battle for another day, perhaps when I had her boyfriend in a cargo container headed to Antarctica. "Sure. Fine. Whatever. Just like you and Jacob. Is that okay with you? Me and Willow being together."

"Are you going to get married?"

It was my turn to shrug. "Eventually, some day."

"*Caven*," Willow breathed, but it was breathy and no longer scolding.

"Will she live here forever?"

"When we get married. Yeah."

"Can she sleep on my tremble?"

"No."

She crinkled her nose adorably. "Sometimes? *Please.*"

I rested my hand on her jaw and grazed my thumb back and forth across her cheek. "Okay, fine. Sometimes she can sleep on your *trundle*. Will that make it okay for her to be Daddy's girlfriend?"

"Sure," she chirped with a white and crooked grin. "Wait, if you get married and Willow has a baby, will it come out of her butt?"

I grinned and swung my gaze to my new *girlfriend*, who was standing on the other side of the counter, sporting a look that fell somewhere in the middle of adoration, amusement, and horror. I waited for her to answer, but she lifted her hands in surrender and turned back to making pancakes.

Chuckling, I partitioned my mouth off and leaned in close to whisper, "God, I hope not."

Rosalee mirrored my position and replied, "Me too. That would be so gross."

"So, *so* gross."

She smiled.

I smiled.

Willow continued to shake her head.

But I felt like I was on top of the world.

And just like that, telling my daughter that Willow and I were dating was done. With as much as she loved her, I hadn't been expecting much push back. Though I probably had Jacob to thank for prepping her for some of that. And for that reason alone, I'd considering mailing him to somewhere in the Caribbean instead of Antarctica.

With my hands under her arms, I lifted her off the stool, stealing a quick hug and kiss before setting her on her feet. "Why don't you go get dressed and I'll help Willow finish cooking."

"Are we going somewhere?"

"Maybe?"

She bounced on her toes. "Can I wear a dress?"

I scoffed. "Uh… Absolutely. I insist."

She giggled and then she was gone, sprinting up the stairs.

"Hold on to the rail!" Willow called after her.

And I'll be damned if I didn't fall in love all over again.

"Hey," I murmured into the back of her hair as I wrapped my arms around her from behind.

She clicked the burner off before turning in my grasp. "I can't believe that's how you told her. I had this entire elaborate story, step-by-step *what to expect when you find a woman sleeping in your dad's bed* ready to go."

"Then why'd you wait on me to tell her?"

"Because she's your daughter."

I grinned and pecked her lips. I loved that she'd waited. I loved that she had always been careful about boundaries and keeping Rosalee's best interest in mind. Mainly, I just loved her. "Well, I appreciate that. And to show my eternal gratitude, why don't I take my beautiful ladies out to brunch. Alejandra is coming over to keep her while we meet the police at your house, but after that, there's this amazing place in the city that has mimosas for you and ice sculptures that Rosalee loves."

"That's probably a good idea. She's not going to eat these. I tried to sneak carrots and oats into the pancakes, but I think she caught me."

I curled my lip. "Dear God, why would you do that?"

She glared up at me. "It's healthy. Vegetables are good."

"Yes. But this is pancakes. They aren't supposed to be healthy. Literally, it has the word *cake* in the name."

"But that doesn't mean—"

The buzz at the gate interrupted her. It was nine a.m. on a Sunday; no one should have been standing at my gate. Even Ian knew better than that. "Go get dressed, I'll get rid of whoever that is, and we can meet back down here in twenty, yeah?"

"It might be Beth. She probably heard you mention the

words *brunch* and *mimosas* and teleported herself over here by sheer force of will."

I chuckled. "She allows me to invest in her discovery of teleportation and she's more than invited to join us for brunch."

She giggled and pressed up onto her toes for a kiss, inhaling with the same content reverence I felt at the core of my soul.

The damn buzzer sounded again.

"Go," I said, giving her ass a gentle smack. "Check on Rosalee too. She's probably tried on seventy-four dresses by now, leaving them all over her floor. "

"Only seventy-four?" She laughed.

We walked together, splitting off at the stairs. She went up, and I went to the screen showing the front gate beside my door.

And that was when my smile fell and my stomach soured.

Trent and Jenn were sitting in his SUV at the gate.

I loved my brother, but it was not time for a visit. He lived hours away; it wasn't like he just happened to be in the neighborhood and decided to stop by. The last time he'd shown up, he'd cornered Willow and scared the piss out of her. Granted, he'd had some pretty valid concerns, but that shit was not going to fly again. Which was why, after punching the button to open the gate, I walked outside rather than inviting him in.

Jenn was out of the car first, jogging up the steps. "I'm sorry," she whispered as she pulled me into a hug. "I'm *so* sorry."

"For what?"

She chewed on her bottom lip and glanced over her

shoulder as my brother folded out of the vehicle. "I talked to Ian about getting some things together for your birthday and he mentioned that Willow was staying with you. I thought it was a good thing and I...shit...*may* have mentioned it to Trent. And he *may* have gotten pissed. And he also *may* have insisted we drive up here to talk some sense into you."

I groaned internally. Fucking Trent. The man spent years at a time avoiding anything and everything to do with me and our past. Then I find a woman who makes me happy, knows and accepts every fucking skeleton in my closet, and loves my daughter as her own because in a way she *is* her own and he suddenly feels the need to drive his ass up to ruin it all?

Fuck. That.

She made an eek face. "Heads-up: He's *really* pissed."

"Well, he's going to have to *really* get over it. This is not his life. Not his concern."

She nodded and then bolted off to the side as Trent made his way up the steps.

"You keep popping up like this, I might start to think you actually miss me," I said, positioning myself in front of the door. If he was there to be an ass, he wasn't going to do it inside with my woman and daughter.

He sauntered toward me, pushing his sunglasses up to his head. "I wouldn't have to keep showing up like this if you were acting like a normal human being, not a pussy-whipped teenager."

"Shit," Jenn whispered.

"So, is that a yes? You missed me?"

"Fuck you. What the hell is she doing here?"

"She?" I questioned, just to be a dick.

"Hadley or Willow. Or whatever the fuck you're calling her now."

"Just Willow. And, currently, she's getting dressed so we can meet the police at her house."

He stopped in front of me and planted his hands on his hips. "Please tell me that's so you can turn her ass in for fraud."

"What fraud?"

"Don't give me that shit, Cav. This is bullshit and you know it. That bitch has been playing you for months, so your solution is to move her into your house and give her unlimited access to your daughter? What the fuck is wrong with you?"

My vision flashed red, and I stepped up until our chests bumped. "You watch your fucking mouth when you talk about her. Do you understand me? This is my goddamn house. You don't get to show up slinging shit you know nothing about."

"You think I know nothing about this? I'm the one who fucking figured it out."

Jenn tugged on his arm. "Trent, come on. Stop."

He roughly shook her off. "Get in the car."

"Why don't we both get in the car and come back after you've had a chance to cool off," she argued.

He turned a murderous sneer her way. "Get in the car, Jenn. This is none of your damn business."

I slid between the two of them. "It's none of *your* business, either."

He stabbed a finger in my chest. "*You* are my business, Caven. Since the day Dad died. Whether you like it or not. And I'm telling you: This woman is bad fucking news. Her sister was a whack job. What the hell makes you think she's any different? It was bad enough you didn't want to press charges. But now you have her sharing your bed? What are you thinking? She's a goddamn pathological liar."

"You want to talk about liars, Trent? Let's go stand in the fucking mirror."

I don't know why I said it.

Maybe because it had been a hot coal in my throat, burning and blistering for eighteen years.

Maybe because I'd finally broken the dam by telling Willow about the pictures we'd found but never reported.

Maybe just because I was pissed that he was acting like such a dick without knowing the first thing about her.

But, regardless of the reason, it was the truth.

"Excuse me?" he hissed.

I loomed closer, forcing him down one of the brick steps. "You want to act high and mighty now. You want to pretend she didn't have her reasons to do what she did. You want to dismiss the fact that she's a good person who made a stupid choice. But after the mall, you didn't give the first fuck about lying when it suited your needs."

His dark eyes narrowed. "That was different."

"Right. Completely different because, last I checked, Willow didn't kill anyone. Neither did she cover for a murderer even though it was gradually dissolving her soul like acid every single day for over half her life. And she sure as shit didn't burn our only proof that Malcom had killed twelve people in the decade before the shooting all while I was still in surgery, fighting to stay alive after taking two bullets from that maniac. And I know you hate talking about this and you think we should just let it lie in the past, but what she did was not even close to the things we've done in the name of self-preservation. So, if you want to stand here, on my front porch, and condemn *my woman* for being a liar, then you're going to have to acknowledge your own damn sins first."

"Oh my God," Jenn breathed. "Malcom killed people before the shooting?"

Trent's entire body swelled, and his eyes filled with rage. "We're just airing this shit out now? Doesn't matter who's around, huh?"

"She's your wife. She should know what we did. You should have told her years ago."

His face flashed downright venomous. "You tell Willow about this?"

I took the step down, forcing him back again. "I sure as hell did. And it was the best fucking decision I've ever made. I have been drowning in what that man did for what feels like an eternity. I've barely kept my head above water. Each time I try to catch my breath, the guilt slams me down harder. I swear to you, if it weren't for Rosalee, most days I wouldn't want to breach the surface again.

"But then came Willow. She doesn't look at me like a monster. To her, I'm not Malcom's son. Or the kid responsible for the shooting. I'm just me. Flawed, fucked up, and gasping for oxygen. And she's okay with that. So you go. Get the hell off my driveway. Go home. Keep your secrets. But don't you dare come here asking me what the hell is wrong with me. You *know* what's wrong with me. And you, of all people, should know that when you find a single sliver of happy you hold on to it." I paused long enough to catch my breath. "Get used to Willow. She's not going anywhere. Not now. Not ever. Do you understand?"

His jaw ticked as he held my stare. "Oh, I understand, *brother*. I understand *completely*. Maybe you deserve her after all." Reaching out, he grabbed Jenn's hand and gave her a sharp tug. "Let's go."

"Trent, wait," she urged.

"Let's. Go," he rumbled, marching away, dragging her behind him.

She caught my gaze over her shoulder and mouthed, "I'm sorry."

"It's okay." I pointed at Trent's back. "I'm sorry you have to deal with that."

She rolled her eyes and trotted to keep up with her husband. She gingerly got into the SUV while he stormed around, complete with slamming the door.

This wasn't our first argument. It wouldn't be the last, either.

But it would be the last until he could figure out how to accept my family.

A family that now included Willow.

TWENTY-ONE

WILLOW

Caven was in a *mood* as we drove to my house to meet the police. He held my hand and tried his best to cover it with a smile, but the pissed-off energy rolling off him was damn near suffocating.

He'd told me that Trent had showed up.

He'd told me that Trent had acted like a dick.

He'd told me that he'd told Trent to leave until he could stop being a dick.

None of these things surprised me, though I was rather excited about the latter because Trent was in fact *a dick*, so I didn't think I'd have to put up with him again any time soon.

This was a huge relief.

So, while we rode to my house with pissed off rolling off Caven, my smile was genuine and my breaths were easy, though this did make me feel a tad guilty.

But only a tad.

As we pulled into my driveway, that relief disappeared and a giant ball of anxiety took its place. There was crime scene tape covering my front door and three police cars in my driveway. I'm sure old man Jerry next door was *loving* this. He'd probably already shoved a letter in my mailbox comparing crime before I'd moved in to crime after, including stats about his plummeting property value because of me. The man didn't know how to recycle, but he could produce a strongly worded letter at the drop of a hat.

"You okay?" Caven asked as he put the car in park.

"Yeah. Though I'm probably going to have to move."

"He's dead, babe. He's not going to come back to cause you any trouble."

"Yeah, but Jerry's not. And he might look old but trust me, his shit-list is a dangerous place to be. There's a reason I got this house for a steal."

He chuckled. "So, you're okay?"

I gave his hand a squeeze. "Are you? After what happened with Trent?"

He kissed the back of my knuckle. "Yeah, babe. I'm good. I promise. Let's get this over with so we can get Rosie and head into the city for brunch."

"Can we maybe hit Central Park too? My dad used to take us there sometimes on the weekends. His old bakery is still off Times Square. I hear the guy who bought it is an asshole, but they still sell bear claws. I'd love to get Rosie one and then show her where Hadley and I used to play out back."

Catching me at the back of the neck, he met me halfway over the center console and kissed me. Chaste and sweet, but it was Caven, so it was also filled with absolute love. "Then it sounds like, after brunch, we'll be getting bear claws and hitting Central Park."

I smiled huge and stared into his blue eyes. It didn't matter that my life was pretty much in total disarray and we were sitting in front of my house with police tape across the front door. I thought maybe Hadley had always been right. I was the lucky one.

"I love you."

"I love you too, Willow."

"You have to call me Hadley, remember?"

He pursed his lips. "I'll call you babe, baby, sweetheart, beautiful, and maybe even gorgeous. But I'm not calling you Hadley. Okay?"

I didn't argue because I liked all of those. "Fair enough."

He kissed me again, and then we both climbed out of the car. He immediately took my hand again as we strolled up the front sidewalk, where three young officers were standing around talking.

"Mrs. Banks," the youngest of the three greeted when we got close.

I was either getting old or the PD was fishing from the junior police academy swimming pool.

"That's me. This is my, um…" I flashed a smile at Caven. "My *boyfriend*, Caven Hunt."

Stoic Caven's lip twitched just like old times and it caused butterflies in my stomach. It wasn't very long ago that he had been standing in that very same spot, angry and worried that I was there to take his daughter. I'd never in a million years dreamed we'd be standing there holding hands, committed and in love, on the cusp of starting a life together.

God, life was crazy sometimes.

"Nice to meet you," he replied, taking the officer's proffered hand for a quick shake. "Is Detective Gains around? He's been my contact for the last few days."

My eyebrows popped. "Your *contact*? Why don't I have a contact?"

He squinted one eye. "Did I say contact?"

"That's what I heard?"

He bit his lip as he winked.

So damn sexy.

"Uh…you just missed him," the young officer said, flicking his gaze between us. "We've finished up inside. Got several prints we matched to Aaron White. Big-time druggy. Small-time criminal. No one you have to worry about anymore. We just need you to take a look around and see what's missing so we can put it on the report and then we'll be out of your hair. Hopefully for good." He shot me a grin and then lifted his chin to the other cop standing by the door. "Let 'em in."

Caven's grip on my hand tightened as we walked up the steps to the door. It was sweet that he was concerned. Unnecessary, but sweet.

"I'm okay. Really. It's just stuff, remember?"

He nodded. "Maybe. But in case that changes, I'm gonna stay close."

Gah! Sweet Caven was the best.

I leaned into his side as we walked inside. A smile broke across my face when we found my living room covered in fingerprint dust but otherwise untouched. Hadley's paintings still hung on the walls, and after a few days of staying in Caven's neutral-snoozefest house, the bright pops of colors seemed more intoxicating than ever.

"My house is so much prettier than yours," I told him.

"I'm not sure pretty is the word. *Loud* may be more accurate."

"It's okay to be jealous. It's a natural human emotion. I still love you."

He chuckled and shook his head.

We went to the garage first. It was where I'd been storing all of Hadley's boxes that she'd mailed to me in Puerto Rico. I hadn't gone through them yet, but when I opened the door, it was clear someone had. They'd all been opened, dumped out, and strewn from one side to the other. It didn't appear to be much more than a bunch of clothes and shoes, though I did catch sight of a few of her art supplies scattered around.

I was happy.

I was in love.

I had a big day planned with brunch, bear claws, and Rosalee.

The garage could wait.

"Yep, everything seems to be okay out there," I said, shutting the door.

Caven eyed me warily, but I strategically ignored it. We had time to deal with that later.

Our next stop was my studio, and oh holy fuck. Paint was everywhere. Pictures that had once been stacked against the wall were broken and torn to shreds to the point where I couldn't see the floor. I had insurance. I wouldn't file it though. They were all just a bunch of junk. In a way, it was liberating to see them lying there. At least now I could stop trying to be someone I wasn't.

No. The symbolism wasn't lost on me.

"Damn," I mumbled, pointing to the blank space on the wall where the picture of Rosalee had once hung. It had no doubt met its untimely demise and was hidden somewhere in the rubble.

"Don't worry," Caven said. "That one was just a bad reproduction. I bought the original." He winked.

A loud bubble of laughter sprang from my throat. "Sure you did."

We made our way up the stairs. It was strange the way everything was in its place, not even a crooked painting in the hallway. However, my bedroom was a disaster area. It was a lot like the garage with the exception that *my* clothes and shoes and jewelry were strewn everywhere. How they expected me to know if anything was missing was beyond me.

Though one thing caught my attention. The photo albums that had once been stacked on my dresser were now stacked on the floor.

Not thrown or ripped.

Stacked.

My stomach dropped as I waded into the wreckage. I'd told Caven that it was all just stuff, but those pictures were irreplaceable. I'd digitized everything over the years, but there was nothing like holding the very same image my mother or father had once held. Their invisible thumbprints still graced the corners, and I often held them without even looking at the photo just to feel close to them again.

"Babe?" Caven called as I sat down and cracked open the album on top.

A picture of my father sitting on the couch, reading Hadley and me a book, greeted me on the first page.

"It's okay," I said, blowing out a ragged breath and tracing my fingers over my sister's smile.

That picture had been taken three days before my parents were killed. I'd found it on a roll of film still in my mother's camera shortly after I'd been released from the hospital. I'd cried for hours when we'd gotten the pictures back from the photo lab because the majority of them were of Hadley and me playing outside. I'd had my sister. I hadn't needed pictures of her. What I'd needed was for that roll of film to be filled with new images of my mother and my father. Seconds frozen in time of them laughing and smiling so I could lie to myself and pretend like they were still alive. A familiar coping mechanism for me.

I turned the page. More of Hadley. More of my father. More of me. One page at a time, I flipped to the end, making sure nothing had been damaged.

However, it was the very last page of that album that ruined us all.

"Son of a bitch," I breathed, tracing my finger over the blank spot where the final image of my parents alive had once been.

It was the picture snapped in the mall, literally one second before my father died. My grandfather had gone through hell and back to get that little disposable camera from the police for me and my sister. While that picture had provided me quite a bit of comfort on dark nights, knowing my dad had been happy until the very end, it had destroyed Hadley's life.

"What's wrong?" Caven asked, squatting beside me.

"He stole my picture."

"What?"

I pointed at the empty space. "My picture. The one of my parents the day at the mall."

His brows furrowed. "Are you sure it was there? You didn't take it out or anything?"

"No. It's *always* been right there. I took some of the other ones out to show Rosalee, but I never moved that one."

"Why would anyone want to steal *that* picture?"

"I don't know." I dug my phone out of my back pocket and opened my photos.

It had been a long time, and I didn't keep many photos of my parents on my phone, but over the last few months, I'd saved dozens of Hadley's texts from over the years. Unfortunately, she'd sent that one photo more than anything else. Always circling the blurry woman in the background in various zooms and crops.

I found the image I was looking for and passed my phone to Caven.

There were some things that I would remember for the rest of my life.

How my mother always smelled like Gardenias and honey.

The sound of a gun echoing in a food court.

The feeling of being splintered in half the day I'd found out Hadley was gone.

The beauty of Rosalee bouncing in a sea of bubbles.

And no matter what happened to me from that day on, I would never forget the pure devastation on Caven's face when he saw that picture for the very first time.

"What the fuck," he breathed, bolting to his full height. He furiously pinched his fingers to zoom in on the screen. "What the fucking fuck?" On weak knees, he stumbled back, tripping over a river of clothes, barely managing to stay on his feet long enough to land on the edge of my bed.

"What is it?" I said, scrambling on all fours after him.

He never tore his eyes off the picture as he asked, "Is that the woman Hadley used to obsess about?"

"Yeah. Why?"

His hands shook as he finally lifted his shattered gaze to mine. "Because it's not a woman. It's Trent."

TWENTY-TWO

CAVEN

"**D**o not open that gate for anyone, do you understand me? I don't care who is on the other side. You don't open it. I'm on my way there now. Pack Rosalee a bag, and if Trent or Jenn show up, I want you to call nine-one-one first and then me second. But whatever you do—"

"Don't let them in," Alejandra finished over the phone. "I understand, Caven. I promise. We'll be safe."

"Thank you. I'll be there soon." I hit the end button and raked a hand through my hair as Willow stood at the front of my car, explaining the situation to a group of police officers— men who were probably toddlers at the time of the shooting.

Not a single one of them did anything other than stare at her like she was a mental case.

I couldn't breathe.

Trent hadn't been at the mall that day.

He'd gone to work, picked up his paycheck, and then gone home to pack for our grand escape. There'd been bags for both of us in the trunk of his car to prove it. He'd been questioned by the police numerous times. We both had, and short of the Polaroids he'd specifically left out, I'd had no reason to dispute anything he'd said.

Besides, it wasn't like the cops were out combing the streets for Malcom's accomplice. Every single witness from the mall had reported that my father had worked alone.

Every single witness except Hadley.

His face was blurry in the image on Willow's phone.

But it was him.

Absolutely, one hundred percent Trent.

He was wearing the purple soccer jersey he rarely took off, and back in those days, he'd kept his hair long, almost brushing his shoulders. The lower half of his body was obstructed by Willow's father, but that was no woman.

That was my brother, and it scared the hell out of me because it made no sense.

Sheer adrenaline had forced my legs down Willow's stairs and out to my car. My chest felt like it was going to cave in, but I didn't have time for a heart attack yet. Not until I had my family in one place and could figure out what in the fucking hell was going on.

It was all lies upon lies. And while I didn't believe Trent was capable of the shit that was going through my mind, I'd learned the hard way not to leave anything to chance. He was in the area and pissed at me. I wanted my daughter and Willow safe before I started the what-if game on why Trent had been at the mall that day.

Pressing the button, I rolled the window down and yelled, "Get in the car, babe!"

She broke the conversation mid-sentence, snatched her phone back from one of the cops, and started toward the door. She was cut off by one of the officers.

He propped his elbow on the window and casually leaned in like it was any given Sunday and not the day the entire fucking world had fallen off its axis. "If what you are saying is true, Mr. Hunt, and that is, in fact, your brother in that picture—"

"No ifs," I snapped. "That *is* my brother. And he was at my house less than an hour ago. He's a cop with resources, and we got into a big argument and he left pissed to hell and back. So, if you will kindly back the fuck up, I'll be happy to come up to the station and tell you everything I know about that damn picture, but not until I have my daughter."

He arched a dark eyebrow as Willow tried, unsuccessfully, to squeeze around him. "Do you have reason to believe that your daughter could be in danger?"

"I don't know what to believe at this point!" I roared, slamming my hands on the steering wheel. "I just want to get to my daughter!"

His eyes narrowed, but he slowly stepped far enough from the door to allow Willow to get in.

I had the car in reverse before she shut the door.

He leaned back into the car. "How about I give you an escort to your house? Just to be on the safe side."

I wasn't sure if he was talking about the actual safe side or if he thought I might be an emotionally unstable person he needed to keep an eye on. Either way, I didn't care. I just needed to get home. Fast. "Great. Perfect. Whatever. Just *move* so I can get the hell out of here."

WILLOW

My head was a veritable vortex of swirling puzzle pieces—none of which fit together.

Above and beyond the fact that Trent had been at the mall the day of the shooting, I couldn't seem to make heads or tails of why Aaron White would want that picture from my album. When he'd assaulted me at the grocery store, he'd accused Hadley of stealing a flash drive, not a photo.

It could have all been one big coincidence, but there were too many corner pieces to that puzzle even if the center was a jumbled wreck.

"It's gonna be okay," I whispered around the knot in my throat as we drove—entirely too fast—with a cop on our rear.

"I know," he replied, his voice sounding like it had traveled over a pile of broken glass. "I want you to take Rosalee and head to my beach house in North Carolina. I'll text you the address and have my property manager meet you there to let you in."

I gave his thigh a squeeze. "Maybe it won't come to that. There has to be an explanation for—"

"I want you both out of here!" he snarled, flicking his gaze to mine for only the briefest of seconds, but that was all it took to see the terror in his deep blues.

"Caven," I breathed.

"I don't know what's going on, but I have a bad, bad feeling about all of this. There are a million blinking neon signs pointing in different directions, but if even a single one of them is pointing at you or Rosalee, I'm not going to wait to see how that pans out. God willing, I'm overreacting. We'll all be laughing about this by this time next week. But if I'm not and my gut is right, I don't want you two anywhere near this mess. I fucked up that day at the mall. I'm not doing it again. I'm going straight to the cops and you're going straight to the beach.

Worst case, you have a fantastic vacation. But I need you to do this. I need you to get out of here and take our girl so that she's safe while I figure out the rest. Can you please just do that for me?"

My stomach twisted, and I hated the idea of leaving him to deal with whatever the hell was happening all alone. But he was right. If there was even the slightest possibility that Rosalee could be in danger, it was his—*our*—responsibility to protect her.

"I can do that," I vowed. "Don't worry about it. I'll take good care of her. I swear."

"I know you will."

He didn't relax, not even a fraction. He simply punched the accelerator and gunned it toward his house.

CAVEN

A breath I'd been holding for what felt like my entire life flew from my lungs as my house came into view. The gate was still closed, Willow's car in the driveway, but nothing was out of the ordinary. It was the most beautiful sight I'd ever seen.

I didn't know what was going to happen at the police station; there were so many balls in the air, so many secrets untold. But if I could just get them somewhere safe, nothing else mattered.

The police officer pulled in behind me, parking sideways and blocking anyone from coming up or down the driveway. Then he climbed half out of his cruiser. "I'll keep an eye out here while you get your kid. Don't take too long. The captain is waiting for you at the station. Seems he's familiar with your father."

Of course he was. The majority of the country, especially those in blue, was familiar with the shit Malcom had done that day at the Watersedge Mall.

"In and out. Five minutes max." I rested my hand on Willow's back, guiding her up the front steps. After I unlocked the front door, I pushed it open and called, "Rosie!"

"Right here, Daddy!" She laughed and I swear to God muscles I didn't know I had sagged with relief.

Now to get them out of there.

I passed Willow my keys then typed my code into the beeping alarm. "Take my car. Her car seat's already installed. There are some DVDs under the console. That should keep her busy on the drive. Alejandra packed her bag, but buy whatever else you need while you're down there."

"Okay," she breathed, wrapping her hand around the tattoo on my forearm. "We'll be fine. I promise."

And she would. I knew it with every fiber of my being.

Or at least I thought I did.

The moment we made it to the living room, I realized just how wrong I'd been.

We must have seen him at the same time, because I threw an arm out to the side to stop her just as she fisted the back of my shirt, pulling me up short.

"Oh, God," she croaked.

Twenty-four hours earlier, it would have been a welcome sight. A surprise visit from my brother—Rosalee's favorite uncle. But in that moment, finding Trent on the couch with his arm draped around my daughter, who was sitting beside him with a book open on her lap and a smile on her face as she turned the pages…

It was the most terrifying thing I had ever witnessed.

And that was before I saw the gun in his hand.

And it was definitely before I caught sight of Jenn and Alejandra lying facedown, unmoving, in the hallway.

WILLOW

My heart stopped, and the oxygen became too toxic to breathe.

It was too much.

I'd never get used to how much he looked like Malcom.

Especially now that he had a gun.

And Rosalee.

And…

My head began to spin and the past roared in my ears when I saw Jenn and Alejandra lying in the hall. It wasn't the food court. But it was too close. Too similar. Too devastating. My vision tunneled and I couldn't tell if they were breathing. They were so agonizingly still.

My legs began to shake and it was all I could do to stay on my feet, but falling was not an option.

He had her.

He had my Rosalee.

"Hey, Daddy! Hey, Willow," she chirped. "Look, Uncle Trent bought me a book about animals. It has llamas and everything."

He grinned at Caven, slimy and baleful. "I sure did. Uncle Trent's the best. Right?"

"Right," she replied.

"Rosalee, come here," Caven rumbled, taking a long stride forward. "Right now. Come here."

She started to slide off the couch, but all at once, Trent's arm snaked around her and he slapped a hand over her mouth. As he stood up, he leveled the gun on his brother's chest.

"Please stop!" I cried, darting forward as she dangled in his arms like a rag doll.

His gun swung to me, and just as fast, Caven sidestepped in front of me.

"No!" Caven boomed, lifting his hands in surrender. "This is not about them. This is about me and you. Let them go and I'll give you whatever you want."

He cocked his head to the side. "What I wanted was for you to keep your fucking mouth shut." He jerked his chin toward the hall. "Do you see that? *You* did that. You told Jenn about the goddamn pictures and left me with no fucking choice. My own wife and you fucking killed her."

My pulse thundered in my ears, the fear from the past almost as debilitating as the panic in the present.

This wasn't happening.

Not again.

Not again.

When I heard Rosalee's muffled scream, I moved around Caven, unable to hide for a second longer while she was in the arms of the beast.

Tears were rolling down her face as she kicked her legs and had both arms outstretched for Caven. Her eyes. Oh, God, the confusion and terror in her bulging eyes were like a million arrows falling from the sky. I didn't want this for her. I'd have given my life right then and there if it meant she never had to know a fear like that.

"It's okay, baby," Caven choked out. "It's okay. Daddy's right here. Just relax."

His reassurances only made her fight even harder, and my chest constricted as Trent's fingers bit into the side of her face.

"Please. You're hurting her," I pleaded.

"And you," Trent snarled, his gun once again training on me. "You and your fucking sister have been nothing but a pain in my ass for years. If I'd known there were two of you, I'd have killed you both at the same goddamn time."

"What?" I gasped, his confession penetrating my brain one syllable at a time. "You…you killed her?" That wasn't possible. It'd been a car accident.

An accident just like the first of Malcom Lowe's first twelve victims.

I blanched as his verbal knife slid, slow and violent, into my gut.

"She was a cokehead who deserved far worse than what I gave her. The crazy bitch was constantly asking for me at the station and following me home from work. She and that worthless piece of shit, Aaron White, camped out in front of my house, taking pictures like they were at a fucking zoo. I've never had a dead woman blackmail me before. Or man for that matter. Good old Aaron can attest to that from the morgue."

He shifted Rosalee in his arm and cracked his neck. "Everything would have been fine until you, like a cockroach, came back. I knew you were a liar from the moment I saw you. I'd already killed Hadley Banks. There was no fucking way she was sitting in my brother's house, waiting to blow out her birthday candles. You should have stayed gone, Willow. You should have fucking stayed gone. And none of this would have happened."

He suddenly turned the gun to Rosalee's temple.

I screamed, tears springing to my eyes, but Caven lurched forward. His jaw so hard that it was magic that his teeth hadn't crumbled.

"Stop! Stop. She's Mom, Trent. She's the only part of Mom we have left. Just give her to me. I'll give you all the cash you need, and this can all be over."

He swung the gun back on Caven. "Fuck Mom! She liked to run her mouth too. Dad warned me over and over again that you were just like her and you would flip on us the first chance you got."

"Dad was a fucking psychopath."

"But he was right about you. You were all set to turn him into the police with those Polaroids. You didn't give a damn about your family. You didn't care about me. You've always been such a selfish prick. And you're the worst fucking kind because you won't die. I'd chained every door at the mall that day. And you still somehow made it out alive. I gave you every benefit of the doubt. I told you to keep your fucking mouth shut, but you can't do it, so your mountain of bodies just keeps growing by the day, little brother."

Bile clawed up the back of my throat as I watched his every word slash across Caven's face and strip him bare.

But it wasn't Caven the boy, the one from the mall, broken and defeated.

It wasn't the helpless kid so filled with anguish and guilt that he could barely breathe.

It was Caven the man who would do absolutely anything to protect his family—even at the risk of his own life.

"You helped him?" Caven whispered, inching closer.

Trent grinned with honest-to-God pride. "Couldn't let the old man take all the glory."

"You were just like him. You always have been." It was almost imperceptible, but with every sentence, Caven closed the gap between him and his daughter. "I don't know how I was so blind all these years."

Suddenly, Trent moved the gun back to Rosalee. "If I were you, that would be the last step you take toward me."

When I was eight years old, lying as still as possible on the floor of a bloody battlefield in the middle of a mall food court, I'd sent up my very first prayer that someone, anyone, would save me.

It was Caven who'd arrived that day.

But in his house eighteen years later, while I was at the risk of losing my entire family all over again, a different kind of savior appeared.

"Mr. Hunt," the young cop called, pushing the front door open. "Is everything—oh, shit!"

Trent's gun exploded.

The sounds echoed in my ears, and everything in my body tried to shut down. From my knees buckling to my vision blurring, the memories of the past threatened to take over. But just as Caven had told me all those months earlier, the one thing that would always override my fears was *making sure Rosalee was safe*. And the second I saw Trent drop her, instinct took over and I dove across the room, scooping her up as Caven finally tackled his brother.

Gathering her in my arms, I scrambled to my feet just in time to dodge the two men crashing to the floor.

"Go!" Caven grunted, his fist colliding with Trent's jaw. "Get her out of here. Go!"

I hated to leave him, but Rosalee needed me more. Racing as fast as I could, my chest heaving with every step, I ran out the back door with Rosalee sobbing in my arms. I'd made it all the way around the house, my throat raw and on fire from screaming for help, when I heard the unmistakable sound of another gunshot.

Rosalee's grip around my neck tightened to match the vise in my chest. I had no idea who had fired the shot. Or who it had hit. But I didn't stop running. There was nothing I could do to help Caven at that point, but all he would have wanted was for her to be safe.

I could give him that. I could give us that.

Sirens screamed in the background as I raced toward the end of the driveway. "It's okay, sweet girl. I got you. We're gonna be okay."

"I want my daddy," she cried into my neck.

Truth be told, I wanted him too.

I smoothed the top of her hair down and spun in a circle as blue lights flashed in the distance. "He's right behind us, baby. I promise."

It was a promise I prayed I could keep.

It couldn't have taken more than a minute for police cars to fill his driveway and officers to storm inside with guns drawn. But as I stood across the street, staring at the front door, with a hysterical little girl in my arms and my heart in my throat, I felt no relief.

I felt like I was lying on the floor of that mall again. My life wasn't in danger, but I was on the edge of extinction all the same.

Ambulance after ambulance arrived, still no sign of Caven, and with every second that passed, I died inside a little more.

I hadn't had him long. Life couldn't take him from me too. Not like this. Not after everything we'd been through.

"Willow?" Rosalee choked out, sitting up, her eyes so red that they almost matched her hair. "Where's Daddy? I want to see him."

That time, I didn't even have to lie. Because in the most amazing *second* of my life, Caven appeared in the open doorway of his house.

My heart exploded in time with my legs as I took off at a dead sprint with Rosalee bouncing in my arms.

He was staggering and covered in blood. It was exactly what I assumed my worst nightmare would look like.

But he was alive. Therefore, never had Caven Hunt been more beautiful.

"Daddy!" Rosalee screamed, fighting her way out of my arms.

He'd barely collapsed into a sitting position on the bottom step before she careened into his open arms.

"Hey, baby," he murmured, shifting her to one side and reaching for me.

As much as I wanted to fall into his arms and never leave, there was too much blood to set my mind at ease. "Oh my God, Caven. Are you okay? I heard a gunshot. I thought... Are you hurt?"

His face paled. "It wasn't me."

Three whispered words had never been louder.

He was okay.

Trent was not.

He was nothing but a coward whose final act of emotional terrorism was to leave his death on his brother's conscience.

"Oh, Caven," I breathed, dropping to my knees in front of him. I hooked one arm around his neck, my other around Rosalee's shoulders.

"None of that matters. It's over. It's finally over. We're living in the seconds. And nothing matters except for this second *right now*. We're safe. We're okay." His voice cracked, but he still managed to force out, "We're going to be just fine." He kissed my forehead and then Rosalee's. "Okay?"

"Absolutely." I squeezed them tight. "We're a family. We'll get through this too."

He nodded, and as I peered up at him, I saw that all-too-familiar storm brewing in his eyes.

"Don't say it," I whispered. "Don't you dare apologize. Not now. Not for this. Not ever. You did not do this, Caven. None of this."

He nodded again, but he didn't believe me. He was a good man with a heavy conscience. It was going to take a long time to convince him that he couldn't carry the weight of the world.

Luckily for me, I had forever.

TWENTY-THREE

CAVEN

One month later...

"What's taking them so long?" Willow asked, the sound of waves crashing in the background. Rosalee was a few yards away, giggling and racing the waves up the beach.

I shrugged, digging my toes into the sand. "Royal Rumble off the balcony?"

"God, I hope not. We don't have enough ice for Ian's balls."

The side of my mouth curled. "And what makes you think Beth would win?"

She shot me a pointed glare. "You've spent the last week with Beth. Tell me you seriously think Ian could take her."

"Take her? No. Handle her? Absolutely."

She rolled her eyes. "I kinda wish they would have sex and get it over with already so they'd stop bickering all the damn time."

I glanced back at the beach house. "Who says they're not?"

Willow lifted her phone and flashed the screen my way. "No texts. Trust me, I'll know if Beth is getting laid before Ian does."

I let out a loud laugh and brought her hand to my mouth to kiss the back of it.

A wise woman had once told me that we aren't given a hundred years all at once. Time was doled out one very manageable second at a time. If all you focus on is the big picture and worry about tomorrow, you lose the happiness that can be found in the seconds.

And God, had we earned some good seconds.

After Willow had rushed out of my house with Rosalee in her arms, my anger had broken through the all-encompassing fear. A raw betrayal had branded my soul. I hadn't been able to hit Trent hard enough to make myself feel better, and while he'd landed a few blows of his own, it was when he fumbled the gun that I knew it had to end once and for all. I pulled the trigger on my own brother. And after seeing him hold that gun to my daughter's head, there would never be a day when I regretted it.

I'd sworn to Willow that Trent wasn't my father. And he wasn't.

He was worse.

When the police searched his house, they found not just my father's stack of Polaroids—the ones Trent had claimed to have burned all those years earlier—but a stack of Trent's own victims, including a picture of Hadley dead in her car.

From what the police could piece together, Hadley had figured out Trent was the woman in the picture and had been hell-bent on exposing him. Files from Aaron White's computer showed surveillance footage he and Hadley had taken during one of their stakeouts. It was a very clear, very damning video of Trent disposing of a body. The authorities surmised that these were what he'd been so desperate to get off the stolen flash drive that had never been recovered. Though we couldn't be sure because, while Aaron White had been found OD'd on a park bench after he'd trashed Willow's house, a Polaroid of him dead had been recovered at Trent's house.

In some ways, nothing made sense.

In others, I was a fool not to see it earlier.

My father had beaten Trent every day of his life. But he'd never hated Malcom the way I had. He'd been the one to convince me that we needed to get our paychecks and leave town, but his real motive had been to buy himself time so he and his fellow sociopath could get a plan together. And considering that Malcom hadn't seemed to care if he lived or died in the mall that day, maybe Trent had been the mastermind all along.

For years, he'd pretended to be the doting brother and uncle. He'd sat at my dining room table and taken my daughter on vacations. If I hadn't seen his madness firsthand at my house that day, I'm not sure I would have believed he was capable of killing dozens of people. Let alone his own wife.

Jenn died that day. Recordings from my security cameras revealed that Trent had choked his loving wife with his bare hands. In a miracle, Alejandra survived. She'd sustained quite a few injuries, including a broken cheekbone, cracked ribs, and swelling on her brain. She'd put up one hell of a fight, but she was no match for Trent. An oblivious Rosalee had interrupted him before he'd been able to ensure she was dead. It was quite possibly the only thing that saved her life.

The minute Alejandra had come to in the hospital, she'd burst into tears, asking if Rosalee was all right. She was a good woman and while she was still on the mend, the doctors expected her to make a full recovery. We'd gone to visit her in the hospital, and for as many times as she'd admonished me for lying to Rosalee, I gave her hand a squeeze when she told my girl that she'd taken a tumble down the stairs. We all got a good laugh when Rosalee told her she should have held on to the rail.

There wasn't much I could do to make up for what my brother had done to Alejandra. So I did the only thing I could think of—I fired her. Well, it was more like a retirement with full medical and a pension plan. It included a car and a house of her choosing with all utilities paid for the rest of her life. She took the pink slip in stride and negotiated that she still got to pick Rosalee up after school and got first refusal to keep her on nights and weekends when I was working or had plans. So, basically, we were back at square one, only her house was no longer in my backyard.

This was probably a good thing because I was never going back to that house.

Willow and I had both put our houses on the market, and we were staying at the beach house in the Outer Banks for a few weeks until we could find a place we could buy together. And, yes, it was going to be *Willow's* name on the deed when it finally happened.

With an absolute clusterfuck of information flying through the Leary Police Department and national news banging down their doors, it had taken Doug and Beth less than one conversation to draw up paperwork to have Willow's death certificate declared invalid. They had also ensured that any possible fraud charges against her would not be pursued on the grounds that she had been fearful of her life after Trent Hunt, a serial killer, had murdered her sister. Willow had been adamant about no more lies, but that was our chance—the out we desperately needed to be free forever. I'd all but gotten on my hands and knees, begging her to agree. Standing in front of a judge with Beast Mode Beth at her side, she'd finally let Hadley rest in peace and perjured herself right back into being Willow Banks.

I'd never been prouder of breaking the law in my life as I was when I walked out of that courthouse hand in hand with the woman of my dreams.

"Daddy, look!" Rosalee called, holding up two fingers.

Willow pushed her sunglasses up and squinted. "What is that?"

It was nothing. Or at least that's what it appeared to be.

I tilted my head to the side as if it might make it easier to see. "Uhhh… Dad experience tells me it's the the tiniest speck of a broken shell." I looked at her and grinned. "Or possibly a booger."

"Ewww," she groaned. But she'd been getting a lot of parenting practice as well recently. So she gave her a thumbs-up and called back, "Oh my gosh, that's so pretty!"

I'd died every single second that Trent had been holding Rosalee with that gun in his hand. It had been burned on the backs of my eyelids and carved into my subconscious. I'd woken up almost every night since it'd happened in a cold sweat, the sound of gunfire and her cries reverberating in my head. Willow was always there, whispering reminders that it wasn't real and we were all okay. I didn't know what I would have done without her that day. She'd saved my life when she was just a kid, but that day, as she took off out of the house with Rosalee, she saved me all over again.

I'd lived through a lot. But if anything had happened to Rosalee, I would have been stuck in hell forever.

We were all struggling in our own ways. Willow had

jumped into caretaker mode, baking and cleaning as if having sparkling countertops could cure everything. And Rosalee, my poor sweet Rosalee—she was also waging war with nightmares. And the questions. Oh my God, all the questions. I didn't know what to say when she asked why Uncle Trent had become a bad guy. Above and beyond wanting to shield her from the harsh reality, I had no explanation for why Trent had done what he'd done, either.

But not having an answer or sugarcoating it in the name of protecting her weren't going to cut it after what she had been through.

We all started therapy within a few days. Individual sessions. Couples sessions. Family sessions. Any session I could get us into. Malcom had ruined her mother's life. I was not going to allow Trent to do the same to my daughter. She was adjusting and coping as best as a four-year-old could. I'd noticed that she was a lot clingier and more cautious than she had once been, but that was okay. I was there for her. And so was Willow. If she wanted to sit in our laps or sleep in the bed with us, that was A-okay because we needed her just as much as she needed us.

I'd asked Willow to marry me as we were driving to the beach.

I had no ring. No plan. No grand proposal. No getting down on one knee.

All I had was her smile lighting one of the darkest hours of my life and the overwhelming need to keep her forever. Life was short and unpredictable. Sometimes, the seconds were all you had. And, dammit, I was going to make the most of them.

She told me no.

We argued about it. Her stating that the timing wasn't right. Me stating that I loved her, so the timing didn't matter.

But then that night, only moments after I drifted off to sleep, I woke up to hear her counting to ten.

"Yes," she whispered in my ear.

I couldn't even be mad that she'd waited for the splice. It was a new day. And she was going to be my wife. I would never love anyone like I loved that woman. And while she believed that the world was dictated by unorchestrated coincidence, I had not a single doubt that she had been sent to me from someone up above.

I didn't deserve her. And our lives, as twisted and tangled as they were, would never be easy.

But she was mine.

They were mine.

The rest would fall into place.

"Have you given any thought to if you want more kids one day?" I asked.

She hummed and smiled out at Rosalee. "I just wanted a family. She's enough. We're enough."

I stared out at Rosalee splashing in the ocean, the tide rolling in, my guardian angel and soon-to-be wife sitting on my left, and I had to agree with her. Though some doors were better left open. "You change your mind, I want to be the first to know."

"Absolutely. Right after I see if Ryan Reynolds is available to father my children, *you* will be the first to know."

She giggled as I stared at her with a gaping mouth.

God, I loved that woman.

"If you scream, you're going to scare her," I stated, standing up.

"Huh?"

I put my hands on either side of her chair and repeated, "If you *scream,* you're going to scare her."

"I don't—"

But that was all she got out before I dipped low and tossed her over my shoulder. I had to give her credit; she barely let out a squeak.

"Hey, Rosie Posie. I think Willow needs to cool off. The sun has gone straight to her head. Let's get in the water."

"Yay!" Rosalee squealed. "Let me get my floaties." She trotted over to our chairs and riffled through Willow's beach bag, throwing everything out in her furious search.

"Caven, put me down."

"You got any more Ryan Reynolds jokes?"

"Not at the moment. But I reserve the right should one pop into my head at a future date."

I chuckled and set her back on her feet, the water biting her ankles. She could make whatever jokes she wanted as long as she was making them with me.

"I love you, Willow. In this second and all the ones to come."

I hooked her around the waist, dragging her into my chest, and kissed her hard and completely indecently.

EPILOGUE

WILLOW

Five years later...

"Willow!" Rosalee called down the hall. "Keira's diaper stinks."

I looked at Caven, who was sitting beside me on the couch. He had his legs kicked up on the leather ottoman, mine draped across his, a football game playing in the background.

"Rock, paper, scissors?" I asked.

"Are you going to cheat and use the atomic bomb again?"

I popped one shoulder. "Probably."

"Then no."

I laughed and shoved at his shoulder. "Come on. I'm tired. I did the last one."

"No, you didn't. You took the girls out back and drew on the sidewalk for an hour, blew bubbles for another hour, painted their hands and feet then stamped them in their baby books for a half hour after that. Which, babe, I know I don't have to remind you of this, but Rosalee is almost ten. You can probably stop the baby book before she becomes college-age. But then, after you did all that, you brought them back inside and asked me to change Keira's diaper before you went up to take a shower. But what you failed to mention was that, before I removed that diaper, I was going to need a hazmat suit."

I laughed again. This was all very, very true.

It had taken two years and watching Rosalee graduate kindergarten for me to catch the baby bug. For as many times as Caven had asked me if I'd changed my mind about kids, I think he'd caught it long before then—possibly even before our wedding.

We had given a lot of thought to how we wanted to finish our family. Caven was concerned his family history would prevent us from adopting, so we both agreed to give IVF and surrogacy a go. However, we had no idea the emotional rollercoaster we'd signed up for.

First, it took over six months to find a surrogate we both trusted. I liked several of the women the agency had matched us with. Caven wasn't so sure. And when I say he wasn't so sure, I mean he threw their folders into the trash and told me that they were all unacceptable. By the fifth *perfect* candidate, who he ruled out because she was a coffee drinker, I realized he was just scared.

After everything we'd been through, trust was not his strong suit. And trusting a stranger with his unborn child was more than he could handle.

Eventually, Beth volunteered to be our surrogate, and while Caven was ecstatic, Ian lost his mind. They weren't together at the time. Or maybe they had been. Who the hell knew with those two. But when she showed up to break the news to Caven that she couldn't do it, she was wearing an engagement ring the size of Rosalee's head (slight exaggeration, but only slight.)

That night as we lay in bed, we talked a lot about how we'd met and how far we'd come. Caven was a firm believer that we'd been destined to be a family from the start. So, with that in mind, I told him that there was a surrogate out there who was already meant to carry our son or daughter. He just had to keep his eyes and his heart open long enough to see her.

I woke up the next morning to find the file of the dreaded coffee drinker on my nightstand. Her name was Hope.

After that, things only got harder. Holy shit, getting someone else pregnant was rough.

With only one damaged ovary, it took months of shots, medication, ultrasounds, and failure upon failure for my body to finally produce one mature egg. While our one little fighter successfully fertilized, the quality of the embryo was poor and every doctor who spoke with us begged us not to get our hopes up.

It was the impossible.

But we had been the impossible from the very start.

Keira Marie Hunt was born nine months later. When we'd found out she was a girl, we'd expected another redhead who looked just like Rosalee. But life once again proved it worked best with the element of surprise. At eighteen months, Keira looked just like her father—brown hair, blue eyes, and all.

"Okay, so what if I promise not to use the atomic bomb?" I asked.

He arched a challenging eyebrow. "Volcano?"

I bit my bottom lip. "No."

"Meteor?"

"No."

"Tsunami?"

"Damn," I muttered.

He barked a laugh. It could be said that diaper duty was not my favorite.

I started to move my legs, but he stood up.

Leaning in for a kiss, he rumbled, "I'll get it. Relax."

"Have I ever told you how much I love you?" I breathed against his mouth.

"A time or two. But maybe you could show me tonight?"

"As long as the girls fall asleep before I do, I'm all yours."

He chuckled and pecked me again before lamenting, "Great. I'm never having sex again."

"Ew, gross. Stop kissing all the time," Rosalee groaned as she walked into the room, covered head to toe in sequins.

It was what I recognized as Hadley's flapper Halloween costume. Keira was holding her hand in nothing but a diaper, a long pearl necklace, and white elbow-length gloves.

I smiled, my heart overflowing with love. While packing up all of Hadley's things from my old house, Caven and I had divided some of her stuff into age-appropriate boxes to one day give to Rosalee. There was everything from dress-up clothes and purses, to high heels and prom gowns, to a few pieces of nicer jewelry she hadn't sold. Every so often when I was feeling particularly nostalgic, I'd ask Caven to bring one of the boxes down from the attic and we'd give it to Rosalee.

Hadley was gone from our lives, something I'd tearfully accepted the day we'd had the headstone at my family plot changed, but Caven had promised me she would never be forgotten. And that wasn't just because Rosalee was looking more and more like her mother every day, but rather because he went out of his way to help me keep her alive through stories and laughter.

He didn't have much to contribute in the way of memories, but he was always the first to randomly ask for a story about Hadley or my mom or dad. And I loved him more than words could ever express because of it.

Hadley and my family could have been a strained topic we were forced to tiptoe around forever. Caven's guilt was still very real, though it had been fading over the years as our therapist had him transferring more of that guilt to his father's and brother's shoulders. It was still there. I could see it in the almost imperceptible winces while I spoke about happier times, but there wasn't much that man wouldn't sacrifice for his wife and his children. So he smiled and usually held my hand as I told Rosalee all about the amazing Banks family.

"Wow! You look gorgeous," I told her.

Caven wasn't so fond. "You look twenty-five. Take it off."

Rosalee rolled her eyes, ignoring his order completely. "I think Keira stole your wallet. I found it hidden in one of my mom's purses."

It was like a slow-motion statement. The words all came out, floated around in the air, and went in through our ears, but it took several seconds for Caven and me to absorb them.

His eyebrows drew together as he slapped his back pocket. I could already see the bulge, so I knew whatever she had found wasn't his wallet—at least not currently.

She extended a leather bifold out in front of her and I swear I felt a bolt of lightning hit Caven. The hairs on the back of my neck stood on end.

He stared at her outstretched hand for a long minute, but he never moved to take it from her.

"Here," Rosalee said, pushing it toward him again.

But my husband, stunned into silence, just stood there, staring. His face was unreadable, which to me was the most concerning of all.

I stood up and took the wallet from her hand. "Hey, why don't you take Keira to her room and get a diaper out. I'll be there in a minute to change her."

"Okay, but hurry. I can't take the smell much longer." She fake gagged and then started down the hall with her sister in tow.

The minute they were gone, I moved in front of my husband, who had turned into a statue. I rested my hand on his pec. "Is this the one Hadley took?"

He nodded.

My lips thinned, and I started to flip it open. His hand came up so fast that I never even saw him move.

He clamped the wallet shut. "Don't do that. Not yet," he rumbled.

I slid my hand up his chest, curling it at the base of his neck. "Caven, what's going on? Talk to me."

He scrubbed his hand over his face. "I accepted that it was gone."

"Your wallet?"

"No. My mother's necklace. It was tucked in the front pocket. And I know Hadley, and I know she sold off pretty much anything of value. But now, I'm standing here, staring at that wallet, knowing it's yet another impossibility but hoping like hell that maybe it's still in there."

I pushed up onto my toes and kissed his plump lips. "So maybe we should open it and find out."

He shook his head. "It's not going to be in there. There's no way."

251

"But what if it is? Think of how spectacular that would be. You never expected to see that necklace again, right? So if it's not in there, nothing changes. Rosalee still has the matching one that you had made for her. Keira has the matching baby bracelet you had made for her. And we go on about our lives, knowing that pieces of your mother are living, breathing, and waiting on a diaper change just down the hall. We have everything we need, Caven. Necklace or not. We have everything."

His blue eyes searched my face for a long second. "You're right. You're absolutely right."

He took the wallet from my hand and sat on the couch, motioning for me to join him.

Together, side by side, we held our breath as he opened the wallet. His driver's license was still in the front, and a few random credit cards lined the other side. There was a yellow piece of paper folded up in the cash compartment in Hadley's handwriting that read:

IOU-$167 Damn, cabs are expensive in the city.

Yep. That was Hadley. I laughed as I took it from his hand and traced my finger over her handwriting.

He sucked in a deep breath and looked at me one more time.

"I'm right here, Caven. Always and forever."

He smiled weakly and then dug his finger into the small pocket. I waited, staring at him, searching for any sign of what, if anything, was inside. But his forehead crinkled as he pulled out another small, folded piece of yellow paper.

My heart sank when I thought it was another IOU, this time for the price of the irreplaceable necklace. But Caven made hurried work of opening it.

A heart-shaped necklace fell out onto the palm of his hand.
I gasped, gripping his forearm.

I waited for the relief and joy to hit him, but as he read the paper, it was a loud laugh that sprang from his throat. He handed me the paper and then immediately got busy untangling the chain.

The note read:

You know who would love a hideous necklace like this? My sister. You saved her life once. So in a way, you saved mine too. Sorry I thanked you by stealing your wallet. I'm complicated. Willow's not though.

And then, at the bottom, she'd left him my name, my address in Puerto Rico, and my phone number.

She was right. Hadley had been complicated. And I had no idea why she'd left that note because she'd never given Caven his wallet back. Or how it had gotten into a purse I had personally gone through years earlier.

But then again, maybe Caven had been right and everything—even the timing of us finding that necklace—happened for a reason.

Or maybe we had always just been two players in serendipity's greatest game of all.

Because the smile on my husband's face as he looped that necklace around my neck was one of the most spectacular things I would ever witness.

"I love you, Willow," he murmured against my temple.

I sucked in a deep breath and squeezed the heart charm hanging at my throat, relishing in the wonderful life that man had given me. "I love yo—"

"Willow!" Rosie yelled. "Are you coming? She really stinks!"

Yeah. That was our life. And I wouldn't trade it for anything in the world.

I laughed, tears of pure happiness filling my eyes.

He kissed me again and then put his fist on his flat palm. "Rock, paper, scissors."

I grinned and mirrored his position as we both counted off, "One, two, three... Go."

THE REGRET DUET

THE END

OTHER BOOKS BY ALY MARTINEZ

ABOUT THE AUTHOR

Originally from Savannah, Georgia, *USA Today* bestselling author Aly Martinez now lives in South Carolina with her husband and four young children.

Never one to take herself too seriously, she enjoys cheap wine, mystery leggings, and baked feta. It should be known, however, that she hates pizza and ice cream, almost as much as writing her bio in the third person.

She passes what little free time she has reading anything and everything she can get her hands on, preferably with a super-sized tumbler of wine by her side.

Facebook: www.facebook.com/AuthorAlyMartinez

Facebook Group: www.facebook.com/groups/TheWinery

Twitter: twitter.com/AlyMartinezAuth

Goodreads: www.goodreads.com/AlyMartinez

www.alymartinez.com

42421482R00149

Made in the USA
Lexington, KY
16 June 2019